A Love Not Lost

A Love Not Lost

Jeanne McCann

Writers Club Press
San Jose New York Lincoln Shanghai

A Love Not Lost

Writers Club Press
an imprint of iUniverse, Inc.

For information address:
iUniverse, Inc.
5220 S. 16th St., Suite 200
Lincoln, NE 68512
www.iuniverse.com

All characters in this book are fictional and hve no relation to anyone of the same name or names. None of the characters or events have been inspired by anything other then the author's imagination.

ISBN: 0-595-20599-2

Printed in the United States of America

Dedication

To my partner, a generous, loving woman, who laughs at my jokes, encourages me to write, and has been my happy ending for over fifteen years. Ms. P, you have, and always will be, someone I admire and respect —thank you for your patience, your encouragement, your faith in my abilities, and most of all your love.

Acknowledgements

I would like to acknowledge my editor Kristin Kirby, who continues to teach and guide, to my family who continues to read each page I write, and to the people who are reading my stories. If there is one woman out there, who after reading my book believes in happy endings, I have done my job. Because once you believe in happy endings you will find your own.

Chapter One

"Aunt Jessie, guess what?"

Jennifer's enthusiastic teenage voice echoed loudly throughout the house. She had the habit of talking as soon as she came through the front door. It didn't matter if anyone was in earshot, she would just yell louder until she located you. Every day was an exciting new challenge to Jennifer, and she loved to share her news with her family. This was a character trait she had exhibited as a young child, and while at times it irritated her brother and aunt, it was also one of her most endearing qualities. She lived life completely and at full speed, enjoying everything that came her way. Nothing slipped by her inquisitive mind and she would always share with the people she loved the most.

"I'm in my studio, Jennifer," Jessica called to her as she continued to sand her current carving. She was almost finished with it, and she was very proud of how the figure turned out. She just needed a few more minutes. "What happened?"

"Our new Police Chief is a woman, isn't that cool!"

Jessica couldn't help but smile as her niece burst through the door of her studio, grinning from ear to ear and bouncing up and down with excitement. Jessica was amazed at how grownup and beautiful Jennifer was becoming. Her long blond hair and golden brown eyes were a gift from her mother; her dimples, generous smile, and her almost six-foot height came from her father. Her older brother, Thomas, could be her twin. He had the same hair, eye color, and dimples, but his height topped out at six-feet-four. They were both good looking kids but what made them special was the loving, generous natures that both parents had nurtured in them as small children. It was a testament to their parents that they were becoming such special young adults. Jessica couldn't have been more proud of them if they were her own children. She wanted to think she might have contributed to their becoming such wonderful people.

It was over seven years since Jennifer and Thomas's parents were killed in a plane crash while returning to Cascade from a business trip, and Jessica took over the raising of her niece and nephew. Jessica had lost a sister and brother-in-law, and Jennifer and Thomas, a mother and father. It was a horrible tragedy that the three of them were forced to overcome. Two small broken-hearted children and a grief-stricken woman alone and bewildered, it had been a very difficult time for all three of them. It could have made any one of the three of them bitter or angry but that didn't happen. It strengthened their bonds, and the early influence of their loving parents had helped all them to heal and grow together as a family.

"Can you believe it?" Jennifer exclaimed as she fidgeted in front of Jessica. She moved quickly, her young athletic body in constant motion.

Jennifer fervently believed that women could do anything they put their minds to and she celebrated each time she heard of one doing the work that had historically been held by a man. This was due in part to her parent's early encouragement and of late, her brother and aunt's guidance.

"That is cool. I knew the council had hired someone."

"I got to meet her, Aunt Jess, Chief Buck introduced her to me. She's real nice and she's so pretty. She's sort of small, though. It's hard to believe she is strong enough to be a police officer." Jennifer barely took a breath as her words tumbled rapidly out of her mouth. "Her name is Caterina Andolino but she told me to call her Chief Andy."

Jessica put her tools down and cleaned up her worktable as she listened. She knew this bundle of energy she called her niece would calm down after she shared her day's activities. She just needed to dissipate her excitement.

"I imagine she has to be pretty well trained to be hired as a Police Chief," Jessica commented as she covered her latest carving.

Jessica had finally tapped into the hidden beauty of the wood and was intent on completing it. Her vision of a woman with the elusive, sexy look of someone who knew her own power was there. Jessica's goal was to capture the magic and excitement a young woman feels as she learns to love and be loved. Jessica knew she had caught that look and much more in the full torso and bowed head. Now all she had to do was complete the final detailed carving and a whole lot of sanding to finish the piece. She was very satisfied with it. It was one of her best works. Jennifer caught her attention again.

"She used to be an FBI agent. Can you believe that? She trained at Quantico, Virginia where they send all the agents. She is an expert in martial arts." Jennifer followed Jessica out of the studio and into the kitchen, practically bouncing of the walls.

Her niece continually amazed Jessica with how quickly she found out every little detail about someone she found interesting. Jennifer had an innate ability to charm someone while at the same time drilling him or her with question after question until she got all the information she wanted. She was charismatic and relentless. "I asked her if I could interview her for the school paper and she said yes." Jennifer grinned.

"Congratulations, honey."

"Way cool, huh!" Jennifer hugged her tightly.

"Way cool, doll." Jessica returned the hug. "It should be a good article."

"I thought I would write about her training and then how she came here to work. Hey, what's for dinner? Can I do something?"

"I fixed a taco salad and French bread. Since you have volleyball practice and I'm going to the town council meeting, we can eat early. I just need to warm the bread. Why don't you set the table?"

"Okay, I bet they are going to introduce the new Chief of Police tonight."

"You're probably right. Do you want to drive me to the meeting and pick me up afterwards?"

"Sure, can I pick up Vicki, she needs a ride?"

"No problem, I just need to clean up before we leave and you need to pick me up on time, no running around after practice." Jessica warned her niece with a lift of her eyebrows.

"I promise I won't. And I think you look just fine Aunt Jess, pretty J. Crew-ish." Jennifer grinned as she flitted around the kitchen table laying out two place settings.

Jessica grimaced at her niece as she placed foil-wrapped bread in the oven. Her choice of attire while working in her studio was faded torn blue jeans, a T- shirt, and deck shoes. Her niece loved to tease her about her clothes only because they shared similar tastes. The only thing that kept Jennifer from borrowing them was the fact that Jessica was no taller then five and a half feet and two sizes smaller.

"I need to fix my hair." Jessica's hair, unlike her niece's, was dark mahogany brown, and wavy. She wore it short and layered more for convenience than style. She was not one to worry about fashion statements and strived for comfort and functionality; it suited her personality and her lifestyle.

"Are you coming to the volleyball tournament this weekend?"

"I wouldn't miss it." Jennifer was a star volleyball player of her high school and Jessica tried to attend all of her matches.

"Good, it starts at ten o'clock Saturday morning."

"I'm working Saturday afternoon at the gallery so Loren can have the afternoon off, but I'll stay as late as I can."

"Do you need me to help out at the gallery after the tournament?"

Jennifer loved to work at the business. It had been her mother's dream to open an art gallery in the small town of Cascade and she had built the business from scratch. Jennifer found that working there kept her memories of her mother alive. She loved to wander through the artwork and talk to the customers. She had grown up along with the gallery.

"You just concentrate on your tournament, doll face, I can handle the gallery this weekend, but thanks for the offer." Jessica tweaked her on the cheek, with a grin.

"Yes, boss." Jennifer smiled as she placed the taco salad in the center of the table.

"Now, sit down and eat." Jessica put the heated bread on the table and followed her own advice.

The two of them comfortably chatted about Jennifer's school day and weekend plans, while Jessica discussed with her the progress she had made on her current carving. It was over an hour before Jessica rushed upstairs to clean up while Jennifer promised to take care of the kitchen.

Thirty minutes later Jennifer was uncharacteristically waiting at the base of the stairs. "Aunt Jess come on, we've got to go. We are going to be late!"

"I'm coming, I'm coming," Jessica reassured her impatient niece as she hurried down the stairway and met her by the front door. It was rare that Jennifer was ever on time. Actually, they were both running late.

"Cool outfit, Aunt Jess," Jennifer commented as Jessica hurried down the stairs.

"Thanks, sweetie."

Jessica had to agree with her niece, it was one of her favorites. She was wearing a turquoise silk shell with a sarong style calf-length skirt in swirling turquoise, cream, and black, and a lightweight black linen blazer. Black shoes completed the outfit. Jennifer, on the other hand, was dressed like a typical seventeen-year-old girl on her way to volleyball practice.

Baggy sweats hung from her slender waist; a torn, stained sweatshirt, and untied high top tennis shoes added to her look. To top it off, she had on a baseball cap from her brother's college, a gift he had sent her his first quarter away from home. Tommy was currently attending college at California University in Berkeley. The hat was one of her prized possessions and she wore it often with her long hair pulled through the back in a ponytail.

"Now don't forget to pick me up in front of the town hall right after practice," Jessica reminded her niece, whose one flaw was her inability to arrive on time to anything.

"I will, I promise," Jennifer pledged as she pulled the car to a stop in front of the building. "See you later, Aunt J." She grinned.

"Good luck at practice, dolly."

Jessica hugged her tightly as Jennifer returned the affection. Even as young children, both Tommy and Jennifer were very close to their Aunt Jessica. Their mutual grief had only strengthened their bonds as they grew into the close family they now were. They were very affectionate and loving to each other. Jessica waved at her niece as she drove away before heading up the stairs leading to the town hall. Jessica walked through the open doors of the town hall and was immediately accosted by the town gossip, Mrs. Ruth Boylston. Ruth was on older woman in the small community of Cascade and involved in everything.

"Jessica, my, don't you look pretty tonight. You know this is a good time for you to meet the new postmaster. He is so handsome and I believe he is about your age."

Ruth not only repeated everything she heard or saw, but also considered herself the town matchmaker. Knowing that Jessica was a lesbian had not stopped Ruth from trying for the last seven years to set her up with any available male, young or old. In a town of less than fourteen thousand people, Ruth made it a point to know everything, and what she didn't know she just plain made up. Jessica had learned to politely brush her off over the years, finding her behavior more of a pleasant nuisance. It was easier to ignore Ruth than watch her flush with acute embarrassment while Jessica redefined the word lesbian to her. Just as she started to lose patience with Ruth, they were thankfully interrupted.

"Jessica, one of my favorite persons." A large older gentleman with silver hair and the tan face of an outdoorsman enveloped her in a hug.

"Buck, how are you doing, enjoying retirement?" Jessica grinned as she hugged him in return.

Buck was one of Jessica's closest friends. He had been the Chief of Police for the town of Cascade for many years. He had also been the one to call her with the devastating news about her sister and brother-in-law's deaths and he had jumped in and helped her take care of all the legalities and funeral arrangements. Buck had actually kept her from falling apart while she dealt with everything, including two small, grieving children. After Jessica became the children's guardian, it was Buck who helped her move in and get settled. He had been a wonderful friend when Jessica had needed one, and was still one of her closest now.

Buck was also no stranger to tragedy and sorrow. After losing his wife fifteen years earlier, his only son, an FBI agent, was killed in the line of duty just four years ago. His twenty-seven years as a police officer, with the last eighteen as Chief of Police, had earned him the right to retire. He was planning to spend his retirement doing the things he enjoyed best; fishing and hiking on the river and mountains he had grown up in. He also acted as surrogate grandparent to both Jennifer and Thomas and loved them very much. He taught Tommy how to fish and treated him like the son he had lost. He also spent many nights and weekends watching Jennifer play volleyball. He was a loving and valued member of their very small family.

"I haven't retired just yet. The town council has asked me to assist our new Chief of Police while she gets her feet wet." As he spoke Buck turned toward a small woman standing slightly behind him. "Jessica, I would like you to meet Chief Caterina Andolino. Andy, this is one of the most talented artists you are ever going to meet and one of my very best friends."

"Hello, welcome to Cascade." Jessica turned to the woman and smiled. Her breath caught in her throat as she found herself looking directly into deep violet eyes, a color she had never seen before. The woman had coal black hair pulled back into a French braid and was drop dead gorgeous. Her niece was right, this woman couldn't be any taller than five and a half feet and slender, not at all what Jessica would have expected in a police officer. She just didn't fit the image of a tough law enforcement officer.

"Thank you, it's nice to meet you."

The tiny woman smiled as she spoke and moved toward Jessica to shake her hand, her voice deep and hoarse. Jessica found herself leaning toward her while she shook hands. The woman's grip was sure and strong; Jessica could feel the power in her grip. Jessica's stomach fluttered and flipped as she gazed at the incredibly beautiful woman. What was she doing reacting to a straight woman? Jessica knew better then that. She straightened up and away and avoided looking directly at her, trying to settle her nerves. She never, ever flirted with straight women; it would only get her into trouble. Besides, she had just met the woman; what was wrong with her?

"Jessica owns the Riverside Gallery in town and is our resident artist."

Buck didn't notice the blush that warmed Jessica's face. She glanced at Caterina and flushed even more. The woman was watching her intently; a slight smile on her face, her eyes sparkling, her long black lashes surrounding her unique eyes. Jessica felt like squirming, she was so uncomfortable.

"What type of art work do you do?"

"I carve in wood from pieces I find laying around on the mountain," Jessica responded. This woman was going to cause quite a stir in this small town. Her looks by themselves would set her apart, let alone the fact that she was the new Chief of Police. She would create quite a bit of activity and gossip.

"I'll have to make sure and see your work."

"It's well worth the trip," Buck remarked. "Well ladies, it looks like the show is about to start. Andy, we need to sit up in front, and Jessica, I'll catch up with you later.

"It was nice meeting you. I'll make a point of getting to your art gallery." Caterina spoke.

"It was nice meeting you and welcome again. You couldn't have picked a better town." Jessica smiled.

"I'm beginning to believe that."

Jessica could swear the woman was flirting with her. Either that or Jessica was looking for any reaction. She needed to get out more; she was overreacting in a big way and imagining things. She was so enthralled by the woman's looks that she hadn't even noticed what the woman was wearing. Jessica turned and watched her move to the front of the room with Buck. She had on a navy blue flannel pants suit, obviously tailored to fit her slender frame, as it fit her to perfection. Jessica couldn't help but watch her walk away and she was sure she wasn't the only one in the crowd who was appreciating her very fine figure.

"Please, everyone, let's settle down and take your seats, we have a lot to cover tonight," Mayor Little announced, as the noisy crowd of nearly seventy people took their seats along with Jessica.

"Hey Jessica, how are you?" Amanda Sanford, a very pregnant neighbor of hers spoke as she sat down beside her.

"Amanda, how are you doing? I'm just fine." Amanda was due to have her first child very soon.

"I'm good, big, but good." Amanda patted her stomach as she chuckled good-naturedly. "I'll be glad to get this part of the pregnancy over with," she whispered as the meeting began.

"The first order of business tonight up for discussion is our summer festival. Last year Jessica Newcomb did a terrific job of organizing the event. Now, we need a volunteer for this year's event. Are there any nominations?" Mayor Little addressed the crowd.

"I nominate Jessica again. She did a fantastic job!"

"I second the nomination."

Jessica wasn't sure who was speaking but she didn't mind. She had enjoyed working on the festival. It was a pleasurable challenge. Besides, the whole town pitched in to help.

"Anymore nominations?" No one else spoke up.

"Well Jessica, are you willing to take the job on again?"

"Sure, Mel, I'll do it," Jessica answered, with a quick smile. Her sister and brother-in-law had been very active in the festival and Jessica had continued the family tradition, involving Tommy and Jennifer in the activities. They looked forward to it every year.

"Good, that settles that. Jessica, will you let us know when the first planning meeting will be?" The mayor requested.

"I will, Mayor Little."

"Okay, on to other business. As you all know the town council approved the hiring of a new Chief of Police to replace Chief Buck, who retired this year after many years of wonderful service to our town. All of you attended his rather festive retirement party. This evening though, I have the pleasure of introducing our new Chief, Caterina Andolino. Ms. Andolino comes to us with over sixteen years of law enforcement experience, first with the FBI, and most recently with the San Francisco Police Department. Please put your hands together and welcome her to our nice town."

Jessica watched as Caterina gracefully stood up and acknowledged the applause from the audience. Her smile was genuine as she nodded her head in thanks to the enthusiastic welcome.

"She doesn't look like a cop," someone whispered from the back of the room. Jessica had to agree with the comment. She certainly was not what Jessica or anyone else expected.

"Chief Andolino, could you speak to the crowd?"

She nodded to the mayor and stepped up to the podium. "First of all, I would like to thank all of you for the warm welcome. You have a beautiful town and I am looking forward to living and working here. I realize that Chief Buck has done a wonderful job for many years and no one can replace him. I will rely on his expertise and advice as I learn this job and I am sure I have much to learn. Thank you for this opportunity and I look forward to serving all of you." She shook the mayor's hand and sat down.

Jessica found herself staring again. She wondered if the new Chief of Police was having the same effect on all of the men in the room. She was one of those women that oozed with innate sexuality. Her voice alone could turn a person inside out. She certainly was having an immediate affect on Jessica.

"Thank you, Chief Andolino, the town and I are very happy to have you here in Cascade."

The rest of the meeting went quickly as several items of town business were dispensed with. Jessica found it very hard to pay attention listening half-heartedly to the discussions as she watched the back of this new woman. It was an hour and a half later before the meeting finally ended and people prepared to leave.

"Looking forward to helping out on the festival this year."

"So am I, Abe." Jessica responded as she joined the milling group as they headed for the door.

Abe and his wife Tammy ran the local hardware store. They worked very hard every year at the festival and donated many of the supplies to insure its success. They had lived for over thirty years in the town of Cascade, raising three children. They were now the proud grandparents of five grandchildren who visited them quite often. They were founding members of the small community.

Many others came up to offer their assistance with this year's celebration, as Jessica made her way out of the hall, and she promised to notify everyone of her first planning meeting. She temporarily forgot her fascination with the new, gorgeous, Police Chief as she looked for Jennifer. As usual, she would be running late, so Jessica resigned herself to a little wait on the front steps of the meeting hall. She was used to waiting for her niece.

"Jessica, do you need a ride home?" Chief Buck asked as he walked over to her. Jessica could have groaned when she saw who was with him.

"No thanks Buck, Jennifer is coming from volleyball practice, and as usual, she's running a little behind."

"We'll wait with you. I'd love to say hello to Jennifer. Andy, she's the young woman you met yesterday who asked if she could interview you for the high school paper."

"I remember, tall, blond, full of energy, and very inquisitive. I understand she's your niece."

"Yes." Jessica looked at Chief Andolino as she spoke, and the now familiar flutter began in her stomach. She needed to get a grip, this was ridiculous. She couldn't react like this every time she ran into the woman. Jessica couldn't remember the last time she had felt such a strong reaction to a woman, and it certainly wasn't very appropriate.

"Jessica moved here seven years ago to raise her niece and nephew, and she's done a damn good job. Tommy is a junior at Cal-Berkeley and is getting straight A's. He's studying environmental science. Jennifer, you have had the pleasure of meeting. She is graduating this year from high school." Buck sounded very much like a proud parent.

"They sound like terrific kids." Chief Andolino smiled as Buck bragged.

"They are, sometimes despite my raising them." Jennifer chuckled. "I had to learn as I went along, I wasn't very well prepared." She grinned, as she remembered all her mistakes.

"There's Jennifer now." As Buck spoke, Jessica found herself smiling at Chief Andolino. She really was incredibly beautiful. Buck walked over to speak with Jennifer.

"Well, I'd better get going. Good luck, Chief Andolino," Jessica said.

"Please, call me Andy, and thank you, I am looking forward to making a life here." Jessica could swear the woman's eyes twinkled at her. Jessica was in deep trouble!

"Come on, Aunt Jess!" Jennifer yelled from the car.

"Well, I'll see you around." Jessica spoke over her shoulder as she headed toward the car. "See you later, Buck."

"Bye, sweetie." He hugged her tightly. "I'll give you a call next week, maybe we can get in a hike and pick up some wood."

"That would be perfect, Buck." She climbed into the Bronco.

"Bye, Buck!" Jennifer yelled as she pulled away. Jessica took one last glance toward Andy. Andy was gazing directly at Jessica as they pulled away and it made Jessica blush, heat rushing to the center of her body.

"Well, what do you think of her? She's pretty cool huh, and she's so pretty."

"Yes, she is that." Jessica agreed with her niece. "How was volleyball practice?"

Jessica's question succeeded in changing the subject, as Jennifer chatted about volleyball and the upcoming tournament. Jessica was grateful. For some reason she did not want to discuss what she thought about Chief Andolino. She wasn't sure how she felt about this new woman. Jennifer managed to carry on her one-sided conversation the whole way home, allowing Jessica to absorb her reaction and settle her nerves.

"Are you going to work in the studio tonight?" Jennifer inquired as they both entered their home.

"I thought I would. What have you got planned?"

"I've got to finish some homework. Can I come work in the studio?"

"Of course you can, I'd love the company."

For the past seven years both children would do their homework in the studio while Jessica worked on her carvings. She loved their company and it was how they had formed their family as they spent their time together. It was when they talked about everything, made family decisions, and shared their lives. Jessica treasured her remaining time with Jennifer because she knew it would be ending soon. Once Jennifer left for college she would have her own life, just like her brother. They were both growing up so fast to Jessica and the feeling was bittersweet. She was so proud of both of them; they were becoming wonderful young adults. On the other hand, she would miss their company. They would both be gone to college and Jessica would be alone in the very large house.

"Go get your pajamas on and meet me in the studio. I'll make us some tea."

"Okay, and Aunt Jess?"

"What, honey?"

"I love you," Jennifer exclaimed as she raced up the stairs to change her clothes.

"I love you too!" Jessica called after her niece, smiling.

The remainder of the evening was quiet as Jennifer worked on an English paper and Jessica put the final touches on her latest work. She wanted to put the carving in the shop on Saturday. The woman's features glowed as Jessica polished the wood bringing out the grain. It wasn't often that Jessica found the perfect wood to match her vision. This was one of those times. The work had taken many months to complete while it had taken on the image that Jessica had previously committed to paper. It was a very special piece, one that Jessica was extremely proud of.

"Aunt Jessica, I think this is the best carving you have ever done." Jennifer had taken a break from her paper and was quietly watching her aunt work.

"Thanks, Jen. I agree with you. It turned out better then I expected."

"She looks mysterious and knowing."

"Thanks, honey." Jessica smiled at her niece. She couldn't have described it better. Jessica had captured the look of womanly awakening in the bowed face, grinding and polishing it until it gleamed.

The next morning, Jessica rose early to get a run in before she ate breakfast with Jennifer. Some mornings, Jennifer joined her as she jogged a couple of miles along the river's edge. Not only was it a beautiful setting with the river noise in the background, and the magnificent mountain behind it with old growth timber looming tall into the sky, she also rarely met anyone on her runs. It was her solitary time when she could relax and let everything go as she enjoyed the beauty around her. She put on a hooded sweatshirt, shorts, laced her shoes, and was out the door, after reminding Jennifer it was time to get up. The first mile was nice and slow as she warmed up from the slight chill in the air. Even though it was early March, there was still a winter feel in the morning and a mist hung heavily over the river casting everything into a dreamy state. Jessica loved running; she could think while she ran, her thoughts clear and uncluttered as she felt the rush of adrenalin course through her body.

While she ran, her mind filtered through memories of her life and the few relationships she had been involved in. It had been several years since she had seen anyone seriously, and even that had been a very short involvement. Jessica had met the woman at the home of a friend of hers' where she had been invited for dinner. The woman was a high school guidance counselor and for several months Jessica would drive into Seattle to see her. It continued until Jessica had been forced to make a decision. They had stopped seeing each other because of Jessica's self-imposed rule. As long as her niece and nephew lived at home she would not have anyone over to the house to spend the night. It wasn't that she was dishonest with the woman, she was always up front with anyone she dated. She just hadn't felt it was fair to the kids when they were younger to bring someone else into their newly formed family. They had enough to deal with in keeping their small family together.

After several years of following that rule, she continued to live that way because it was easier. Over the years, she had introduced a couple of women to her niece and nephew but, to be honest, Jessica had not met anyone she had fallen in love with. She knew she needed that passion in her life, she just wasn't sure where she would find it, and it had been secondary to raising Jennifer and Tommy.

Jessica's solitary run cleared her mind of any worries and she headed for home. She would get Jennifer off to school, catch up on some paperwork from the gallery, and finish her latest carving. It would be ready for display on Saturday, as she had planned. She walked through the front door kicking her shoes off and heading for the kitchen.

"Jennifer, hurry up, you are going to be late for school, and please take the car. I need the Bronco."

"Okay, I'll be right down." Jessica could hear her tripping down the stairs as she laid out a bowl of cereal for herself and Jennifer.

Her niece had on a short jean skirt and a red sweater, her hair pulled back into a ponytail, like any typical teenage girl. She reminded Jessica so much of her mother, it brought tears to Jessica's eyes. Jennifer had the same coloring and height and some of her mannerisms were so similar that at times it made Jessica very sad. She still missed her sister very much.

"Will you be home for dinner tonight?"

"Yes, but I have a date, remember?" Jennifer responded as she rapidly ate her breakfast.

"How could I forget? It's that good looking one, what's his name? There have been so many." Jessica teased her niece affectionately.

"Aunt Jess, his name is Todd, you know what it is." Jennifer laughed. "See you later, and have a terrific day."

"You too."

Jessica fondly watched her niece go out the front door, her pack on her back. Jessica straightened up the kitchen and went to her office. She had lots of paperwork, and she had put it off long enough. It was a thoroughly pleasant day as she worked steadily until late afternoon.

Friday night was fairly quiet for Jessica. Dinner with Jennifer went by very quickly, as preparations for her date were Jennifer's biggest priority. She and Todd had been dating sporadically for several months, due to the fact they both were extremely busy their senior year of high school. Todd played football, basketball, and baseball, and worked part time for the local hardware store. He was earning as much money as possible for college. He was counting on earning a scholarship but still needed to make sure he wasn't a burden to his family. His parents had three other children they would have to get through college. He was a very responsible, hardworking young man and Jessica was very impressed with him.

Between Jennifer's volleyball and busy schedule, she and Todd went out two to three times a month. Lately, they had been seeing more of each other and Jessica knew Jennifer liked him very much. Jessica thought very highly of Todd but she also knew that Jennifer was not ready for anything too serious. She and Jennifer talked about her feelings in depth. She and Jennifer could talk about anything, and Jessica was continually impressed with Jennifer's maturity about most things. Jennifer didn't want anything to interfere with her first year of college and she was single-minded in that goal. Even though Jennifer acted like a young adult a lot of the time, she could still behave like a young teenager, silly and immature, but most of the time she was just a great kid.

After Jennifer left with Todd to catch a movie, Jessica turned on a CD of her favorite music, poured a glass of wine, and began sketching her plans for a new carving. She had several nice pieces of wood to work with, but she needed to replenish her supply. Buck's offer of a hike in the hills was timely. His knowledge of the mountains and hiking paths was legendary, and Jessica knew that they would find many good pieces to work with. She and the kids had spent many days and nights hiking and camping with Buck in the woods. She closed up the studio when Jennifer came home from her date, and prepared for bed. Both of them had a long day Saturday with Jennifer's volleyball tournament and Jessica's working at the gallery for the afternoon and evening.

Chapter Two

"Jennifer, get yourself down here. We need to go now!" As usual, her niece was running very late.

"I'm ready, I'm ready." Jennifer laughed as she raced down the stairs in her volleyball uniform.

"Are you sure you can get a ride home?"

"I'm sure, don't worry. Vicki's parents are going to give me one. Actually, Vicki asked me to stay overnight with a couple of other girls from the volleyball team. Can I?"

"I don't see why not. I'll be working until nine at the gallery. What about dinner?"

"I think we're going to order pizza and watch movies at Vicki's."

"Okay, let's go before you're late for the tournament," Jessica reminded her as she headed for the door.

"Aunt Jessica, you look very pretty."

"Thanks, doll."

For some reason, Jessica had felt like dressing up. She had on a long flowing navy blue dress with bright red and yellow splotches of color, a red blazer, and matching red sandals. Whenever she worked at the gallery she made a point of looking a little on the professional side. Her sister had always insisted that her customers deserved her looking her very best, and it didn't matter if she had one customer or fifty. Jessica was continuing the tradition in her own way and whenever she worked, she too tried to dress up. The only noticeable difference in the gallery from her sister's running of it and now, was that instead of one or two of Jessica's carvings on display, she usually had four or five at any given time. Her sister would have loved it that Jessica was able to show more of her work. She had been Jennifer's most loyal fan and ardent follower. She had always encouraged Jessica to put more effort into her carving.

"Aunt Jessica, would you help me fill out my college scholarship application? I need to get it to the coach by next week. He needs all the information by the beginning of next month."

"Certainly, but Jennifer, I don't want you to worry about your college money. Your parents put money in a college fund for you and Tommy."

"I know, but if I can get this scholarship, it will help."

Jennifer would always do anything to contribute anyway she could. She had been working part time at the gallery since junior high to earn spending money. It had always been important to her to help out the family and Jessica welcomed the effort.

"Have I told you today what a terrific kid you are?"

"Not today, and thanks. There's Vicki and her parents," Jennifer remarked with a quick grin as they pulled into the high school parking lot.

"Good luck, sweetie."

"Thanks, Aunt Jess. I'll see you later." Jennifer hugged her quickly and bolted out of the car.

"You girls be good tonight!" Jessica requested loud enough for her niece and Vicki to hear.

"We will, promise." The two girls ran into the gym, giggling as Jessica joined Vicki's parents.

"Jessica, how are you doing?" Jack Jergens, Vicki's father inquired. "Can you believe those girls? It's hard to believe they're graduating in a couple of months. It seems like just yesterday they were little girls." It was a refreshing thing to see a six-foot-five, two hundred and thirty-pound contractor showing such sweet sadness concerning his daughter.

"Jack wants to believe he can hang on to our daughter as long as possible. It's hard for him to realize she's becoming a young adult." Nancy smiled as she slipped her arm around her husband's waist, hugging him tightly as she gazed lovingly at him.

"I know what you mean. Every day I look at Jennifer, I am astounded at how quickly time flies. We sure are lucky to have them grow up to be such terrific young women. You sure should be proud of Vicki. Jennifer told me she is applying to the University of Washington."

"Vicki wanted to go out of state for college but she really wants to go to medical school and the University has a great reputation. I'm hoping she gets in to the University, it will keep her closer to home." Vicki's father was very proud of her. Jessica could hear it in his voice. He had good reason to be. She was a very smart, beautiful, young girl, and Jennifer's best friend.

"Where is Jennifer going to college? Has she decided?" Nancy asked, as the three of them entered the crowded and noisy gym.

"She is applying to Berkeley so she could go to the same school as Tommy, and she also applied to the University. She is currently being considered for a volleyball scholarship at both schools. I'd hate to have her move to California but if that's where she wants to go, I guess I will have to accept it. I'll sure miss her."

Jessica felt lonely already. It had been very hard on both Jennifer and Jessica when Tommy left for college. She had no idea how she would deal with the both of them being gone.

"I know what you mean," Nancy agreed patting Jessica on the arm. Nancy was as affectionate and loving as her husband.

"Well ladies, let's worry about that later. We're here to watch a volleyball tournament," Jack reminded them. "Let's find some good seats."

Jessica followed the two of them up into the bleachers, but her thoughts were still on their conversation. She really would miss Jennifer. She and Tommy had been such an enormous part of her life. She wasn't sure how she was going to fill the void with the two of them gone.

The rest of the morning sped by, as the three of them became enthusiastic fans of volleyball. It was a close-fought match that went right down to the bitter end, but Jennifer and Vicki's team lost the last game by three points, a disappointing battle. The next match didn't start until three, so the five of them decided to get a bite to eat before Jessica had to go to work. The girls moaned a little over their loss and then, as the two of them were known to do, talked about their next match, school, and boys, mostly boys. The three adults listened with much amusement as the two girls chattered, oblivious to the adults at the table.

"Good luck, Jennifer, Vicki. Jenn, call me later and tell me how you guys do." Jessica requested as she prepared to leave for the gallery. "And don't drive Jack and Nancy crazy tonight."

"We won't. I promise, Aunt Jess, and I'll call you later for sure. Love you."

"Love you too, be good, doll." Jennifer hugged her quickly.

While Jessica drove the three blocks to the gallery, she couldn't help but smile. The two, almost grown-up women, had acted like typical happy, very young girls at lunch and it warmed her heart.

"Hey boss, how goes the volleyball tournament?" Loren Blakely asked, as Jessica walked in the front door of the gallery, her latest carving in her arms.

"Not too well, they lost by three points in the final game. They played very well though, and it was fun to watch. Their next match is at three, and depending on if they win or lose they either play another match later tonight or early tomorrow morning."

"I'm sorry they lost. Is that your latest work? Let me see." Loren loved Jessica's carvings and was almost as excited as Jessica when she finished one.

"Yes, help me find a spot for it."

"Right here on this pedestal."

"What happened to the vase?"

"A young couple purchased it this morning. The gallery has actually been busier than usual today. We sold some jewelry earlier, the vase, one painting, and two of the pencil sketches."

"That is busy, Loren, good job."

"Let me see it, please?" Jessica placed her work on the pedestal and pulled the cloth covering away. "Oh my, Jessica it is fantastic! You are amazing!" Loren exclaimed as she slowly circled around the carving.

Loren continued gazing at the piece, her eyes taking in the work of art. Jessica had carved the upper torso of a woman in relief on a large block of wood. She had left the bark on in places to use as shadow and accents, the woman's arms wrapped around her upper body, and her head bowed in prayer. The hair of the woman was close cropped and curly emphasizing her facial features, her mouth carved with a slight smile, almost as if she had just been told a pleasant secret. Jessica had sanded and polished the wood to a smooth finish so the carving glowed when the light hit it, glistening with beauty.

"I think it's my favorite!"

"It's one of mine, too," Jessica admitted as she grinned. "Okay, tell me what price I should put on it and then get out of here, your husband is waiting."

"Let's see, your last one sold for twenty-eight hundred dollars, so let's put thirty-five hundred and see what happens."

"Thirty-five hundred seems pretty steep but I'll make up a label. Now, you go home, you are officially off, beat it!" Jessica grinned as she pushed her partner toward the door.

"Okay, okay, I'm gone. I'll be back tomorrow." Loren laughed as she left.

Jessica's sister hired Loren when she had first opened her gallery. Between the two of them, they had built up the business until they were making a profit. Loren's children were now grown and out on their own and the gallery had become one of her passions. When Angela was killed, Loren grieved as heavily as Jessica, and the two of them had healed together. It hadn't been a year later that Jessica had turned the management of the business over to Loren, and she had taken to it like a duck to water. Due to Loren's efforts, the gallery had remained very successful despite the remote location. Jessica constantly congratulated herself for the smart business move, though she could hardly take full credit for it.

Jessica did work two to three days a week to give Loren some time off to spend with her husband. She didn't need to work, but found the time at the gallery very enjoyable. The death of her sister and brother-in-law had been devastating but, due to the gallery and the foresight of her brother-in-law, Jessica and the children had been left financially well off. Thankfully, Jessica's career as a lawyer in San Francisco had paid well for over twelve years and she had invested wisely. This also added to their financial stability. Quitting her career as a lawyer to raise the children had not been a tough decision and she had not hesitated in making it. Periodically, she did a little law work for people from town- wills, contracts, and other things just to keep from getting rusty, but she didn't miss being a full-time lawyer.

Her change of lifestyle had actually freed her up to pursue her carving full time. Up until then it had been little more than a part-time hobby. The years of work on her carvings were starting to pay off as more and more of her artwork was in demand by collectors from Seattle. Several of her pieces were prominently displayed in the buildings of major corporations. Out of tragedy and sadness had come much happiness for Jessica and her small family, and she thanked God every day for taking care of them.

The opening of the gallery door disturbed her thoughts as a small group of young college students entered who appeared more interested in browsing than buying. Jessica labeled her piece, hesitating briefly before writing the price of thirty-five hundred dollars. She then settled down at the desk and began working on a stack of paperwork. She was good at keeping the books and paying the bills, so she and Loren had decided that was what she would do while Loren would handle the day-to-day details around the marketing side of the business. It was a very successful partnership for the two of them and for the gallery.

The afternoon proved to be a quiet one, with an occasional browser and two sales, which was pretty usual for early spring. The tourist season would officially begin in about a month and sales would be much more numerous. Tourists provided over three-quarters of the total sales. Summer weekends could get pretty heavy as people from the city browsed through the gallery looking for bargains. The telephone ringing in the background disturbed her concentration.

"Riverside Gallery, Jessica speaking."

"Guess what, we won!" Her niece's voice announced, bursting with excitement.

"Congratulations. When is your next match?"

"Tonight at seven."

"I doubt if I can get there in time to watch. Good luck honey, and let me know when you play tomorrow."

"I'll call the answering machine at home."

"Great, play well, and have a good time tonight. Get some sleep, Jenn."

"I will, see you tomorrow, love you."

"Love you."

Jennifer sounded excited and full of energy but Jessica knew her well; Jennifer did not function with too little sleep. She would be exhausted by Sunday night with all the volleyball and the slumber party. Jessica settled back down to work on the books. Since she was going to be there until closing at nine o'clock, she might as well finish what she was doing.

Around seven, Jessica began to get a little hungry. She was just about to go next door to the deli for a sandwich when the front door opened. Jessica did a double take when she realized who was walking in, her stomach jumping nervously. Wearing a faded pair of jeans, a blue silk blouse, and an old letterman's jacket, the new Chief of Police entered the gallery. Her hair was down, reaching just above her shoulders, a shiny curtain of blue-black color. Again, Jessica's stomach flipped as she stared straight into the deep violet eyes of the gorgeous Police Chief.

"Hello, I saw you from the window and I decided to stop in." Her soft husky voice floated across the room as Jessica stood rooted to the same spot.

"Come in, please have a look around. Are you beginning to get settled?" Jessica responded, trying very hard to keep her voice calm. This was ridiculous, she wasn't a teenager. Reacting to this woman like that was certainly unacceptable and uncomfortable, but she seemed to have no control over her reactions.

"I am. I am taking a break from unpacking to pick up some groceries. The one thing I don't have yet is food." A warm chuckle followed this remark as Andy grinned.

"Where are you living?" Jessica asked as Andy wandered around looking at the art on display.

"I am renting a house. I believe it's called the Jenkins Place, on the river."

"The tree house, it's beautiful. I live about a quarter of a mile away. You couldn't have a better view the mountains and river."

"The tree house?"

"That's what everyone in town calls it. It looks like it has been built high in the trees. When it was first being constructed, it was quite a show place. Everyone from town would drive by to see the progress."

"It still is pretty spectacular. I was surprised at how inexpensive the rent was."

Andy stepped up to Jessica's new carving. "This is yours." It wasn't a question, it was a statement, as she slowly circled the piece, her eyes locked on the graceful carving.

"Yes." Jessica blushed with embarrassment. She normally didn't care that much about the opinion of others she didn't know, but this one was different. "I just put it on display today." Jessica resisted the urge to ask her if she liked it.

"Buck told me you were good, but this is not just good, it's incredible." Andy's voice didn't rise above a whisper, and Jessica could barely hear her, but the affect on her was explosive. "Can I touch her?"

Jessica didn't realize that she was holding her breath as she moved to stand next to Andy, whose eyes were still on the carving. "Sure, go ahead."

Jessica watched as Andy's right hand reached out to touch the face of the statue, where she ran her index finger down the cheek. Jessica's face flooded with warmth. It was as if Andy had touched her directly. She could almost feel the finger sliding down her cheek, heat rippling through her body. It was all she could do to keep from moaning out loud.

"It's amazing," Andy whispered as she pulled her hand away.

"Thank you, it's one my very favorites."

"You have other pieces of your work here?" Andy turned to Jessica, her violet eyes large and luminous.

"There are three others in the back of the room." Jessica jumped as the gallery telephone rang. "Feel free to wander around." Jessica hurried to answer the telephone, irritated with the interruption. She wanted to watch Andy as she looked at Jessica's other works.

"Riverside Gallery, may I help you?" Jessica tried to follow Andy with her eyes, but her view was blocked, increasing her level of impatience.

"Jessica, it's Loren, I forgot to tell you something important. The McGraw Corporation is sending a designer over Monday afternoon to look for display pieces to put in their lobby. They are interested in purchasing one or two of your carvings. Would you like to be there?"

"Loren, you're supposed be off this evening. If you need me to be there, I certainly will."

"I'm sure they would like to meet the artist. They are coming at three."

"I'll be there. Now go have some fun with that husband of yours."

"I plan on it. See you Monday."

Jessica had her back turned away from the main gallery as she spoke. She turned around to find Andy watching her intently, not three feet from her. Jessica flooded with new warmth as she gazed at Andy.

"You have a nice place here. Your collection of artwork is impressive." Andy smiled at Jessica. "Being this far away from Seattle, do you get a lot of business?"

"During the winter and early spring it can be a little slow, like now, but come summer there's a steady stream of tourists and it gets extremely busy. We also have our fair share of corporate clients." Jessica's stomach growled as she spoke. "Excuse me, I haven't eaten since early this morning." She laughed nervously. "I need to step next-door and get a sandwich. Care to join me?"

"I'd love to."

"Great, let me get my keys and put the sign up." Jessica grabbed her wallet and led the way to the front door. "You are going to love the food next door at the Cascade Deli. It's one of my very favorite places." She locked the door behind them.

"Your favorite place, huh?" Andy's eyes and voice told Jessica that she was being teased. Andy's eyebrows rose as she entered the very tiny shop.

"You just wait," Jessica teased her back. "The food here is better than sex." As the words came out of Jessica's mouth, she froze. Where had that come from? She could have just died of embarrassment; here she was bantering with the Chief of Police.

"Oh, I doubt it's better than good sex." Andy chuckled, as she looked directly at Jessica.

Jessica refrained from comment; embarrassment flooding her face as she jerked her head away from Andy. Was this woman really flirting with her? Did she know Jessica was gay? Jessica could usually tell if a woman was a lesbian; it was a sixth sense that some lesbians thought they had mastered. She always thought she had it until tonight-it was failing her big time.

"Hello Jessica, what can I get for you today?"

"Hi Rachel, how is business?"

"It was busy earlier, but it's slowed down a bit now. I've only got one other person working tonight so I'm glad we're not swamped."

Rachel looked harried as she pushed her dark brown hair back into her bun. Short and stocky, Rachel and her partner Denise had owned the delicatessen for over eighteen years. Denise worked during the week as an architect in Seattle, and on the weekend she could be found in the deli helping out. The place had been a dream of Rachel's, and Denise worked hard to make sure it would happen. They were two of Jessica's closest friends and two of the nicest people in town.

"Rachel, I'd like you to meet our new Police Chief Catarina Andolino, Andy this is Rachel Viachi."

"A fellow Italian. Welcome, what a beautiful name." Rachel grinned.

"Thank you, my friends call me Andy. It's nice to meet you."

"Denise, we have company, can you come out here?" Rachel called.

"Just a minute, I'll be right there." A voice could be heard echoing from the kitchen.

"What can I get for the two of you?"

"I would like your chicken salad sandwich and a bowl of your barley soup to go, please." Jessica ordered her favorite meal. "And a cup of your great coffee."

"You got it. And how about our gorgeous Italian Police Chief?" Rachel didn't blink an eye, as she looked Andy up and down with obvious pleasure.

"Hey Jessica, how are you doing?" Rachel's partner burst through the kitchen doors, a large white apron tied around her waist. Where Rachel was short and stocky, Denise was tall and slender, with short gray hair and wire frame glasses. She looked like the architect that she was.

"Terrific Denise, how are you? Is Rachel working you too hard?" Jessica was glad for the interruption, Andy's face had blushed with embarrassment when Rachel had made her remark and Jessica had turned red for her.

"Like a slave." Denise grinned at Jessica.

"Give it up, girls," Rachel advised with a shake of her hand. "Okay Chief, what can I get for you? These women won't give me a rest."

Andy grinned with humor. "I'll have a bowl of the same soup and a turkey breast sandwich. I'll take some iced tea if you have any."

"We've got it. I'll have your orders ready to go in ten minutes. Have a seat while you wait."

"So you're the new Chief of Police. Welcome to Cascade, you'll love the place." Denise spoke to Andy as she and Jessica sat down to wait. She also checked Andy out but not quite so obviously.

"Thank you. My name's Andy, and I think I'm going to love it here. Everyone is so friendly and the place is beautiful."

"That's why Rachel and I moved here. We fell in love with the place over twenty years ago, and we have been here ever since. I guarantee you once you live here you won't want to leave. Besides, where else would you find such a talented, beautiful artist and a New York deli all in one town?"

Jessica's face flushed with warmth and embarrassment as Andy looked directly at her. "I couldn't agree more." Jessica's stomach was doing flips.

"Here is your food, ladies. I put a couple of extra things in there for you. Enjoy your dinner."

"What's our bill, Rachel?" Jessica inquired, still rattled by Andy.

"Let's see, that total is twelve eighty-seven."

"This should cover it, thanks Rachel, Denise." Jessica handed over several bills. "What time are you two closing up shop tonight?"

"I think we'll shut the doors at eight." Rachel answered. "Denise and I have a date with each other tonight, and nothing is going to interrupt our plans."

"It's been three weeks since we had our last date," Denise informed them.

"Well, we'd better get out of here so you can lock up." Jessica laughed. She was used to these two and their dates. "Thanks again."

"It was nice to meet the two of you, enjoy your evening." Andy smiled.

"Thanks, we plan to," Denise responded. "It was nice meeting you."

"They seem like very nice women," Andy remarked as she and Jessica returned to the gallery.

"They are. Everyone loves them. I consider them two of my best friends." Jessica unlocked the door. "Let's eat over here at the desk."

"Here, let me help," Andy volunteered, taking their bag of food from Jessica.

"Thanks, let me clear these papers out of the way."

The two of them worked in silence, as Jessica moved things around and Andy pulled items out of the bag, setting their makeshift table. Their fingers brushed against each other as they worked, and Jessica was extremely aware of Andy. She found it hard to look at her.

"This soup smells delicious," Andy said as she removed the lids from their bowls. What do I owe you for dinner?'

"You don't owe me a thing, and the soup is delicious. Everything at the deli is good. Whenever I work late I sneak over there for something."

"Do you work late often? Oh, look at what we've got here." Andy grinned as she held up two very large brownies. "Chocolate."

"Oh, my favorite! Thanks Rachel."

"Mine, too. Chocolate is my biggest vice." Andy grinned wickedly at Jessica.

"You have vices?" Jessica couldn't help but tease her back. " Maybe I should take mine now." She leaned over the desk, reaching for one the brownies.

"I have a couple of other vices. Don't you have any?" Andy put her arms behind her back so Jessica would have to reach for the goodies. She had leaned over to respond to Jessica, their faces inches apart.

"I have a few that I like to indulge in occasionally." Jessica boldly flirted with her. Andy's violet eyes were flecked with silver specks, her dark lashes thick and long. Jessica was amazed how bold she was being but what she really wanted to do was kiss Andy's luscious lips. She straightened up quickly before she followed through with her thoughts. Making a pass at the town's new Police Chief was not a smart move. "Are you going to share those brownies with me?"

"I guess I should share since you bought dinner. It's the least I can do." Andy grinned impishly as she handed one of the brownies to Jessica. Boy, Andy was some charmer.

"Thank you, let's eat." Jessica smiled, sat back in her chair, and started eating her soup. She was too nervous to do much else. Andy did the same.

"You were right, this is the best soup I've ever tasted."

"Rachel used to be a chef in Seattle before she and Denise started the business here. I've tried almost everything she makes and it's all terrific."

"What does Denise do for living?"

"She's an architect in Seattle."

"That's a long commute every day."

"I think she works at home a lot. There are many people from Cascade who make the commute to Seattle. Living here with all this beauty makes it worthwhile."

"I can't wait to do some hiking. Buck has always bragged about this place."

"He would know. He's lived here for over forty years. How did you meet Buck? He told me he has known you for quite a long time."

"I met him sixteen years ago when I was going through the FBI academy. His son, Ben, and I went through the academy together. Ben and I eventually became partners and worked together for a little over three years. We were best friends until he was killed. Buck and I have remained friends."

"I'm so sorry, I didn't know you knew Ben. He was such a good man." Jessica couldn't help but empathize with Andy. She knew what it was like to lose someone you love and she had liked Buck's son very much.

"He was my best friend and my partner. He was such a good person, and a great agent." Andy stopped speaking for moment, her eyes showing her sorrow. Jessica reached out and clasped her hand in her own.

Andy acknowledged her by gently squeezing in return, her fingers wrapped around Jessica's.

"The worst of it was, I wasn't there when it happened. I had taken the night off to go on a date, of all things. Ben and three other agents responded to a call for assistance with the San Francisco Police Department. They had found what they thought was a group of gun smugglers. It ended up in a gun battle and Ben was shot in the neck. He bled to death before he made it to the hospital. I should have been there. Instead, I was trying to save an already doomed relationship."

"It certainly wasn't Ben's fault or yours. You take risks in your line of work. It goes with the job." Jessica gazed at the beautiful woman who obviously still grieved.

"My mind knows that, but my heart still tells me differently."

"That's because you loved him." Jessica smiled at her.

"I did love him, and I miss him. I could talk to him about anything." She smiled back. "Enough about me, tell me about yourself."

"Oh, there isn't that much to tell," Jessica responded self-consciously, pulling her hand away from Andy's. "I moved here seven years ago to take care of my niece and nephew. My sister and her husband were killed in a plane crash here in the mountains." Jessica could speak about it now without much heartache.

"You do know what it's like to lose someone you love. I'm sorry for your loss, you have obviously done a terrific job of raising your niece. According to Buck, both kids are wonderful."

"They're both fantastic, despite my mistakes. Tommy is doing well at Berkeley. He's in his junior year of college and is studying to be an environmental scientist and an engineer, getting almost straight A's, I might add."

"Good for him. Berkeley can be a tough college."

"Then there is Jennifer. She's graduating from high school this year and has applied to Berkeley and the University of Washington. She will likely be receiving a volleyball scholarship since they have been recruiting her. We are waiting to hear. She wants to be a journalist, as you will find out when she interviews you for the school paper. She's ruthless when she wants answers to her questions and she has lots of them. She was very excited to meet you, the first woman Police Chief for the town Cascade."

"She won't find my life too exciting, I'm afraid."

"I don't know about that, a woman Police Chief, and you look pretty impressive to me," Jessica teased Andy.

"Why thank you, ma'am," Andy responded with a southern drawl.

"Oh my, look what time it is. It's nine-thirty. I can't believe it! I had better lock up."

"Can I help?"

"Sure, could you grab our dinner stuff and put it in this bag. Loren will kill me if I leave this place in a mess."

"Who's Loren?"

"She's my partner and she manages the gallery for me. She usually works on Saturdays but took the night off to go out with her husband. I usually work two to three days a week so she can have some time away from the gallery. I work more hours when the tourist season starts."

"Saturday night must be date night in Cascade. Everyone seems to be on a date."

"Everyone but you," Jessica reminded her.

"I don't know about you, but I had a terrific evening, good food, and great company. It beats unpacking boxes any day." Andy's violet eyes twinkled at her. Jessica was beginning to love those eyes.

"I had a wonderful time. I hope I didn't keep you from anything too important." Jessica walked Andy out the front door. She locked it behind them.

"What could have been more important than this." Andy slipped her arm through Jessica's and squeezed.

"I can't think of anything right at this moment." Jessica was telling the truth. She really liked Andy and it might become a very serious problem.

"This is my car. Where's yours?" Andy inquired.

"Right over there. Thanks for having dinner with me."

"You're welcome. Maybe we can do it again some time, my treat."

"I'd like that."

"Goodnight, then."

"Goodnight, Andy."

Jessica hurried to her car. She needed to get away from this woman before she made a fool out of herself. As Jessica drove home she chided herself for responding to Andy. She must be out of her mind! Once she pulled into her driveway, she watched Andy's car drive past her home. Not only would Jessica see her around town but she lived a quarter of a mile down the road from her. She would need to get over this attraction and quickly.

Later that evening, after spending a couple of hours in the studio, Jessica crawled into her bed. Her thoughts immediately turned to earlier in the evening and her reactions to Andy. If she didn't have Jennifer to worry about, she would probably think of pursuing something with Andy and just take her chances to see what might happen. She had always been so careful and discreet about her relationships in order to protect the kids from any gossip. Besides that, their grandparents on Thomas's side had made it very clear how unhappy they were with the decision of her guardianship of the kids. Even though it had been legally taken care of, they had threatened to take Jessica to court and fight for custody if she gave them any reason to, like a very obvious lesbian relationship. She had bowed to their wishes in order not to make waves.

It was amazing to her that those two people had raised such an open-minded loving son. He and Angela would have been very angry over their demands. Both Angela and Thomas had been supportive of Jessica, encouraging her to bring a partner with her on visits, and their children had always been told the truth. Jessica raised Jennifer and Tommy in the same open and honest way that their parents had. In fact, the last time Tommy had come home for a visit he had encouraged

Jessica to get out more. He felt she needed someone to share her life with. She promised him she would, but time and that underlying threat from their grandparents had done the job. Even though they had both passed away, Jessica still felt compelled to keep her promise. She would do nothing while Jessica was at home to jeopardize her security.

However, that wasn't the only reason Jessica avoided involvement. She began to panic whenever a woman wanted more from the relationship than she was willing to give. What if she fell in love with someone and something happened to them? She didn't think she could stand the loss. She still grieved over the loss of her sister and brother-in-law. She didn't think her heart could survive losing a woman she loved above all else.

Jessica's love life, if you to could call it that, was limited to short unfulfilling episodes. If a woman asked for anything more than a casual encounter, Jessica walked away. She had not met anyone that made her want to change her life or her behavior and she wasn't sure she ever would. The woman would have to be very special.

Her immediate attraction to Andy told her something, though. It would not be a casual encounter with her, if by some chance Andy were gay. Jessica needed to ignore her reactions and let it go. Nevertheless, even as her mind told her that, her body spoke differently to her as she drifted off to sleep while visions of Andy in various stages of undress kept her restless and unable to stop tossing and turning.

Chapter Three

It was several weeks later and Jessica had, true to her word, avoided any encounters with Andy besides the occasional glimpse of her car. The truth be told, according to the town talk, Andy had been spending long hours getting to know her small police department and all it required of her. She had even spent the last five nights working the graveyard shift in order to understand what her small crew went through. She had made it clear from day one that she would be put on rotation for all shifts. This was new to all of them, since Buck had only worked in the daytime. After working all night on patrol, Andy would spend several hours in her office learning to deal with any paperwork or other office requirements. Her assistant, Marta Rasmussen had immediately adopted Andy, reminding her to eat and to go home for some much-needed sleep. Marta was also very competent and organized, and Andy recognized early on that Marta actually ran the place like clockwork.

There were three officers who comprised the full-time department and six part-time officers. One full-timer was Jeff McPherson, a retired Seattle police officer for more than twenty years before he came to Cascade. He loved small town life and also enjoyed being a member of its police force. His calm demeanor and laid-back personality made working with him a pleasure. At six-feet-four two hundred and fifty pounds, he was a force to reckon with, and his experience made him a valuable resource.

Randy Stevens was a young, shy police officer, who had been in uniform less than five years. He had spent three years as a King County officer but when an opening became available in Cascade he had worked very hard to get the position. Buck had hired him because he had seen a compassionate and dedicated police officer. Andy could also see the same qualities in Randy, and despite his shyness with her they were developing a good working relationship. He was becoming a very important member of the department and Andy had high hopes for him. Now all she had to do was keep him from blushing beet red whenever she spoke to him.

Len Stubben was a different matter. The very first day of work Len countermanded several of her orders to the others until Andy had asked to speak to him in private. She could still remember the conversation.

"Len, I know you have been with this department for many years and my making changes the very first day is hard to understand. I just ask that you do not change any of my instructions before coming and speaking to me."

"Even if you are dead wrong?"

Len's belligerence was understandable. He had applied for the job of Chief of Police and had been rejected. This angered him tremendously. He had worked as an officer for eight years in Cascade and thirteen as a King County officer. This situation made the relationship between Andy and Len adversarial, compounded by the fact that Len had several more years of experience than her, and she was a woman, a small gay woman at that.

Andy had been very open with her small department, on the advice of Buck, and told them that she was a lesbian. She felt that it was important that they not be surprised by it. Len's comments about her sexual orientation had been behind her back but just loud enough for her to hear.

"She doesn't look like a dyke? What a waste!" Andy had winced at the comments but chose not to respond to Len's distasteful comments. She had heard worse. Besides she would deal with it in her own time.

By the end of the first week Andy realized that it wouldn't have mattered who had gotten the job of Chief. Len had wanted it badly and was extremely bitter about it. Her being a woman just made it that much more difficult for Len to understand why he hadn't been promoted.

She had to laugh. He was very persistent at irritating her, including parking his truck in the Police Chief's spot, a petty, but irksome behavior nonetheless. From the very first day, he made it clear he thought Andy would be unable to do a credible job as the Police Chief. He would just bide his time until she failed, making her job as tough as possible. Andy had quietly vowed that she would not react to his attitude and would take care of business despite him. His attitude was familiar. Andy had run into the same feelings during her tenure as an FBI agent and a police officer. Not all men were accepting of women in law enforcement. She wasn't sure how she was going to deal with his behavior but she would find a way.

Andy had just spent eight hours with Len and another four in the office when Marta finally kicked her out. Andy needed to get away, so she didn't put up a fight. She was exhausted and mentally drained. She could use a break.

"Okay Marta, I'm going, I'm going." Andy chuckled, throwing her hands up.

"That's good. You need to get some sleep, Chief. I don't want to see you until tomorrow morning. We can go over the budget before your meeting with the council next week."

"Sounds good, I'll take the files with me."

"Now you are not going home to work, Chief. You can look at the files another time." Marta shooed her out the door. "Go home."

Andy couldn't help but laugh. She was lucky Marta was so good to her. She needed that right now. Her job was her only focus. She had no personal life. Her house was organized, her work life was coming together, and now she needed to take care herself. Buck had reminded her of that fact two days earlier when he called to ask if she wanted to go hiking with him on Saturday. Her immediate response was no, she needed to work. As she pulled into the driveway of her home she changed her mind. She would go hiking on Saturday. Dropping her stuff in the front entryway, she took a moment to enjoy the view of the river below and the mountains in the background. She really liked living in Cascade.

Dialing Buck's number to inform him of her changing plans, she looked around her new home. She had made a clean break when she left San Francisco, leaving a crumbling two-year relationship and an accumulation of shared possessions. The only request she had made of her ex-girlfriend was that Andy got to keep the stereo. It had been her pride and joy and a source of pleasure. She left everything else, taking her clothes and her car, choosing to make an easy financial break. Jana had bought her out of the house so the financial split was clear. Jana had been more than fair, due in part to her guilt at being caught in a year-long affair with a mutual friend of theirs. Andy had a little time to purchase a few things for her new home; a couch, a television, and bed, a few kitchen items, and other essentials, but that was it. Her hardwood floor was bare, as were her walls. She wanted to take her time filling her home, looking for just the right items that she would enjoy. It had been a long time since she been able to do everything on her own, and she was looking forward to it. Buck's answering machine interrupted her wandering thoughts.

"Hello, This is Buck. I am probably out fishing. Please leave your name and number and I will call you back as soon as possible."

"Hi Buck, this is Andy. Are you still going hiking on Saturday? If you are, I would like to change my mind and go with you. Let me know. Thanks, Buck."

Since she might be going hiking, Andy knew she had better go for a run. She was very consistent about exercising before she moved to Cascade but since then she had gotten hardly any exercise at all. She should join a local gym in order to keep her strength up, but she wasn't sure they had one in town. Stripping her uniform off, she grabbed a pair of her shorts and a faded T- shirt, a pair of heavy socks, and her running shoes. Her hair was still braided, but after fifteen hours on the job it was looking a little mussed. It would work long enough for her to get in a run. Slipping her house key in the small pocket of her shorts, she locked her door and began stretching to warm her legs. It was a nice pleasant sunshine-filled spring day devoid of the usual raining drizzle, perfect running weather.

Andy headed down her driveway and turned right. Setting a nice pace, Andy started to feel her body respond. Running had always been something Andy enjoyed, and it always helped to keep her in shape.

At the very same time Andy was beginning her run, Jessica was throwing on her own running shoes, shorts, and a hooded sweatshirt. She had just spent four hours in her studio roughing in her latest carving. This was the most physically demanding part of the process, as she removed large portions of the wood in order for the piece to begin to take on the shape Jessica could see her mind. She had labored nonstop and after four hours had been satisfied with what she saw, but she had worked up quite a sweat. She figured it was a good time to get fifty minutes of healthy running in before she cleaned up. She had some errands to take care of later in the afternoon. Sliding her hair back from her face, Jessica slipped out of her front door and began to jog. She had gone right yesterday and today she would run to the left. The road either way didn't matter, both directions had a full view of the mountain and a nice wide shoulder to run on. Jessica's pace began to quicken as she fell into her rhythm. She had been running on and off for over ten years, and it had become second nature to her.

Andy worked up quite a sweat after twenty minutes and started to turn around, when she noticed a runner in the distance coming her way. From this far away all she could make out was that the runner was small with short wavy brown hair. All of a sudden she recognized the woman as Jessica Newcomb, and she stumbled. Of all the people to run into, looking like this; she could just die of embarrassment. It was hard enough that she was wildly attracted to Jessica and now she was running into her at the worst time imaginable.

The same exact thoughts were crossing Jessica's mind as she recognized the runner coming in her direction; the dark hair and body had given Andy away. Jessica slowed to a stop as Andy approached. Andy spoke first

"Fancy running into you." She chuckled at her own pun, embarrassment making her nervous.

Jessica ran her hands through her hair self-consciously, very aware of her ratty attire. "I didn't expect to see you running in the middle of the day," she responded.

"I was kicked out of my office by Marta and I took her advice. I've been working nights trying to get to know the routine and she felt I needed to get some sleep."

"What are you doing running after working all night? You must be exhausted."

"Actually, I'm still a little wired, and I need the exercise."

Jessica looked at Andy as she spoke. Seeing her in shorts and a T-shirt, there was no doubt she was in extremely good shape. The muscles in her calves stood out and her arms showed definite signs of weight lifting. She looked Andy up and down and finally directly at her grinning face. The T- shirt was moist with sweat and clung to her stomach and breasts. It made Jessica's mouth dry just looking at her.

"You should be sleeping, not running." Jessica tried hard to act natural. It was difficult to hide her reactions from Andy. "Have you eaten anything?"

"I thought I would fix a snack before I went to bed."

"I'm just finishing up my run, would you like to join me for lunch?" The invitation came out of Jessica's mouth before she could think about what she said.

"I'm not really dressed for lunch." Andy looked a little embarrassed. Jessica thought she looked adorable.

"Who cares what you're wearing, I'm not exactly a fashion plate here." Jessica grinned, pulling on her paint splattered and torn hooded sweatshirt.

"I think you look just fine." Any smiled in return.

"Now that we have our dress code decided upon, let's go rustle up something to eat. My house is right over there." Jessica pointed to the house behind them. She led the way down the driveway to the front door, quickly unlocking it. "Welcome to my humble abode."

Andy followed her into the large open living room with a high, open-beamed ceiling. It was flooded with lots of light coming from the large windows and numerous skylights. The room's furniture was brilliantly covered overstuffed couches and chairs. Artwork on the walls reflected the decorator's taste, as they too were filled with wonderful colors. Andy liked the room very much; it was very welcoming. She followed Jessica into the kitchen and the dining area, which was equally as open and colorful, the wood beams extending from one end of the house to the other.

"This place is beautiful."

"Thank you. My sister and her husband built this place from scratch. They used all recycled wood and refinished it themselves. It took them four years to complete it but they did a terrific job."

"It really is something." Andy took in the natural wood moldings and window frames. It made the house appear like it was part of its surroundings, a natural extension of the trees that surrounded it.

"I'll show you the rest of house as soon as I clean up."

"Is there a bathroom I can use?"

"Sure, I'll get you a clean towel and you can use this one." Jessica opened the door to a bathroom down the hall. Reaching into a cupboard, she pulled out a large burgundy towel and washcloth. "I'll use the bathroom upstairs. I'll be right back, make yourself at home." She smiled at Andy.

As the door to the bathroom shut, Jessica fairly flew up the stairway and down the hall to her room. She shed her damp sweatshirt and stepped into her bathroom. Rapidly, Jessica washed her upper body and face with a washcloth and dried herself off. She then rifled through her drawer for a clean T- shirt. She kicked off her running shoes and dirty socks, and contemplated whether to put clean socks and her tennis shoes back on.

"Oh hell, I'll just go barefoot."

Jessica giggled when she realized she had spoken aloud. I'm acting like a teenager and I am thirty-six years old. This is ridiculous. She tripped rapidly downstairs to start lunch. She had no clue what she would fix. Thankfully, she had gone shopping two days earlier and had some choices. Jessica decided to prepare a shrimp salad, a meal she had planned for dinner later in the week. The shrimp were cleaned and cooked so all she needed to do was throw together a little lettuce and tomatoes. As she finished shredding romaine lettuce, Andy joined her in the kitchen.

"Can I help you with something?" Andy's voice had its usual affect on Jessica, sending shivers up her spine.

"Sure, I'm fixing a shrimp salad, if that's okay?" She turned her head to look at Andy, whose hair showed signs of dampness, her freshly scrubbed face shining with cleanliness. She had circles under her eyes betraying her exhaustion.

"Sounds terrific, what can I do?"

"You can cut up these tomatoes and this cucumber. Here's a knife."

"Okay. I have to tell you though, I'm not very handy in the kitchen." Andy's eyes twinkled as she winked. Jessica's heart flipped.

"You look tired." Jessica spoke quietly. She had to physically stop herself from reaching for Andy.

"I am, but I need to make sure I know what is expected by everyone. The only way I can do that is if I work every shift. I have to if I'm going to be successful."

Jessica understood what she was saying. Being a woman Police Chief was tough. Adding the fact that she was in a predominantly male job made it even tougher. She had run into that when she was younger, working her way through the law profession. "How is it going?"

"With the exception of some ruffled feathers with Officer Stubben, everything seems to be going well. Marta has adopted me and seems to enjoy bossing me around," Andy admitted.

Jessica was having a hard time concentrating as she and Andy stood side by side, their thighs brushing against each other. "Marta is a sweetheart. She obviously likes you. She did the same for Buck." Jessica chuckled. "What is wrong with Len? He can be such a jerk!"

"He feels he would have made a better Police Chief then I am. He's a little upset about being passed over."

"He would never make a good Police Chief, he's too much of a hot head. His mouth always gets him in trouble." Irritation bubbled from Jessica.

"I take it you have dealt with him firsthand." Andy turned to look at Jessica, her eyes wide with concern. Jessica felt the physical pull as she gazed at Andy.

"You could say he wouldn't take the word no seriously." Her voice shook with anger. It had been more serious than that, but it happened over five years ago and Jessica had put the episode behind her. Len had pursued Jessica for a date after spending an afternoon at the annual police department picnic. Jessica had been very clear with him when she had turned him down repeatedly. After weeks of telephone calls and unannounced visits, Len had showed up at Jessica's home late one evening after he'd been out drinking with his friends.

"Len, what are doing here?" Jessica didn't open the door too far, she didn't want Len in her home. "It's after ten."

"Ah Jessica, let me in, honey." Len pushed the door open, knocking Jessica against the wall.

"Len, what's wrong with you? Have you been drinking?" Jessica was furious. "Get out!"

"Jessica, why won't you go out with me?" Len's large arms captured Jessica against him as he tried to kiss her.

Jessica began to panic as she struggled to pull away. "Len don't! Let me go!"

"Come on Jessica, just one kiss."

"No!" Jessica shoved Len with all of her strength, knocking him to the ground. Because he was drunk and shocked at her reaction he sat on the floor, unable to move. Jessica immediately ran to the telephone and dialed 911. Len struggled to stand as Jessica made her call.

"Randy, it's Jessica Newcomb. Len's at my home and he is very drunk. Could you send someone immediately to come pick him up?" Jessica wanted Len out of her house. "I'm fine Randy, just come get him, please."

Len was still seated on the floor, his eyes blurry as he tried to focus on Jessica. "Come on Jessica, just a little kiss was all I wanted."

"Len, Randy is on the way. I suggest you don't say another word to me." Jessica was beyond furious.

It didn't take long for Randy to arrive and Buck pulled in right behind him. Jessica wasn't the only one who was very angry. Jessica couldn't remember ever seeing Buck's expression on his face.

"Jessica, are you okay?" Buck immediately went up to her, ignoring Len who sat meekly, still on the floor.

"I'm fine Buck." Jessica allowed Buck to hug her tightly.

"Jessica, I'm going to take care of Len, but I want to know what happened."

"He just showed up here out of the blue and wanted inside. He didn't want to take no for an answer. He tried to kiss me and I knocked him down."

"Good for you honey." Buck hugged her again. "Now, I want you to go sit in the kitchen. I'll be there in a few minutes."

Jessica did as Buck asked but she didn't miss hearing Buck speak. "Randy, I want you to throw Len in the back of your car and take him to the station. Also, I want his truck towed."

"Ah Buck." Len started to speak.

"Len, shut the hell up." Buck's fists picked Len up by the front of his shirt. "I ought to beat you senseless for touching Jessica. As it is, you are going to spend the night in jail while I think of what I might charge you with besides drunk and disorderly. You had better hope that Jessica doesn't want to charge you with assault. You could lose your job, you goddamn idiot!"

Len's head hung in shame as Buck dressed him down. Randy led a very quiet Len out of Jessica's home.

Buck walked back to where Jessica sat by herself at her kitchen table. She was thankful that both Tommy and Jennifer were staying at friends for the night. It was bad enough that she had to deal with this mess.

"Jessica, I am ashamed of Len and I'm sorry." Buck sat next to her and covered her hands with his.

"Buck, it's not your fault. Do you want a cup of coffee?" She got up to pour him one. Buck always liked a cup of coffee.

"He's an idiot! Jess, do you want to charge him with assault?"

"No Buck, I just want him to leave me alone."

"He'll do that honey, or I'll have his head and his job!" Buck was a very nice man but he loved Jessica like a daughter, and that made him very protective.

Len learned his lesson while both Jessica and Buck put him in his place. Actually, Len and Jessica had a casually polite relationship after that episode. He showed up at her house the next morning with Buck to apologize. He'd been a perfect gentleman to Jessica ever since.

"Do you want to tell me what happened?" Andy placed her hand on Jessica's arm, her voice barely above a whisper.

"It was a long time ago and I took care of it." Jessica responded softly, Andy's hand was still on her arm. "It wasn't that big a deal."

Jessica was having a hard time concentrating. She really wanted to kiss Andy and she was fairly sure Andy wanted to kiss her. They stared at each other for several seconds and Jessica felt Andy's hand slide up her arm. Jessica turned toward Andy and started to lean toward her when the telephone rang, interrupting them. Jessica answered it with quite a bit of irritation.

"Hello."

"Jessica, this is Loren. I have great news! We got that corporate account. They want us to fill their building, all ten floors, with artwork, and you wouldn't believe the budget!"

"Congratulations, I know how hard you worked on this project. When do we start?" Jessica's irritation evaporated.

"Next week we start looking at the site. We need to have all the pieces in place before their anniversary in May. That gives us only a couple of weeks to come up with over thirty pieces of art."

"Terrific. I'll be in tomorrow and you and I can start planning. You make sure and celebrate with Chuck. Congratulations, Loren." After visiting with Loren for a few more minutes, Jessica hung up the telephone.

"Good news?" Andy asked as she finished tossing the salad together.

"Yes, it's fantastic! It seems we have acquired another corporate account. A business in Seattle wants us to fill all ten floors of their building with art, around thirty pieces."

"That is amazing, congratulations. You should celebrate." Andy was genuinely impressed.

"I think I will. Here, let me finish the salad. I invited you for lunch." Jessica removed the shrimp from refrigerator and rinsed them, blotted them dry, and tossed them into the salad. "What kind of dressing would you like? I have a Raspberry Vinaigrette, Thousand Island, and Uncle Dan's?"

"The vinaigrette would be fine. How about I get glasses of water for us."

"Perfect, glasses are in the top cupboard over there."

Jessica finished the salad and placed it in the middle of the dining table, as Andy set glasses of water at each place setting. Jessica continued preparing several slices of fresh French bread and butter, while Andy completed setting the table with silverware, plates, and napkins. They worked in silence as they prepared for lunch.

"Let's eat," Jessica announced.

"The salad looks great," Andy remarked, as she took a seat. "Thanks for inviting me for lunch, but I think it's my turn next time. This makes twice you have fed me."

"I'm glad we ran into each other."

Jessica was feeling a little shy. She was beginning to have doubts about their exchange earlier. Maybe she had misread the signals and she had almost kissed Andy! She was more than a little bit embarrassed.

"I've got an idea. How about I return the favor and take you out to celebrate your good fortune. If you want to, that is?" Andy asked, a shy smile on her face.

"I would like that." Jessica smiled in return.

"Good, how about Friday night?"

"Sounds perfect, I have to work at the gallery until four so it will have to be after five, if that's all right?"

"I can pick you up at six, will that give you enough time?"

"Plenty. Is this something I should dress formally for?" Jessica grinned at Andy.

"I don't think that a long dress is in order, but it won't be a jeans kind of place." Andy grinned back, her now familiar violet eyes flashed.

"I guess I'll have to leave my beaded purse at home." Jessica twinkled her eyes right back.

"This is a great salad, thanks again for inviting me for lunch. I would probably have fixed myself a peanut butter sandwich, my usual choice for lunchtime fare. I'm not much of a gourmet."

"Before I moved here to take care of the kids I existed on takeout and fast food. I couldn't very well raise the two of them on junk food so I learned to fix three good meals a day. The first few months I prepared some pretty awful food." Jessica laughed as she remembered the expressions on the kid's faces while she tried to convince them that a little black on their pork chops was good for them. "It took a lot of practice."

"Maybe you could give me cooking lessons?"

"I'd love to." Jessica thought the verbal sparring meant something, she just wasn't sure what.

They finished their lunch with light-hearted conversation about all the characters in town. It was amazing to Jessica how many of them Andy had managed to run into in two weeks. They shared a little laughter over the resident town alien, as Nick called himself. He routinely would drop into police headquarters and inform them that he had been beamed up to the mother ship. Nick had been doing this for many years and otherwise was harmless, working part time at the local gas station. What amazed Jessica even more was Andy's explanation of how she had dealt with Nick's story. She actually sat him down in her office and filled out the police report herself, promising him she would look into it. Nick left satisfied that he had done the right thing.

"Why did you write up a police report?" Jessica really wanted to know.

"He just needed someone to pay attention to him. He's lonely." Andy's explanation impressed Jessica with its compassion. Jessica was beginning to like this woman very much. "Well, I'd better get going, I'm sure you have better things to do." Andy smiled.

"And you need to get some sleep, you must be exhausted." They both stood up as they spoke.

"Here, let me help with the cleanup." Andy picked up her dishes and walked them over to the counter.

"I can take it from here. Would you like a ride home?"

"No, I can use the exercise. Thanks again for lunch, and I'll see you on Friday."

Jessica walked Andy to the front door. "I'm looking forward to it."

"So am I." Andy turned to speak. "Goodbye."

"Bye." They both stood there for a few moments staring at each other.

"See you." Andy turned and began to jog toward the end of the driveway. Jessica watched her as she left, enjoying the view, when Andy turned at the end of the driveway and waved. Jessica returned the wave with a smile, and shut her front door. This woman was having a major effect on her. Jessica fanned her face as she leaned against the closed door.

Jessica finished washing the dishes and went upstairs to clean up. She had to finish some errands and she wanted to stop by the gallery and congratulate Loren in person. That one corporate account would pay them over twenty thousand dollars a year; it was a tremendous account. She also needed to clear her day. Tomorrow she was going to Seattle to do some shopping. She wanted something new to wear Friday night.

Chapter Four

The rest of the week flew by while Jessica anticipated her dinner with Andy. Andy called Thursday evening to confirm that she would pick Jessica up at six on Friday. They didn't have much time to talk because Andy was still in her office and something came up. By Thursday Jessica hadn't mentioned her dinner with Andy to anyone else, and she worried about how to tell Jennifer. She thought long hard about it, but it wasn't until Friday afternoon that Jessica made her decision.

"Hey, Aunt Jess, where are you?" Jennifer's voice preceded her through the gallery.

"Back here, sweetie." Jessica had to smile. When Jennifer was excited about something, she had to share it with her family, and she was definitely full of something. She was grinning from ear to ear, bouncing on her toes.

"Guess what?" Jennifer asked as she hugged Jessica tightly.

"What honey?" She hugged her snugly in return.

"I got it!" Jennifer jumped around with excitement.

"Got what, honey?" Jessica had no idea what she was talking about.

"The volleyball scholarship at the University, I got it!"

"Oh Jenn, that's fantastic. I'm so happy for you." Jessica felt tears fill her eyes as she hugged her niece tightly.

"Isn't it totally cool!" Jennifer's face was lit up with happiness.

"Totally."

"I wanted to tell you first. I just found out from Coach Burns."

"I'm glad you did Jenn. I'm so proud of you. You've worked real hard. If your parents were here, they would be too." Jessica hugged her niece tightly again. She was such a sweet kid and it brought tears to her eyes. "Do you want to celebrate tonight?" She hoped Andy would understand when she canceled.

"Can we celebrate on Sunday? A bunch of us want to go to the dance at the Grange Hall, it's a swing band!" Jennifer loved to dance.

"Actually Jennifer, Sunday night would be just fine, but you need to call Tommy and tell him. He would love to know about your scholarship. Do you have a moment, I'd like to talk to you about something else?"

"Sure, what's up? And I will call Tommy before I go out," she promised.

"Good. Jennifer, I thought I would go out to dinner tonight with Andy Andolino, if it's okay with you?" Jessica watched Jennifer closely. If she showed any sign of discomfort or embarrassment Jessica would cancel the dinner and explain it to Andy.

"That's cool, Aunt Jess. She seems really nice, and she is very pretty. Where are you going? What are you going to wear?" Jennifer sounded as excited about Jessica's dinner as she was about her scholarship. Jennifer loved her niece more each day.

"I don't know where we're going, and I'm wearing a new outfit I bought yesterday." Jessica grinned at her niece. "It's cool, you'll like it."

"I want to see it! What time are you going?" Jennifer danced around her.

"Andy is picking me up at six."

"Great, I'm not leaving until seven-thirty so I can say hello to Chief Andy and see what you are wearing," Jennifer responded with a smile. "I'm going to head home now. I have to figure out what I'm going to wear to the dance, and call Tommy. See you later."

Jennifer flew out the door as rapidly as she arrived. Jessica could only grin and laugh quietly. Her niece was one of a kind and she wouldn't trade her for anything.

Jessica settled in for the rest of the afternoon. Only two hours more and she could go home and get ready. Her stomach was already full of butterflies in anticipation of her date. A last-minute flurry of business at the gallery had Jessica in a state of panic when she finally made it home a little after five.

"Aunt Jess, you better hurry you only have forty-five minutes to get ready," Jennifer reminded her as she passed Jessica's open bedroom door.

"I know. I'm going to hop in the shower, honey. Have you eaten?"

"Yep, I had a chicken pot pie for dinner. Can I help you with anything?"

"No sweetie, I just need to get organized, but thanks for offering. Did you talk to Tommy?"

"Yes, and he said hi."

"Good, now I have got to hurry."

Jessica rushed into her bathroom, removing her clothes as she went, she didn't even have time to get nervous. The hot shower was a welcome relief as she washed her hair and shaved her legs. After ten minutes she toweled herself dry and began to dress. For some reason this dinner felt special to Jessica. She slipped on her new navy wool slacks, cream-colored silk blouse, and matching blue silk vest. Glancing at her watch she knew she had twenty minutes before Andy was to arrive, unless she showed up early. Quickly, Jessica applied her makeup and began to dry her hair. She was down to five minutes when the doorbell rang.

"Damn." She muttered aloud. "Jennifer, can you get the door please? I'll be right down."

"Okay, take your time, I'll keep Chief Andy company."

While Jessica slipped her shoes on she could hear Jennifer inviting Andy in. The conversation got faint, and Jessica assumed they must have gone into the kitchen. She went to her dresser and applied perfume on her neck and wrists. Taking one last look at herself in her full-length mirror, she left her bedroom and walked down the stairs. As she reached the kitchen she heard laughter. Her niece's high-pitched giggle was recognizable, the other one a deep full laugh. As she walked through the kitchen door she took in the back of Andy's trim figure. She had on a pair of snug black pants and a royal blue cashmere sweater, a pair of black boots finishing the outfit. She looked like she had just stepped right out of Vogue magazine. Her glossy black hair was pulled back into a barrette at the base of her neck. She was standing next to her niece, who was giggling hysterically.

"Wow, Aunt Jess, you look terrific!" Jennifer exclaimed, grinning.

"Thanks, sweetie. Andy, I apologize, I'm running a little late."

"No problem." Andy turned to face Jessica. "Your niece was sharing a funny story with me."

"Really, what story?" Jessica looked at Jennifer who was showing signs of guilt. What was she up to?

"She was telling me about your first camping trip."

"Jennifer." Jessica groaned with embarrassment.

"I didn't tell her everything!" Jennifer giggled.

"There's more?"

"Wait until I tell you about the skunk!" Jennifer volunteered. She was having enormous fun teasing her aunt.

"Jennifer, let's wait for another time, please." Jessica warned her with her eyes, while Andy looked on with humor. "Are you ready, Andy?"

"Sure, thanks for sharing camping stories with me." She smiled at Jennifer, who responded by grinning back.

"No problem, Chief Andy. What you doing Sunday night?" Jennifer inquired.

"I have nothing planned, why?"

"Would you like to come over for dinner? It's a celebration, I got a volleyball scholarship from the University of Washington!" Jessica was so surprised by Jennifer's invitation, her mouth dropped open.

"Congratulations! You must have worked very hard to be offered a scholarship. I would love to come, as long as it's okay with your aunt?" Andy spoke directly to Jennifer so she couldn't see Jessica's expression of surprise.

"It's okay, isn't it, Aunt Jess?" Jennifer pleaded.

Of course it is. It's your party." Jessica smiled, trying to hide her reaction from Andy. "Have you asked Todd?"

"He has to work. It's all settled then. Andy, you can come over at five, okay?"

"I'll be there," Andy reassured her.

"Okay Jenn, put the alarm on when you leave, and remember your curfew." Jessica grabbed her purse.

"I will, have a good time." As Jessica followed Andy out the front door, Jennifer called to her, "Aunt Jess, remember your curfew." Jennifer's giggles followed them as she closed the front door.

While Andy grinned at her, Jessica grimaced. "My niece can be a brat."

"Oh, I found her pretty entertaining. I can't wait to hear the skunk story," Andy teased. "Besides, I think she's right, you do look terrific!" She smiled.

Jessica acknowledged the compliment with a smile of her own. "Thank you, you look pretty nice yourself."

"Why thank you, ma'am," she drawled. "Much better than my shorts and T- shirt the other day."

"I don't know about that. I kind of liked you in your shorts." Now it was Jessica's turn to tease.

Andy chose not to respond as the two of them got in her jeep. She just smiled at Jessica; her violet eyes flashing, causing Jessica to flush with warmth. Their conversation for the first twenty minutes remained light, as first Andy and then Jessica described their day. Andy's description of the day's activities at the small rural police station had Jessica laughing. The major crime of the day was Mrs. Ames' report that Mrs. Otis was stealing flowers from her yard. This major crime had been called in on the town's emergency line. Because it wasn't one telephone call but seven, it forced Andy to drive to the home of Mrs. Ames to investigate. It took forty minutes of discussion with the two women before Andy came up with a solution. After a short trip to the local hardware store, a simple wood fence section placed strategically between the two women's gardens did the trick. Jessica's sides hurt from laughing, when she informed Andy that Mrs. Otis and Mrs. Ames had been feuding for over ten years.

"I can't believe our Chief of Police installed fencing today."

"Hey, we are a full-service police department." Andy laughed with her. Jessica appreciated the fact that Andy took everything in stride. She was adjusting to small town life very quickly.

"Maybe I should ask you where we're going?"

"I thought we could have dinner at Snoqualmie Falls Lodge, if that's all right? I've never been there but I've heard it has a spectacular view and great food."

"Sounds perfect. I've never eaten there either."

"Then it will be a first for both of us," Andy responded. "Jessica, Buck told me you were a lawyer before you moved here. Why aren't you practicing law now?"

"I was a partner in a fairly big law firm in San Francisco for several years. My specialty was defending large companies from their own employees' lawsuits, not exactly defending the poor and the needy." Jessica's guilt could be heard in her voice. "You know the old saying, everyone deserves a good defense."

Andy reached over and clasped Jessica's left hand. Her smile encouraged Jessica to continue. Jessica lightly squeezed Andy's hand in return, responding with a smile of her own.

"Needless to say, I made a ton of money while working six days a week, ten to twelve hours a day. It was not conducive to a healthy, happy relationship, of which mine was not. I can't blame my career as the cause of any bad relationship, but it certainly didn't help," Jessica ruefully admitted.

"You can't blame yourself for having a career," Andy reminded her.

"I know, but I was never sure that if I had spent less time on my career and more time on my personal life I might not have made so many questionable decisions."

Andy squeezed her hand in support. "We all make mistakes and bad decisions. That's how we grow. Boy, I have made a few big ones in my day."

"When my sister and her husband were killed, it changed everything. I realized that I needed to make some major changes in my life. I still practice a little law in town, the usual will or contract review for friends and neighbors, and I act as the legal adviser for the town council. I enjoy that kind of work, but my career now is taking care of Jennifer and Tommy, and my carving."

"I'd say you're pretty successful at your new career, judging from how Jennifer turned out, and I've heard from Buck how terrific Tommy is, but your artwork is beyond a career. There's so much passion captured with your carvings."

"Thank you." Jessica blushed.

"I've always been amazed by people like you who are so creative. I don't have a creative bone in my body," Andy admitted.

"Well, considering all the skills it takes to be a police officer, I can believe you have a whole lot of talent. I know you have an innate ability in dealing with people and their problems. That's a talent I envy."

"Thank you. I guess it's true then, we all wish for something we don't have."

"That's for sure."

"I believe we are here." Andy squeezed her hand and let go. "Our reservation is for seven-fifteen. Do you want to go look at the falls before it gets too dark?"

"I'd love to."

The two of them followed the path past the restaurant entrance to the lookout point. "Wow, that is beautiful!" Andy exclaimed as she stared at Snoqualmie Falls.

"It is, isn't it? I didn't know how incredible the view of the Falls would be." Jessica was as overwhelmed as Andy.

The waterfall was impressive as water thundered over the top of the dam into a huge pool. The air was filled with mist as you looked out over the river, almost three hundred feet below. Many considered Snoqualmie Falls a sacred place, and as Jessica and Andy stood in awe, you could swear that the place crackled with power and magic. The two of them stood silently for several minutes absorbing the site as dusk turned slowly into night. It was a perfect way to start the evening. Jessica moved closer to Andy as they stood side by side, and slipped her arm through hers. Andy turned and smiled at Jessica. They gazed at each other silently, their eyes speaking volumes as they recognized their mutual attraction.

"You're the most beautiful woman I've ever seen," Jessica admitted softly.

"I think you're the sexiest woman I have ever met." Andy reached up and stroked Jessica's windblown hair from her face, her voice barely above a whisper, as Jessica moved even closer.

"Thank you."

A crowd of people came up the walkway and Andy reluctantly pulled away. "Let's go in for dinner, before we freeze." Neither one had a coat on, but until that moment they had not noticed.

"May I help you?" The hostess inquired as they entered the restaurant.

"We have reservations for two under the name of Andolino."

"Yes, here we are, please follow me." The table they were led to had a breathtaking view of the Falls. Even at night it was romantic.

"Your waiter will be right with you." While they were seated across from each other Jessica stared directly into Andy's beautiful violet eyes. She could have looked at her all night.

"A penny for your thoughts?" Andy asked, smiling.

Taking a big deep breath, Jessica answered her truthfully. "I was thinking that I could stare at you all night." Jessica could feel her heart pounding.

"I know the feeling. I hate sitting across from you, it's too far away." Jessica shivered with anticipation. She wanted to hold Andy so very much. "You need to stop looking at me like that. I can't touch you here." Andy spoke quietly, just for Jessica's hearing.

"Can I get either of you something to drink?" The waiter intruded on their private moment.

Their dinner was quietly elegant, as they laughed and talked about little things, like their favorite songs and the food that they enjoyed. It was a time for sharing the intimate details that two people who are attracted to each other share. It was as close to touching as they could get in public. Each look was a caress, each smile a promise, as they lingered after dinner enjoying a cup of coffee.

"We had better get going before they charge us rent," Jessica joked.

"The waiter has been giving us the evil eye for the last half hour." Andy winked at her.

The walk to the car was done in silence, each holding onto their thoughts. Awareness of each other was foremost in both of their minds. After they were seated in the car, Jessica turned to Andy to find her staring directly back at her. Slowly they leaned toward each other until their lips met for the very first time. Jessica sighed heavily as Andy's soft lips caressed hers. She tasted so good. Her lips parted and she put her hand around Andy's shoulders to pull her closer. Andy moaned and wrapped her arms around Jessica until their upper bodies were pressed tightly against each other. Jessica could feel Andy's breasts against her own and her nipples began tingle. They broke apart slowly, both breathing heavily.

"I've wanted to kiss you since the first night I met you," Andy admitted. "I've never felt this way before." She had taken both of Jessica's hands in her own.

"I've never felt this way before either. I'm so glad you kissed me and that you feel this way," Jessica responded, smiling.

"Are you seeing anyone else?"

"No, what about you?"

"I'm seeing a woman with gorgeous dark brown hair, and chocolate eyes, who carves beautiful sensuous pieces of art, and is absolutely the sexiest woman I have ever met." Andy smiled.

Jessica's answer was to pull Andy into her arms again and kiss her thoroughly in response. Andy melted against her and returned her kiss, sending shivers through Jessica's body. It was several minutes before a car leaving the parking lot interrupted them.

"I guess we can't park here all night." Jessica laughed softly.

"I would if we could get way with it, but I don't think it's the safest place for us to be necking."

"I'm with a strong, tough, police officer. I couldn't be safer." Jessica teased.

"I think this would be more fun in my living room. Do you need to go right home?"

"I can stay out a while longer."

"Would you like to come over to my place for awhile?"

Jessica marveled at how this highly capable woman could sound so vulnerable. "I would love to." She smiled.

"Good." Andy smiled at Jessica.

Andy pulled out of the parking lot and once they were on the road took Jessica's hand in her own. Jessica stared at Andy's profile as she drove, admiring her beauty. It was a pleasant forty-minute drive back to Cascade, as Jessica and Andy continued to share stories of when they were younger and single. It was important that the two of them share the smallest bit of information about each other. They were building the beginning of a relationship.

While Andy drove by Jessica's home, Jessica checked to make sure the lights were on and whether Jennifer was home. She didn't expect her before the curfew time of one a.m. on weekends. Jennifer would be, as usual, about ten minutes late; you could count on it.

"Are you worried about Jennifer?" Andy asked, squeezing her hand.

"Not at all." Jessica laughed. "I can bet you money she won't be home until a little after one. She has managed to be late to everything since she was a little child."

"She's just a typical teenage girl with too many things going on at the same time," Andy reassured her.

"When that girl turns forty she will still be running late." Jessica chuckled.

"Let's hope I'm still around," Andy teased.

Jessica looked at Andy as she spoke. This woman was turning out to be very special and Jessica found it easy to imagine her being in her life for a very long time. "Let's hope you will still want to be around me when you see what I look like when I wake up in the morning. It is not a pretty sight."

"I'll take my chances." Andy chuckled, as she pulled into the driveway of her new home. "Here we are."

"You know I've always loved this house. It fits so well into the surrounding trees."

"The name fits the place. You do feel like you are in a tree house when you look out of the living room windows. And wait until you see my view."

Jessica followed Andy as she unlocked the door and entered her new home. "Its pretty empty right now. I haven't had a chance to get much in the way of furniture yet. I thought I would take my time and get something nice." She spoke apologetically.

"Look at this wood, your floors are beautiful. It would be fun to pick out new rugs and pictures." Jessica smiled at Andy who stood in her empty living room. She looked so vulnerable standing there that Jessica went immediately to her.

"Maybe you could help me look around for stuff?"

"I'd love to, but right now I can think of lots better things to do with our time." Jessica slid her arms around Andy, who responded by hugging Jessica in return.

"And what better ideas have you got in that pretty head of yours."

Jessica's answer was to kiss Andy lightly on her lips once, twice, and Andy responded. Her kisses flooded Jessica with warmth, as Andy's mouth and tongue coaxed Jessica into opening her lips to Andy's tongue, lightly sucking. Andy's moan matched Jessica's as passion flared between the two of them. It was several minutes before they pulled away from each other. Jessica shivered with feeling as she looked into Andy's eyes. She looked as shaken as Jessica felt.

"Jessica, would you like something to drink? I'm sorry I'm not being a very good hostess."

"I think you're a perfect hostess and no, I don't want anything to drink." Jessica laced her fingers with Andy's and pulled her over to the couch. "Can we sit here for awhile?" She smiled to reassure Andy. They both took a seat on the couch and Jessica kicked her shoes off, tucking her legs up underneath her.

Turning until she faced Andy, she spoke. "I am finding this evening a little bit overwhelming. I have to admit that I find myself extremely attracted to you. I don't know if I have ever reacted like this before."

"I know what you mean. From the very first night I met you, I haven't been able to get you out my mind. You're not at all like I expected." Andy's fingers played with Jessica's hair as she spoke.

"What you mean, not what you expected?" Jessica's face revealed her puzzlement.

"For the last two years Buck has been telling me about this town and your family. I think it was his way of convincing me to move here. He talked about you and your niece and nephew like you are family. You are one of his very favorite people. He loves you, Jessica." Andy smiled as she spoke and leaned closer to her, pushing her hair out of her face. "Do you know how beautiful you are? Your eyes are exactly the same color as your hair."

Jessica felt herself blush. "Buck is family. I just can't believe he has been talking to you about us. I know he considers you like a daughter."

"To tell you the truth, I think you were part of the reason why I finally said yes to Buck and came here to live." Andy's eyes began to sparkle.

"What do you mean?"

"Well, you know I had to come here and be interviewed by the town council before they would consider me for the position of Police Chief?"

"Yes, I remember Buck telling me about it. I was working like mad on a carving when he asked me to have dinner with the two of you, but I told him no."

"And to think you could have gone on your first date with me months before this. Think how much time was wasted," Andy teased.

"That still doesn't explain your statement about my being part of the reason you moved here." Jessica swiftly kissed Andy several times.

"If you keep kissing me I won't be able to explain." Andy chuckled.

"Tell me." Jessica settled with holding Andy's hand while she talked. She was finding it hard to keep her hands to herself.

"The night of the interview Buck and I drove around town so he could show it to me. You were coming out of the grocery store when we drove by. Buck wanted to stop but I had a late flight out of SeaTac and we were short on time. You had on a pair of old ripped jeans, hiking boots, and a bright red flannel shirt, with the sleeves rolled up. Your hair was shorter then and you ran your hands through it as you walked to your car. We were stopped at the light and Buck honked and you looked up and waved. You looked so cute and a lot younger than I expected. I had the same reaction that evening as I did the night Buck introduced us. I felt like we were supposed to meet, and I can't explain it."

Jessica sighed as she listened. She had reacted to Andy from the first moment she met her. "It doesn't need explaining."

She wrapped her hand around Andy's neck, slipping her shiny black hair through her fingers. She pulled Andy to her and they kissed. It was a searing, overwhelming kiss. Andy slid her arms around Jessica, pulling her tightly to her. Andy's breasts flattened against Jessica's as her hands slid down Jessica's shoulders and back. Jessica's mouth left Andy's, and she left a trail of kisses along her jaw to her neck, nuzzling and kissing along the edge of Andy's sweater. Jessica could feel Andy's heart along with her own, beating wildly in her chest. Finding Andy's lips again, she kissed her thoroughly, tasting her lips and tongue. Andy returned her passion as she slipped her hands under Jessica's shirt and vest, running them up her back. Jessica's skin tingled everywhere Andy touched her as she arched her back in response. Andy pulled Jessica gently toward her until she lay on top of Andy. Andy continued to run her hands along Jessica's back and hips while kissing the breath out of her. Their legs intertwined and their upper bodies pressed tightly together. Taking a breath and sighing, Jessica leaned back on her arms and looked down at Andy. Her eyes glowed a deep dark purple, her lips plump and moist from being kissed.

"I could do this all night," She admitted, smiling down at Andy.

"Wouldn't that the nice," Any teased, rubbing Jessica's back.

Jessica slipped over to the side of Andy and leaned on her elbow, her left leg draped over Andy's and her left hand resting on her stomach. "Andy, I have to tell you, if I just wanted a one night stand with you I would stay here all night, but I want more than that."

Andy smiled and turned to face Jessica, placing her finger against her lips. "Jessica, I would love to have you stay all night with me, God knows I am very attracted to you. The evening we had dinner in your gallery I knew I wanted to ask you out. You are special and I don't want to rush things with you. I want to take our time and I want you to fall madly in love with me."

Jessica lightly kissed Andy's fingers as she spoke. She was already falling in love with her. "Then it's okay, if we take everything a little slowly and do things right?" she asked as she ran her fingers along the neck of Andy's sweater.

"It's okay as long as you don't devour me with those eyes of yours. I don't think I could ever say no to you if you look at me with those eyes." As Andy spoke she leaned toward Jessica and kissed her deeply.

Jessica responded by sliding on top of Andy and kissing her back, her breasts resting tightly upon Andy's, tingling with sensation. It was all Jessica could do not to strip Andy of her sweater at that moment and feast on her breasts. She could feel Andy's hands on her waist pulling her closer, their hips clasped against each other. Jessica could feel herself becoming wet as she lay on top of Andy. She was amazed how easily she reacted to Andy's touch. It was quite awhile before either one of them looked at the time.

"Oh my God, it's after two in the morning!" Jessica exclaimed after looking at her watch. "I should get going."

"I'll drive you home. I'm sorry it's so late, I lost track of time."

"I certainly have had a wonderful time tonight. When can we see each other again?" She kissed Andy before she sat up and slipped her shoes on.

"As soon as possible, I hope. What does your week look like?"

"Let's see, I have a planning meeting for this year's festival on Wednesday night. You'll be there won't you?"

"Yes. Maybe we can do something afterwards."

"I think that would be perfect. I'll be working most of the week in my studio. Do you think you could get away for lunch one day?"

"I will make a point of it. How about I call you tomorrow night? I'm going hiking with Buck tomorrow."

"You poor girl, I should have gone home hours ago. You need to get some rest."

As they went to the door together, Jessica placed her hand on Andy's arm to stop her a moment. As Andy turned to Jessica, she stepped into Andy's arms and hugged her. "I'm already starting to miss you." She kissed Andy thoroughly.

"I'm going to miss you, too." Andy hugged Jessica tightly in return. "Now let's get you home before your niece grounds you for missing curfew." Andy grinned.

With their arms around each other they walked to the car. It was a short drive to Jessica's home and, as she prepared to get out, she leaned over and hugged Andy quickly.

"Sweet dreams."

"You too, I'll call you tomorrow night."

"Okay, goodnight."

Jessica walked to her front door, unlocked it, and turned the alarm off. Jennifer had done as she asked, turning the alarm back on when she was home alone. Jessica turned in the doorway to wave at Andy, who was still waiting in the driveway. She didn't know if Andy could see her but she smiled anyway as Andy pulled out of the driveway and drove away. Jessica quietly shut the door and turned the alarm back on.

She climbed the stairs and slipped into her bedroom. Even at the lateness of the hour, Jessica was anything but tired. She pulled her clothes off, washed her face, and climbed into bed. She lay there quietly trying to relax her body, still reacting to the evening's activities. Just thinking about Andy had a wonderful affect on her. This woman was already slipping into Jessica's heart. Her combination of capable police officer and vulnerable woman was so appealing, and her open affection and teasing nature was an added pleasure. Jessica was already falling big-time for Andy.

At the very same time, Andy was having similar thoughts. She had never felt like this before. It was not her usual behavior to jump immediately into a physical relationship. Andy believed in total emotional commitment before embarking on the physical part. She had been the brunt of a lot of joking and teasing from her friends over the years, calling her old-fashioned. It had also been the reason for many of her problems with dating; that, and her career choice. Not many women wanted to date a police officer that worked long weird hours, carried a gun, and didn't want to sleep with them on the first date.

The few affairs Andy had been involved in had been committed long-term relationships. She believed in working things out and doing whatever it took to have a healthy, happy relationship. Her first one ended rather abruptly when Andy found out her girlfriend and lover for over a year could not nor would not move with her to Dallas, Texas, when the FBI transferred Andy. Andy understood why Tracey had made her decision, but it didn't make it any less painful. It had taken several years and a transfer to San Francisco before she could open her heart up for another relationship.

She and Gina lasted for almost four years. It was everything Andy wanted in a relationship and, until her partner Buck's son Ben was killed, it had been perfect. The death of Ben devastated Andy and had a profound effect on Gina. She was unable to handle the fact that Andy might be killed in the line of duty. She became increasingly paranoid and, if Andy didn't get home on time or she didn't call, Gina would become frantic. They tried counseling but that hadn't helped. Gina finally asked for some time alone, and they had separated. They never got back together and it had broken Andy's heart.

Within a year, Andy resigned from the FBI and became a San Francisco Police Officer. It was a position as liaison between the FBI, the ATF, and the police department, and it was perfect for Andy. The hours were more predictable and allowed Andy to become more skilled in the politics and public relations part of police work. She met her last girlfriend this way. Rachel was a cameraperson for a local television news station.

Rachel and Andy dated for four months before Andy succumbed to Rachel's charms and tumbled into bed and a shared apartment. They were together for a little less than two years before Andy found out Rachel had been sleeping with another woman for over a year. To add pain on top of the injury was the fact that it had been a mutual friend of theirs. That was the ultimate betrayal to Andy and forgiveness was not an option. It was a major deciding factor in her considering the job as Police Chief in Cascade, Washington. It was a challenging job and far away from Rachel and San Francisco. Rachel had wanted to work things out and put forth an amazing effort to convince Andy to stay. Andy labored long and hard over her decision but recognized she no longer trusted or loved Rachel enough to make it work. She left everything behind her and moved, committing herself to a new job, and a new home.

Here it was a month later, and she was already becoming involved with Jessica. Lying in bed, she tried to rationalize her response to her. Jessica was so beautiful, with her short, wavy, copper hair, and matching eyes. She was about two inches shorter than Andy, and was smaller in size. She was very slender, but her arms and hands betrayed her strength, her muscles clearly defined, obviously from her carving. Her face had high cheekbones to accent her eyes and heavy lashes, her nose was straight and small, but it was her mouth that captured Andy's attention. Her lips were full and a luscious natural pink color, and when she smiled she had very slight dimples on either side. Her coloring was golden and matched her eyes and hair perfectly. Even with her sexy looks, it was a completely different reason why Andy found her fascinating. It was Buck's description of how Jessica had dropped a promising law career and life in San Francisco to move to Cascade to raise her niece and nephew.

She not only gave up her career but, as Buck stated, "she doesn't have a life of her own." He worried about Jessica, especially since Jennifer would be going off to college. Andy knew Buck loved and respected Jessica very much and, from the first moment, Andy recognized Jessica's responsible and loving commitment to her niece and nephew. That one trait told Andy how Jessica would treat any relationship she would become involved in, and Andy wanted that type of commitment with someone. On top of everything else she was such a passionate person. It showed in her carvings, and Andy was unbelievably attracted to her.

Her body reacted to Jessica the very first time she met her and it was only getting stronger. It made her want to forget her cardinal rule of no sex for the first two months when she began dating someone. If Jessica had tried to seduce her tonight, she might have succumbed. She didn't seem to have any will power. It took every bit of self-control she had not to give in to her body's urgings. She really liked this woman. Sleep was not coming quickly to her and she groaned at the thought of hiking with Buck. She knew he would not take it easy on her and she would probably be sore for days. The telephone ringing next to her bed startled her. It was almost three o'clock in the morning.

"Hi." It was Jessica.

"Hi." Andy's heart beat wildly.

"I didn't wake you, did I?"

"No, I was lying here thinking about this evening."

"I was, too. I just wanted to tell you I had a really wonderful time tonight. But most of all I just wanted to hear your voice before I went to sleep."

Andy's heart leaped and she smiled as Jessica talked. "I'm glad you called. It was a perfect evening, except that it ended too early."

"You have to go hiking real soon with Buck and I know what those hikes are like."

"I can guarantee I'll be sore tomorrow night." Andy chuckled.

"How about I come by tomorrow night and give you a backrub? I want to make sure Buck doesn't hurt you." Jessica giggled wickedly.

"Well ma'am, I would surely appreciate your kindness." Andy spoke in her best Dallas, Texas voice.

"Why don't you call me when you get home and get settled, and I will come up."

"I will, and Jessica, I like it that you wanted to hear my voice before going to sleep. I wish you were here so I could kiss you goodnight."

"I'm afraid, Andy, that if you kissed me right now you wouldn't be going to sleep any time soon."

"I'll take that as a promise for another night."

"Goodnight."

"Goodnight, Jessica, thank you for calling."

The two of them lay awake in separate beds wishing that wasn't the case. It was a long time before either of them fell asleep, and then it was restless and frustrating.

"Aunt Jessica, telephone!" Jennifer's yell vibrated up the stairs. Groaning, Jennifer rolled over and glanced at the clock. Amazingly, she had slept in until after nine. She was normally up early on Saturday, ran a minimum of two miles, and took care of everything she had been unable to take care of all week. It was also a day where sometimes Jessica allowed herself to loaf around, stay in her pajamas, and generally eat whenever and whatever she wanted to. She was hoping to have one of those days today.

"Hello."

"Jessica, it's Rita. What are you up to today?"

"I've got a lot of errands to take care of. Why, what's up?" Rita was one of Jessica's friends who lived in Seattle with her girlfriend Kathy. They were also two people who couldn't it stand that Jessica was still single, and were constantly arranging blind dates and opportunities for Jessica to meet women.

"We were invited to a barbecue today and we want you to come with us. There will be lots of single women there."

"Thanks for thinking of me, but I'm really busy today." Jessica didn't need to meet anyone else. She had found a woman she wanted her in life. She just wasn't ready to talk about it yet.

"Jessica, you need to get out more, and meet more women."

"I know, I know, but I can't today. How about I give you and Kathy a call later in the week and make a date to get together."

"Okay, but if you change your mind we won't be leaving until around one, so call us."

"Okay, and Rita, thanks for calling."

"No problem Jessica. Call us, please."

"I will." As Jessica hung up the telephone, she dragged herself out of bed. She quickly brushed her teeth and washed her face. Glancing in the mirror, she was surprised to find herself looking so rested considering she hadn't gone to sleep until after four in the morning. She grabbed her bathrobe and slipped it on, wrapping it around her body as she walked down the stairs into the kitchen.

"Hey, sleepyhead how was your date?" Her niece was sitting in front of the computer in her office.

"Just fine, thank you. What are your plans for today?" she responded as she headed for the coffeepot. Her niece came out of the office, wearing a pair of shorts and T- shirt, her feet bare.

"I'm going to play tennis and have dinner with Todd's family, if that's okay?"

"That's fine with me. Say hello to Todd's parents for me." She grabbed her favorite coffee cup and filled it to the brim.

"So tell me, how was dinner? Chief Andy sure looked hot. I should ground you for coming in after curfew. What time did you get home, anyway?"

Her niece fairly flew around the kitchen. The only time she wasn't moving was when she slept. It always amazed Jessica when she watched her niece sleep as a young girl that the same body sleeping so heavily in her bed would hours later be moving at the speed of light.

"Honey, I can only handle one question at a time. We went to Snoqualmie Falls for dinner and it was delicious. Yes, she looked very nice and I'm sorry I was so late, we were talking about the town and her job. The time just got away from us." Jessica sipped her coffee slowly, hoping to discourage Jennifer from continuing to question her.

"So tell me Aunt Jess, did she kiss you goodnight?"

Jessica looked up at Jennifer with a startled look. "Excuse me?" She was very uncomfortable talking about this with her niece.

"Well, did she?" Jennifer grinned at her.

"Jennifer, I don't remember quizzing you about your first date with Todd," Jessica reminded her.

"Aunt Jess, we talk about everything. Don't be embarrassed," Jennifer reminded her, and she was right. Normally she wouldn't be so reticent, but this woman was special.

"Yes, we shared a kiss last night, now enough with the questions."

"Are you going out with her again?"

"I imagine we will."

"That's terrific!" Jennifer hugged her aunt. "You guys make a cute couple. I have to run. See you tonight."

Jessica sighed as her niece bolted out the front door. What she needed today of all days was peace and quiet, and some time to think about her feelings for Andy. Just thinking about her made her body flush with heat. Jessica spent the bulk of her day sketching in her studio; she had several ideas just waiting to be put on paper.

Andy and Buck hiked for several hours before Jessica even crawled out of bed. They traveled along the riverbank and then climbed higher up into the mountain, through a meadow filled with wild flowers.

"Buck, this is incredible."

"It is, isn't it? I thought we could head up higher on the ridge before stopping for lunch. There are some waterfalls I'd like to show you."

"Sounds good."

"How's your job going?"

"Good. Other then Len, I think everyone else has accepted me."

"He's angry about being passed over. He'll get over it."

"There is more to it then that. I'm a gay woman."

"A very well trained, intelligent, gay woman."

"It's going to be a while before he trusts me."

"My money's on you, kid. Now tell me, how was your dinner with Jessica?"

Andy blushed as she prepared to respond. She wasn't used to sharing that part of her life with many people. "It was very nice."

"Are you going out again?" Buck asked as he steadily led the way up the mountain path.

"Yes. Buck, are you playing matchmaker?" Andy grinned as she struggled to keep up with him.

"You couldn't do better with Jessica and I know you would be good for her."

"Why Buck, you old romantic, you." Andy laughed.

"Hey, quit yakking, and start hiking." Buck grumbled good-naturedly. Andy wisely remained silent but couldn't keep from grinning as she followed him through the forest.

It was just after five when the telephone rang while Jessica sat drawing in her studio. "Hello."

"Hi. I hope you know how to do CPR. Buck hiked the legs off me." Andy laughed. "Why didn't you warn me?"

"You poor baby, have you eaten yet?"

"No, I just walked in the door."

"How about I pick up something for dinner?

"Perfect, I'll leave the front door unlocked for you. I've got to clean up."

"I'll be there in about twenty minutes."

"Jessica, I'm looking forward to seeing you."

"I can't wait to see you, Andy." Jessica smiled.

"Hurry."

"I will."

Jessica had cleaned up earlier and was wearing a pair of faded old jeans, a red bulky knit sweater, and a pair of moccasins. She checked herself quickly in the hall mirror, running her hands through her hair. She wrote a quick note to Jennifer telling her where she would be, and included the telephone number. Turning the alarm on, she locked the front door and left. She headed for town and the delicatessen, the one place she could be guaranteed to get something good to eat. She ordered soup and vegetable quiche for two and was on her way to Andy's in less than twenty minutes.

The closer she got to Andy's home the more nervous she became. What if Andy didn't feel the same way? Maybe she just wanted something casual. Maybe she didn't find Jessica that physically appealing. By the time Jessica pulled into Andy's driveway, she had talked herself into believing Andy just wanted to be friends. She was extremely nervous. Grabbing her bag of food, she walked up to the front door and knocked. Getting no answer, she entered the house.

"Andy, I'm here."

She spoke loudly in case Andy was in another room. Not hearing an answer, she walked into the kitchen and began to unpack their dinner. She looked through the cupboards and drawers until she found plates, bowls, and silverware, and set the table. She heard footsteps behind her and nervously turned around. Her pulse raced as she looked directly into Andy's violet eyes. Andy was wearing a pair of jeans and a T- shirt with the initials FBI on the front, and was busily drying her hair with a towel. She looked freshly tousled, and all Jessica wanted to do was rush over to her and kiss her. She stayed where she was, smiling and nervously shifting from foot to foot. She was waiting to see what Andy would do.

"So, what are we having for dinner?" Andy moved slowly into the kitchen, her feet bare. She had just stepped out of the shower, and the thought of her in the shower intrigued Jessica very much.

"I brought hot soup and vegetable quiche. Have a seat, it's still warm." She smiled to hide her nerves, feeling very insecure.

"I've something more important to do right now." Andy quickly twisted her hair up in a towel and moved over to stand directly in front of Jessica. "Are you as nervous as I am?" Andy asked as her arms reached out and gathered Jessica close to her.

"Yes, I'm very nervous." She admitted as she slid her arms around Andy's neck. They kissed slowly and thoroughly, and their nervousness subsided.

"I'm glad you came over. I was thinking about you all day," Andy admitted.

"I thought about you, too. I just couldn't wait to see you again. This is so silly, my being so nervous." Jessica blushed as she spoke.

"I don't think it's silly," Andy reassured her, smiling. "I think it's wonderful and that you're pretty terrific."

Jessica's response was to kiss Andy again, as she fitted her body against Andy's. It was several minutes before they pulled away from each other. Andy held Jessica's hand as they walked to their dinner sitting on the table.

"Let me go braid my hair and I'll be right back." Andy leaned into Jessica and kissed her lightly. "Don't go away."

"I'll be here." Jessica reassured her with smile.

It was only a couple of minutes before Andy returned with her hair neatly braided. "Let's eat," Andy announced as she entered. "Jessica, what you want to drink? I think I have some white wine, pop, juice, water, what would you like?"

"A glass of white wine if you'll have one."

"Perfect. As you can see I don't have much in the way of dishes or glassware, but I should have two wine glasses around here somewhere. Here you go." Andy poured two glasses and carried them to the table where Jessica was seated. "Here's your wine. It's not exactly a great year," Andy teased her. "Let me get one more thing and this dinner will be perfect." Andy rummaged through a cupboard and a drawer behind Jessica. "There we go."

Andy placed two candlesticks in the center of the table, and then lit the candles. Quickly she switched off the overhead lights. "Now it's perfect."

Jessica smiled at Andy as she sat down. Jessica had placed their seats at an angle so that they could see each other. She wanted to look at Andy and to be close to her. The candlelight glistened off Andy's shiny blue-black hair, and her eyes sparkled. Jessica, at that moment, fell in love with Andy. This woman had turned a quick takeout meal into a romantic candlelit dinner. Jessica smiled and leaned toward Andy to kiss her deeply.

"Thank you," she whispered into Andy's ear.

"For what?" Andy whispered back, looking into Jessica's eyes.

"For finding me." She kissed Andy with all the passion she felt at that moment.

Andy moaned in response as she pulled Jessica out of her chair and onto her lap, never breaking the kiss. She placed a hand on either side of Jessica's face and began to cover her face with kisses. Finally finding Jessica's lips again, her tongue entered Jessica's mouth, meeting hers and sliding deliciously around her lips. Andy's hands slid down to the edge of Jessica's sweater and slipped underneath. Her hands against Jessica's back felt perfect as they pulled Jessica tightly against Andy's body. Jessica enjoyed the feel of her breasts against Andy's. Taking it slowly was proving to be very difficult with this woman. It was much later before either one of them thought about their dinner.

"I had better put the soup in the microwave. Otherwise we'll be eating cold soup." Andy helped Jessica off her lap and then carried their now cold soup to the kitchen. "It will only take a couple minutes."

"Andy, why are you single?"

"What do you mean, like I'm horrible in bed, I snore, that type of stuff?" She teased.

"You know what I mean."

"My last relationship ended about six months before I moved here. I found out that my then current girlfriend Rachel had been sleeping with a mutual acquaintance of ours for about a year."

"Oh Andy, I'm sorry."

"It's okay now. Rachel wanted to work it out, but I couldn't forgive her. It was not working anyway. It was just a matter of time."

"Why was that?"

"Rachel and I had different goals. It just took a while for us to figure it out. I don't really care much about making a lot of money, I would really rather enjoy my job." Andy brought the heated soup back the table. "What about you?"

"What about me?" Jessica asked. "This soup is good."

"Don't change the subject."

"Okay, I'll talk." Jessica grinned. "When I moved here I had more than enough trouble learning how to raise two children, so I imposed a hard and fast rule."

Andy looked at Jessica, puzzled by that statement. "What rule?"

"I made a promise to myself that as long as the kids lived at home I would not bring a woman home with me. I have always been honest with the kids about my life. They have known I am gay since they were tiny. My sister and her husband insisted upon it."

"Then why did you place that restriction on your life? It must have limited your relationships."

"Boy, did it ever. The minute I mentioned I was raising two children and that no matter how important a woman was to me I would not sleep with her in my home, they were gone. Silly, huh." Jessica laughed uncomfortably.

"I don't think it's silly. Those children depended upon you for everything, let alone your dealing with your own losses. It's difficult to nurture a successful lesbian relationship without all those other responsibilities. Have you been able to have a relationship despite your rule?"

"I would say I have had extended dating relationships and one that lasted several months. She was a school counselor and she kept reassuring me that Jenn and Tommy were almost adults and that they would understand. You could say she gave me an ultimatum, and I made the decision to end the relationship. It was the best thing for both of us, because I realized I wasn't in love with her. I wouldn't have ended it if I was. I would have found a way to make it work."

"Do you believe in love at first sight?" Andy had listened quietly while Jessica talked but her question seemed very important to her. She stared intently at Jessica.

"Yes, I do. What about you?"

"Until recently I didn't, but I've changed my mind." Andy looked at Jessica and smiled. "I'm going to go out on a limb here but I think it's worth it. I'm rapidly falling in love with you, and if that's too serious for you all I ask is that you let me know now before we get any more involved with each other."

Jessica's eyes welled with tears. Losing this woman would not be an option. "Andy, I want this to happen as much as you do. There is no question in my mind that I am falling in love with you. I was afraid you didn't feel the same way."

"I do."

Andy met her coming out of her chair. Their lips touched in a tender kiss, one that held a promise of newfound love. It was several moments before they hugged tightly, neither one wanting to let go. Andy was the first to speak.

"I guess this means when we decide to spend the night together it will be here? I had better purchase a bed." She teased.

"You don't have a bed?"

"Of course I do, do you want to see it?"

Jessica grinned in response to Andy's teasing. "Was that just a trick to get me in your bed?"

"A trick. Did it work?" Andy pushed Jessica's hair out of her face, a gesture that Jessica was beginning to love along with the woman who did it.

"You don't have to trick me, just ask."

"I will remember that." Andy wiggled her eyebrows at Jessica, making her giggle. "Let's put these dishes in the sink, and then I'm going to do my very best to demonstrate to you my gratefulness for bringing dinner."

"Your very best," Jessica requested.

Twenty minutes later, Andy lit her fireplace and brought a blanket for the two of them to snuggle with on the couch.

"You didn't tell me about your hike with Buck."

"It was fun. He showed me a waterfall, and we walked through an old growth forest. It's so beautiful here, I love it."

"Buck knows these mountains and the river better than anyone. He has shown the kids and me many beautiful places."

"Maybe you and I can go on a hike with Buck some time."

"I'd love to."

"Let's wait awhile so I can recuperate from today's hike."

"Are you terribly sore?"

"Let's put it this way, consider yourself lucky you won't be around to see me try to get out of bed."

"I don't know about that." Jessica laughed.

"I promise you, it won't be pretty." Andy groaned.

"I got a terrific idea. Do you have any lotion?"

"Yes."

"You do have a dryer, don't you?"

"Of course, and a matching washer."

"I need two big bath towels, the lotion, and then you go put on a pair of shorts. I am going to give you a rubdown. It will make you less sore in the morning."

"You don't have to do that. I'll be fine. You didn't come over here to take care of me."

Jessica kissed her quickly. "You can take care of me next time, now get me what I need, please." Andy did as Jessica asked and returned with two towels and the lotion. "Where is your dryer?"

"Through that door in the laundry room."

"Go change into shorts."

Jessica went and placed both towels on high in the dryer, then came back into the living room and spread the blanket out in front of the fireplace. She turned when she heard bare feet padding down the hall. Andy had changed into a pair of black shorts as Jessica had asked. She couldn't help but admire Andy's legs. They were well muscled and nicely shaped. Jessica's mouth went dry as raw lust flooded her body.

"Andy, come lay down on your stomach and relax. I'm going to work on your legs."

As Andy did as she asked, she spoke. "Should I ask where you learned your skills?"

"When Tommy was a lot younger he grew too fast for his joints and his legs would ache, keeping him awake at night. The doctor told me this would help with the pain." Jessica put some lotion in her hand to warm it. "Are you ready? This lotion may be a little cold."

"I can take it. I am a tough police officer," Andy bragged, giggling.

It wasn't that Jessica feared the lotion was cold that made her hesitate, it was the sight of Andy lying on the blanket in front of her. She slowly placed her hands on Andy's calf and began to massage the muscles, rubbing and kneading. She spent ten minutes on each calf, first one then the other, using her fingers to smooth the muscles until they relaxed. She then moved to the upper thighs, being careful not to go any higher than where the shorts ended. The muscles of Andy's thighs were well defined, firm, and smooth. While Jessica worked on them she could feel Andy gradually relax as she rubbed.

"Stay right there and don't move, I'll be right back," Jessica instructed. She retrieved one of the now warm towels from the dryer. Returning to the living room she knelt down and laid the towel over Andy's legs.

"That feels wonderful," Andy responded, stretching on the blanket. "I feel better already."

"Now don't move, let the heat soak in. Then I'm going to have you roll over and I will massage the front of your legs." Jessica waited ten minutes before asking Andy to lie on her back. Andy did as Jessica instructed, placing one arm behind her head, watching her very closely.

"Now, we do the front of your legs." Jessica was much more nervous with Andy watching her every move. She began her massage on Andy's lower legs, rubbing and stretching each one completely. She then placed her hands on Andy's upper thigh, glancing up to find Andy's beautiful eyes following her movements. She continued her ministrations until she felt the muscles relax under her fingers. She again retrieved the second hot towel and covered the front of Andy's legs with its warmth. She sat back and watched Andy as she lay silently enjoying the heat.

Andy reached out and gently tugged until Jessica leaned over and kissed her. Andy deepened the kiss by opening her mouth to Jessica's tongue. Andy's arms wrapped around Jessica's neck and pulled her gently down on top of her until Jessica's upper body was leaning fully on hers as they continued kissing. Andy rolled onto her side, sliding her body against Jessica's. She nuzzled Jessica's neck with her lips and tasted her skin with her tongue. She reached the top of Jessica's sweater and then began kissing her jaw line back to her mouth. Jessica's hands slipped under Andy's T- shirt and floated along her ribs until she ran into the edge of Andy's bra. She wasn't sure if Andy would think she was moving too fast and she didn't want to scare her. As if reading her mind, Andy reached down and slid the bottom of Jessica's sweater up until her stomach was uncovered. She leaned over and placed moist kisses on her stomach and lower ribs. Her fingers traced a path on Jessica's skin, causing her to tremble with anticipation.

Andy raised her head and looked at Jessica as she spoke. "Is this okay with you?" Her eyes were a deep dark purple, her lips moist, and a slight smile was on her face.

"Yes, please," She answered her as Andy caught her lips in a searing kiss. Jessica reached down and grasped Andy's T-shirt, pulling it up and off at the same time Andy pulled Jessica's sweater off. They smiled at each other as they lay side by side. Andy's hands reached behind Jessica and unhooked her bra as Jessica slipped it off her shoulders and away from her body. Andy leaned down and left a string of kisses down the center of both breasts, placing her face against the fullness of Jessica. Jessica's nipples hardened in response. More than anything she wanted Andy's mouth on her breasts. She also needed to touch Andy, to taste her. She removed Andy's bra and ran her fingers around Andy's nipple, watching it as it hardened in response to her touch. Andy's breasts were full and beautiful to Jessica and she kissed them lightly. Andy moaned with pleasure, wrapping her arms around Jessica's shoulders, encouraging her to continue. Jessica loved Andy's response as she opened her mouth and sucked lightly. Andy arched her back and clutched Jessica tightly as Jessica's fingers replaced her mouth, and she moved to bathe the other breast with her tongue and lips. She tasted and kissed Andy's breasts, memorizing the flavor and texture until Andy lifted her head up and looked at her. Andy's eyes glistened with passion, her lids heavy, as she continued to gaze at Jessica. Slowly she kissed her, coaxing Jessica's mouth open with her lips as her tongue plunged in, sliding in and out as Jessica's lips suckled. Andy's fingers cupped Jessica's breasts as she spoke.

"You have beautiful breasts," she whispered as she took a nipple into her mouth. Andy's mouth felt hot and Jessica could feel the heat rush through her body, centering between her legs as the familiar throbbing began. She held Andy's head while she smothered both of Jessica's breasts with kisses. Jessica's head was thrown back in pleasure, her eyes closed, as she relished the feelings Andy was stirring in her body. Her hips moved in response as the need began to build. Andy's fingers continued their magic as she rose up and kissed Jessica over and over again. Their passion was becoming unrestrained and overwhelming; their breathing became labored as the two of them barely controlled their bodies. Andy slowed her kisses until the their hearts stopped their rapid beating and they lay quietly in each others arms, their naked breasts pressed together. Their legs had wrapped around each other as they pressed their hips together. Jessica's leg wedged tightly between Andy's, as they savored the feeling they got from lying with each other. It was a long time before either one of them moved, their faces pressed against one another other.

"Andy, I think I should be going. If I don't leave now, I won't be able to," Jessica admitted as she looked at Andy.

"I know." Andy smiled warmly as they sat up. Jessica reached for her bra and sweater to put it back on. "Jessica, you are so beautiful." Andy placed the palm of her hand against Jessica's chest above her heart.

"Oh, Andy, I think you're beautiful." Jessica smiled as she gazed at Andy. "I don't want to leave," She admitted.

"I don't want you to leave, but there will be plenty of time," Andy reassured her as she pulled her T-shirt on. Leaning over, she kissed Jessica lightly on the lips. "I'm not going anywhere." She reached behind Jessica and helped her with her bra.

Jessica pulled her sweater on and then hugged Andy to her. "I feel like I've known you for a long time. This feels right."

"I know what you mean," Andy admitted. "I've never reacted to anyone like I am to you."

"I hate to leave, but I'd better." Jessica grimaced as she kissed Andy again before she stood up.

"Will you call me when you get home? I just want to hear your voice before I go to sleep," Andy whispered to Jessica as she walked her to the door.

"As soon as I get home, I promise," Jessica pledged. Andy hugged her tightly and then watched her leave.

There was no doubt in Andy's mind she was falling head over heels for Jessica, and she was hopeful Jessica felt the same way. She would have no trouble sleeping tonight as long as she dreamed about Jessica.

Jessica resented the short drive home. Her body still vibrated with unfulfilled longing. She was overwhelmed with her feelings for Andy; it had happened so fast. She opened the door to her home and looked around. She loved her life, she was proud of her niece and nephew, and she found great joy in creating her artwork, but until tonight she hadn't realized how lonely she was. In a week, Andy had started to fill in the missing pieces of her life and heart. What was she going to do?

"Aunt Jess, are you okay?" Jennifer came slowly down the stairs in her pajamas, her face showing her concern.

"I'm fine, honey. I was just thinking about something."

"You look so sad. What is it?" Jennifer wrapped her arms around her aunt and hugged her tightly.

"I was just thinking how fast we are all growing up."

"I love you, Aunt Jess."

"I love you, too."

"Where did you go tonight?"

"Out for a bite to eat."

"By yourself?" Jennifer eyed her suspiciously.

"No, I had dinner with Andy," Jessica answered truthfully. She would always be honest with Jennifer.

"Did you have a good time?" Jennifer took a seat on the stairs, her chin in her hands. It was a rare moment when Jennifer sat calmly.

"Yes, I did. I enjoy Andy's company very much." Jessica sat on the stair below Jennifer. Jennifer wrapped her arms around her aunt and leaned her head on Jessica's shoulder. This was something she had done from the first day Jessica moved in to take care of her and her brother. She hadn't done it for quite awhile, and it made Jessica feel wonderful that she wasn't too old to do it now.

"You like Chief Andy a lot."

"Yes, I do," she responded quietly. It felt good to admit it to someone else.

"Does she care as much about you?"

Jennifer thought about her answer for a moment. "Yes, she does." Jessica watched Jennifer as she spoke. "Does that bother you?"

Jennifer smiled at her aunt. "I think it's terrific. She's real nice and she is very pretty, and if she loves you, Aunt Jess, that is all I care about."

"She is beautiful, and I think she does love me," Jessica agreed, smiling at her niece.

"So when will you see her again?

"Sunday night and maybe later this week if our schedules work out."

"Aunt Jess, does this mean you and Chief Andy are going steady?" Jennifer teased.

"Oh, you." Jessica laughed and began tickling her niece. The two of them giggled until Jennifer squealed "Uncle".

"I'm going to go crawl in bed," Jessica announced and stood up.

"Me, too." Jennifer slipped her arm through Jessica's as they walked up the stairs.

"You know, it could be real cool to have the Police Chief as a step mom. Isn't there some dispensation from speeding tickets for the step-daughter?" Jennifer grinned mischievously as she entered her bedroom. "Real cool." Jennifer shut her door before a very surprised and amused Jessica could respond.

Opening the door and grinning, she responded to her outrageous niece. "You are not too old to ground, young lady." Jennifer just grinned as she crawled into bed.

"Goodnight, Jennifer."

"I love you, Aunt Jess."

"Love you too, honey, and Jenn? Thank you."

"For what."

"For just being you." Jessica smiled fondly at her niece and pulled the door shut.

She walked happily down the hall to her bedroom. Fifteen minutes later, her face scrubbed and her teeth brushed, she crawled into bed herself and picked up the telephone on her bedside table. She dialed the number from memory.

"Hello." Andy's voice was as sexy as her kiss, and it had the same affect on Jessica. Her skin tingled, waiting to respond to Andy's touch.

"Hi."

"I miss you."

"I wish you were here."

"With your niece in the other room?"

Jessica chuckled. "She asked me tonight if we are going steady."

"What did you say?"

"I told her you hadn't asked me," Jessica teased.

"Beautiful Jessie, would you please go steady with me?" Jessica had never heard a more romantic request.

"I would be honored. Andy, will you go steady with me?"

"I thought you'd never ask." Neither one laughed or giggled. This was a very serious moment for the two of them.

"I think we need to make this official, Ms. Jessica. Would you go for a walk with me tomorrow night?"

"I would love to." Jessica's doubts had fled completely. "Why don't we go for a walk after Jennifer's dinner."

"That sounds perfect. What time should I be there?"

"Can you get here by five?"

"If you don't mind my being in uniform? I have a meeting with the night shift at nine o'clock."

"We can eat early if you need to."

"I'll get there by five, but I will have to leave by eight-thirty."

"Perfect."

"Could I bring something?"

"Just you. And Andy, I love a woman in uniform, as long as she has blue-black hair, gorgeous violet eyes, and the most luscious lips I have ever had the pleasure to taste."

"And I love a woman named Jessica, with deep copper eyes, wavy copper hair, and a face I could look at for the rest of my life."

"Thank you."

"I will thank you in person tomorrow night."

"Good night. I look forward to your thank you. I believe I have one of my own."

"Sleep tight. I'll miss you."

Jessica smiled as she hung up the telephone. She was truly in love and at this moment she knew Andy felt the same way. She drifted to sleep, her heart brimming with happiness.

By two o'clock the next afternoon, Jessica was cursing her day. Not only had she cut herself while working on a new carving, but also her nicely planned dinner was quickly falling apart. She went shopping earlier for all the ingredients for a nice meal of homemade barbecue spareribs, roasted potatoes, and a fresh spinach salad. Her trip had also included picking up fresh flowers, a card for Jennifer, and a special gift for Andy. Her first tragedy after bandaging her finger was a full bottle of salad dressing leaking in her grocery bag. The second tragedy was a large chip on her favorite vase. Things were still not going the way Jessica had planned. She wanted the evening to be special and she was close to tears when the telephone rang.

"Hello." Jessica's voice sounded harsh even to her ears.

"Jessica, it's Andy. Is everything okay?"

"Hi, everything is fine, how is your day going?" She certainly wasn't going to admit to Andy that her day was crumbling around her.

"Hectic, actually. I can't wait to see you. I just wanted to check again to see if I could bring something?"

"Just you, and I can't wait to see you."

"I'll be there as close to five as possible, if that's okay?"

"Perfect. Andy, I miss you," Jessica whispered.

"I miss you, too."

"See you soon."

"Goodbye."

Andy's telephone call had a calming affect on Jessica. It wasn't like her to get frazzled. The rest of the afternoon ran smoothly and at a little after four Jennifer bounced through the front door. Jessica had reminded her at breakfast that Andy was coming over for dinner.

"Aunt Jessica, I'm home," She announced as she tripped up the stairs.

"Hey, Jenn, how was your day?" Jessica answered from the kitchen.

"Great! I'll be right down." True to her word, Jennifer entered the kitchen moments later. "I'm going to ace my Chemistry final. Vicki and I studied all day." She grinned as she grabbed an apple from a bowl on the counter.

"Good for you, I know you've been studying hard for it."

"Yeah, I studied for my French final too, but I got an A minus."

Jennifer expected to get an A in every subject. She was harder on herself than anyone else could be. Jessica was always reminding her that as long as she did the very best Jessica couldn't ask for anything more.

"Honey, an A minus is very good."

"I know but I want an A. What's for dinner?"

"I'm fixing spareribs. And don't change the subject."

"My favorite. I know if I do my very best you will love it." She grinned at her aunt.

"I know it's your favorite, it's your dinner, honey. Would you do me a favor and set the table for three while I go clean up?"

"Sure, Aunt Jess. What happened to your hand?"

"I cut myself carving, it's just a little thing. Now I am going upstairs. Would you please use the cloth napkins?"

"Yep, Aunt Jess, you want me to put candles on the table? It would make dinner more romantic." She smiled as she placed silverware on the table.

"You set it anyway you want. There are fresh flowers on the counter. I am going upstairs now." She kissed Jennifer on the top of her head and left Jennifer to her own devices.

An hour later, Jessica had just finished dressing when the doorbell rang. She had decided on a pair of khaki pants and a gold silk blouse. Taking one last peek at herself in the mirror, she smiled and walked downstairs. She could hear Jennifer and Andy talking in the kitchen.

"Hi." She smiled and spoke to Andy. The navy blue uniform she wore couldn't hide Andy's trim figure. Her hair was pulled back into a bun at the base of her neck. She looked a little intimidating until Jessica saw her face. Andy's eyes sparkled as she smiled hello.

"Hi yourself."

"Aunt Jess, isn't Chief Andy's uniform neat? She even let me try on her hat. Cool, huh!"

"Very cool."

"I hope you don't mind. I have to wear my gun and I can't leave it in my car. I brought a bag to put it in." Andy was concerned that Jessica would be upset.

"That's not a problem, Jennifer and I have been around guns. We both learned gun safety from Buck and we know to treat each gun as if it's loaded. Right Jess?"

"Yep, Uncle Buck used to bring his gun when we went hiking. He showed it to all of us."

"Buck's one of the safest police officers I know," Andy admitted.

"Can I get you something to drink?" Jessica touched Andy's arm as she spoke.

"I would love a glass of water."

"Jenn, you want something?"

"No thanks, Aunt Jess. Chief Andy, do you wear a bullet proof vest?"

Jessica smiled as she poured both Andy and herself a glass of water. Jennifer was going to get all her questions answered. "Andy, please sit down." Jessica would have loved to hug her hello.

"Thank you. Jennifer, please call me Andy, and yes, I do wear a bulletproof vest sometimes. I'm not wearing it today because I've been in the office all day. When I go on patrol I wear it." She sat down across from Jennifer.

"Have you ever shot someone?"

"Jenn," Jessica admonished her.

"No, I have never shot anyone. It's very rare that police officers or FBI agents ever fire their weapons at someone. I have been very lucky," Andy informed Jennifer, who listened very carefully. "We are not like the police officers you see on television. We all try our hardest to prevent having to use any form of force."

Jennifer smiled. "That's cool."

"I think so," Andy agreed. "Now, tell me about school. Don't you graduate in a couple of months?"

"Yep, in fact, Aunt Jess, I get my graduation pictures back on Friday."

"Great. We will have to get your graduation invitations written and mailed out." Jessica was so glad Jennifer and Andy were so relaxed around each other. She could tell Jenn like Andy.

"Hey Andy, would you come to my graduation? You can sit with Aunt Jess," Jennifer asked, grinning. Jessica was so surprised at her niece she just stared at her.

"I am honored to be invited to your graduation. As for sitting with your aunt, don't you think you should talk to her first?" Andy didn't want to put Jessica on the spot.

"Oh, she would want you there. She likes you a whole lot." Jennifer's face colored as she realized what she said.

"Jennifer!" Jessica could have throttled her.

"Well, Jennifer, I like your aunt very much," Andy admitted, amusement in her voice. Her eyes twinkled at Jessica. Jessica smiled in return. "Jessica, would you show me your studio? I would like to see where you work."

"Sure."

"I'm going to go call Vicki," Jennifer announced.

"Jenn, dinner in a half an hour," Jessica called as Jennifer headed upstairs to her room.

"Okay."

"I hope she didn't embarrass you," Jessica said to Andy. "She tends to be very direct."

"She didn't, and it's nice that she's so honest. So, you like me a lot?" Andy teased.

"She was right about that," Jessica admitted, standing in front of Andy's chair. "I like you in uniform."

"Why, thank you, ma'am. You sure look beautiful." She smiled so sweetly that Jessica couldn't resist hugging her.

"I wish I could kiss you right now."

"Not with your niece upstairs. Now why don't you show me your studio," Andy suggested. "I would love to kiss you, too." She squeezed

Jessica's hand. "What happened to your hand?" Andy asked as she noticed the bandage.

"It's nothing. I just nicked myself carving earlier."

"Did you wash it real well?" Andy looked closely at the bandage.

"I did. Don't worry, it happens once in awhile. Come on, I'll show you where I work." Jessica took Andy by the hand.

She led Andy through the kitchen into her studio. It had been a separate building at one time, but Jessica finished an enclosed walkway on the extended back deck a year earlier. The room wasn't extremely large, not more than fifteen feet by twenty feet, with big windows on all four walls. Jessica's workbench was along the window facing the river with the mountains behind it. The remaining areas contained shelving and tool cabinets. Currently she had four pieces in work, one nearly finished, and three others she had just begun to shape. Shaping was the first part of the process and took the longest.

"I didn't realize you worked with such large pieces of wood," Andy stated as she looked at the workbench. "Is all this wood found around here?"

"Almost all of it. I try and only use wood that is already on the ground. I don't cut any trees down to get a piece. I've used driftwood from the river and a few pieces from the ocean. Most of it I have found laying on the ground in the woods."

"How do you decide what you're going to carve?"

"I have sketches of things I want to carve and I try and match them to a piece of wood. Here are some sketches I'm working on." Jessica opened a large folder and spread around some heavy papers.

"These sketches are just as beautiful as the carvings. Do you ever sell them?"

"No, these are what I work from. No one sees them at the gallery."

"They are just overwhelming. I can't believe how talented you are." Andy continued to stare at the drawings Jessica had laid on the table. "What do you do with the sketches when you're done with the carving?"

"I usually file them with a photograph or two of the work. I keep a record of each one and where it goes. I like to know who has them."

"Is it hard to sell them?"

"Not always. Every once in awhile I do one I feel very connected to and then it's hard to see it go."

"What you do is so amazing. I envy your talent and creativity."

"Just like I admire the skill and talents that have made you a successful police officer."

"While we are out here I have something I want to give you." Andy smiled as she reached in her back pocket. "You have to have something if we are going steady." She handed Jessica a small black jeweler's box.

"Just a minute, I have something for you." Jessica laughed. "I'll be right back."

Jessica retrieved the small box she had in her purse in the kitchen. Returning to the studio, she handed it to Andy, who laughed along with her.

"I guess we both had the same idea."

"Open yours first," Jessica requested, and Andy did as she was asked. Pulling off the box lid, off she revealed a beautiful gold rope chain with a small, stylized gold heart hanging from it.

"I don't know if you wear jewelry, but I thought you could wear this under your uniform." Jessica spoke nervously.

"I love it!" Andy exclaimed. "I'll put it on right now." True to her word, Andy put the necklace on, and slipped it under her uniform shirt. "Now open your gift."

Jessica slowly flipped the lid back on the jeweler's box to reveal a tiny gold signet ring. The face of the ring had the initial J engraved on it. "Oh my."

"You're supposed to wear it on your little finger," Andy explained. "I didn't know if you liked rings, and I don't know if it will fit. You can take it in and get it sized."

Jessica looked happily at Andy. "Thank you, it's beautiful, and so dainty." She slipped the ring on the little finger of her right hand. It slid right on. "It fits perfectly."

"So, is it official then, we're going steady?"

"It's very official," Jessica responded.

"Now, if Jennifer asks you can tell her we are going steady," Andy teased.

"I will, but I still don't believe we both had the same idea." Jessica leaned toward Andy as she whispered. "I don't care if my niece is in the house with us, I want to kiss you." Jessica put her arm around Andy's neck and they shared a brief soft kiss. Andy took Jessica's hand in hers as they parted, placing a small kiss on the ring nestled on her little finger.

"I have to tell you I have never acted like this before. Usually I've dated someone for quite awhile before I know how I feel and know it is real. It just feels right somehow. I hope I'm not scaring you." Andy watched Jessica carefully.

Jessica picked up Andy's hand, turned it over, and brought it to her lips. She kissed the palm of Andy's hand. "I'm not scared. Maybe we both should be, but I'm not. I feel so different with you. I know I can trust you when I tell you how I feel, and it does feel right. It's like I've known you forever," She reassured Andy.

"I know we've seen each other every day but I miss you when you're not around." Andy's finger touched Jessica's mouth very softly.

"I miss you too, but if you have other things you want or need to do I would understand."

"Same for you. I just want you to know that I would love to see you every day but I know you have other commitments."

"Andy, you are one of my commitments." Jessica smiled. "What time are you due back at work?"

"I should be there about eight-thirty. I've scheduled a meeting from nine to ten and then I'm taking the eleven to six a.m. shift." Andy reached out and touched Jessica's cheek. "You are so beautiful. Breathtaking."

Jessica kissed Andy again. "You'll be up for over twenty-four hours, honey. You're going to be exhausted."

"I can sleep tomorrow when I get off. I've got to spend time working each shift so I know what to expect." Andy and Jessica's faces were inches apart as they talked.

"We'd better eat then, so you can get back to work. I know Jennifer was very excited that you were coming for dinner."

"We better go find her, since it's her celebration. I brought her a card."

"Andy, I love you," Jessica whispered.

"Jessica, I love you." Andy smiled and hugged her quickly.

"I love the ring."

"Good, and thank you for my necklace. Now let's go call Jennifer for dinner."

Jennifer answered Jessica's call that dinner was ready and the three of them sat down to a nice humor-filled meal. Andy shared some of the funnier moments of being a police officer and kept both Jessica and Jennifer laughing. It was over an hour before they cleared the table and all went into the living room. Jennifer excitedly shared her plans for college with Andy and even asked her opinion.

"What do you think, Andy, the University of Washington or Stanford?"

"Both are good schools, Jennifer, but if I was granted a full scholarship it would be hard to turn it down. They both have a good program for your major."

"That's kind of what I think," Jennifer revealed.

Jessica just listened and smiled. It was wonderful to see Jennifer respond so positively to Andy. It was another half-hour of conversation and the opening of cards from Andy and Jessica, before a telephone call from Todd captured Jennifer's attention. He called her from work. He was a thoughtful young man and wanted to congratulate Jennifer. He knew how important college was to her and was very impressed with her being offered a scholarship.

"Andy, it was fun talking to you, and thanks for the card. When are you coming over again?"

"It was a pleasure talking to you. Congratulations." Andy replied with a smile. "I'll come over when Jessica invites me."

"Cool. Aunt Jess, when can Andy come over again?"

"Jennifer, Andy and I haven't talked about it yet, but it will be soon. It depends on our schedules," Jessica explained, laughing.

"See you, Andy." Much to Andy and Jessica's surprise, Jennifer quickly hugged Andy goodbye and began to leave the room.

"Jennifer, I asked Jessica to go steady with me." Andy's eyes twinkled.

"That's real cool." Jennifer grinned and ran up the stairs. Jessica and Andy burst into laughter.

"She's a sweetheart," Andy announced.

"Yes, she is. I can tell she really likes you. She doesn't usually ask too many people for advice and she trusts you enough to ask about college."

"I hope I didn't encourage her to do something against your wishes," Andy said apologetically.

"Not at all. Jennifer and I have talked about her choice of colleges many times. It is her choice. I would like to see her go to the University. I don't like the idea of her being so far away even though her brother is at Berkeley."

"It's understandable that you don't want her to go to California. She's still a young girl. I would feel the same way."

"Thanks for listening to her. She needs to talk to someone other then me, and get advice from someone else. Besides, since we are going steady that makes you almost a family member." Jessica grinned.

"I couldn't think of a better family to belong to." Andy was serious as she spoke. "I'm sorry we couldn't go for a walk tonight, but I'd better head back to the office. Officer Stubben is just waiting for me to do something wrong, like showing up late for my own meeting." She frowned.

"If you get a chance, call me tomorrow after you have gotten some sleep."

"I will. Thanks for dinner. I had a terrific time and I love my necklace."

"And I love my ring." Jessica slipped her arm through Andy's as they walked to the front door. She turned to look at Andy before she left and hugged her tightly. "I wish you didn't have to leave."

"So do I. I'll try and call you later." They kissed very softly, both aware of Jennifer not a room away.

"Be careful, and come back to me," Jessica whispered.

"I'll be back, you can count on it," Andy promised. "Jess, I love you."

"I love you too, Andy." Jessica smiled and kissed her again.

"I've got to go."

"I know. Be safe."

Jessica watched Andy's trim figure in her uniform as she walked to her car. As Andy pulled out of the driveway she waved goodbye to Jessica. Jessica returned the wave and then slowly closed the front door. She leaned against the door as she reflected on the last few days. She felt like she had known Andy forever. She really had fallen in love with Andy. She just wasn't sure how to deal with her new relationship and her self-imposed rule. She had never faced bringing someone new into her family, partially because she hadn't found someone until now that she could love unconditionally. Maybe it was time to talk to Jennifer and Tommy and find out what their feelings were about her relationship with Andy.

"Aunt Jess, did Andy leave already?" Jennifer loped down the stairs in her pajamas.

"Yes, sweetie, she had a meeting and then she has to work the night shift."

"Boy, she works a lot."

"She's the new Police Chief and it's going to take her awhile to figure everything out. That requires her to work very hard."

"I like her, Aunt Jess."

"I do too. Do you have a minute? I'd like to talk to you."

"Sure, what's up?" She grabbed a seat on the back of the couch. Jessica sat on the couch below her.

"I need to know what you think about Andy and I seeing each other. Does it make you uncomfortable?"

"I think it's nice that the two of you like each other, and it doesn't bother me at all. Why would it?" She looked at Jessica, puzzled.

"Well, some people might not like it if they found out. You might be teased at school. In fact, some people might get very mad and be extremely rude."

"That's their problem, not mine. I love you, and if you love her that's all that counts. Do you love her?"

"Yes, I do Jenn, but I want to make sure you and Tommy don't have a problem with Andy and I seeing each other."

"I don't have a problem with you and Andy being together as long as you are happy, and I'm sure Tommy would feel the same. Just ask him."

"I have always been honest with you about my being gay, but I haven't brought anyone into our family and I need to know that you both are okay with it."

"Call Tommy, he will tell you the same thing. We have talked about it many times. We both want you to find someone who will love you and take care of you. Tommy and I are both going to be in college and we think you need to be taken care of. You need someone to love you." Jennifer hugged Jessica.

"Well, I guess I'd better call and speak to him. Do you want to talk to him?"

"Sure."

Jessica didn't reach Tommy until a little after ten. "Hi, Aunt Jess, how are you and Jenn?" His voice sounded cheerful.

"We're good Tommy, how are you doing? How is school?"

"Great. I've got a little more then two months to go before I come back home to work. I'm looking forward to it." Tommy worked as a forest ranger in the summer. He had also trained as a mountain rescue expert and had gone out several times to find lost hikers. But he spent most of his time keeping public hiking areas safe and fighting forest fires. It had been Buck's influence and work that had gotten Tommy involved with the forest service. He enjoyed working outdoors in the woods and mountains he loved, and it was evolving into a career.

"We can't wait to have you home. We both miss you very much."

"I miss you guys, too."

"How are your grades?"

"Good Aunt Jess, I think I'm getting close to straight A's. It's been tough, though."

"Good for you, Tommy. I know you work very hard. Are you still seeing Alyse?"

"Yes, I am. Actually, I have invited her to come visit this summer for awhile, if that's okay?"

"Sure it is. She's always welcome." Tommy had invited Alyse home for the Christmas holiday to meet Jenn and Jessica. She was a beautiful, young, woman, very personable, and obviously head over heels for Tommy.

"Great, I'll let her know."

"Tommy, I need to talk to you about something."

"Sure Aunt Jess. Are you and Jenn okay?"

"Yes, we're fine. That's not it. I wanted to know your feelings about my seeing someone, a woman named Caterina Andolino."

"You're seeing someone? That's great Aunt Jess, it's about time! Where did you meet her?"

"Actually, she's our new Chief of Police. She was Buck's son's partner in the FBI when he was killed."

"Chief of Police, huh? I think Buck has talked about her. Didn't she work down here in San Francisco?"

"Yes, in fact, Buck recommended her for the job and the city council voted her in almost a month ago."

"Wow, she must be pretty good if the town council gave her the job. What's she like?"

"She's about my height, black hair, and violet eyes."

"She's a shrimp and she's a police officer?" Tommy teased.

"I wouldn't call her a shrimp to her face." Jessica laughed. He had always teased her about her size.

"Is she good to you, Aunt Jess?" Tommy asked seriously.

"She's very good to me and I like her very much."

"Sounds serious."

"It is. That's why I called. I wanted to make sure you were okay with me being involved with a woman."

"Aunt Jess, I think it's wonderful that you're seeing someone. It's about time and I hope it is serious."

"Thanks Tommy, it's important that both you and Jenn approve of me and who I see."

"What's Jenn think?"

"She's ecstatic. She all but introduced us." Jessica laughed.

"Then I'm sure I'll like her if Jenn does. I can't wait to meet her."

"Thanks Tommy, I love you."

"I love you, too."

"Now your sister wants to talk to you."

"Great, put her on."

"Jenn, Tommy is on the telephone." Jessica called to her.

"I'm coming."

"She's on her way. Tommy, do you need anything?"

"No, I'm fine."

"Thanks Tommy, here's Jenn." Jessica handed the telephone to her niece, who had all but flown down the stairs.

"Hi bro, how's college?"

Jessica left Jenn and her brother to talk. They had always been very close and Jessica encouraged them to stay in touch. She went upstairs to prepare for bed, and changed into her nightshirt, washed her face, and crawled under her covers. She looked at the signet ring on her hand and chuckled to herself. It was amazing that both she and Andy had bought each other a gift on the same day for the same reason. She turned off her light and lay in the dark wondering what Andy was up to. She slid into sleep dreaming of what her life was going to be like with Andy in it.

Chapter Five

Andy was thinking of Jessica at the very same moment. Her shift was beginning and she was sitting in a squad car on the corner of Main and Sutter. It had been a long time since Andy was on patrol, and the night shift had not been one of her favorite parts of the job even then. She would make a loop around the town and make sure all the businesses checked out. The town had very little if any crime, especially during the fall and winter. Spring and summer were completely the opposite. The town tripled in size due to the tourist season, and during some of the busier periods they were inundated with hordes of tourists. The majority of the crimes during those times were related to vacationers that had too much to drink, teenagers driving recklessly, and burglaries. Weapon problems, drugs, and murders had, up until now, not been a problem and Andy wanted to keep it that way.

She drove up and down through the streets of the town that had overnight become her home, and marveled on how comfortable she was with her job. Not only did she love her position as Police Chief, but she had also found the perfect woman. She was beautiful, sexy, and talented, and she was someone Andy could like very much. That was important to Andy. She had always wanted a relationship where she had a partner, someone she could trust for a lifetime. She had finally found that woman in Jessica. She had fallen helplessly in love with her from the first moment. She was praying that Jessica's feelings were just as strong. She thought they were. Driving slowly through town, she forced herself to concentrate on the job at hand, and it wasn't easy.

Three hours later found Andy making another loop through town. Cascade's two bars in town were closing and it was a time to watch out for anyone who tried to drive home while under the influence of alcohol. She slowed down when she noticed a crowd gathered at the door of the Watering Hole Tavern. She checked into the office by radio to let them know where she was, pulled into the parking lot, and parked the cruiser. She stepped out of the car and headed for the door.

The crowd parted enough for her to enter the tavern just in time to see a man throw a chair across the bar. He was yelling, his face a mottled red. Andy stepped up to the bar and asked the bartender what was going on.

"It's Ned Hammer. He's been on a binge and thinks he's back in Vietnam."

Andy approached the obviously angry man as he muttered and knocked over a table. "Ned, can I talk to you a minute?" She asked calmly.

"Hell, no," He bellowed at her.

"I'd like you to calm down so we can let the bartender close the place. It's getting late." Out of the corner of her eye Andy noticed Officer Stubben enter the tavern. She motioned for him to stay back.

"What's anyone know about Vietnam, especially a young gal like you? It means nothing to you young people!" He continued to bellow as he slammed a pool cue against the table.

"Ned gets like this every couple of months. He was injured very badly in Vietnam and his head ain't been straight ever since," the bartender volunteered.

"Ned, what branch of the service were you in?" Andy slowly moved closer to him. He was a large man, about six feet and two hundred pounds. She needed to get him under control before he hurt himself.

"Marines, ma'am, four years." He turned to her as he answered.

"Marines. Chief Buck's son was a Marine. Did you know him?" She was within arm's reach of him.

"I knew him, but he was too young to have served with me. Shame he was killed on the job. He was a good man." He was beginning to relax.

"He was my partner in the FBI. I wasn't working the night he was shot and killed. You're right he was a good man." Ned was finally focusing on her.

"Let's go outside and let this nice gentleman go home."

She gently took Ned by the arm and led him out the tavern door. He had obviously been drinking for quite awhile because he had to struggle to stand upright. She had gotten him about five feet out of the bar when Len decided to assist her, and grabbed Ned by his other arm. Ned was startled and roared in anger, swinging in Len's direction, catching him in the jaw with his fist. Len went down like a ton of bricks. Andy moved quickly, pinning Ned's arms behind his back and using her handcuffs to restrain him. Andy had known that in order for her to be a successful FBI agent with her small size she would have to be an expert at many forms of self-defense. It always came in handy in her line of work, as it had tonight. She had Ned controlled and in the car in less than a minute. After locking him in the back, she stepped over to check on Len, who was standing up and rubbing his jaw in obvious discomfort.

"Are you all right, Len?" She inquired quietly.

"Yeah, he tagged me a good one. How did you get the cuffs on him?"

"I used his size against him. Once I had him off balance, I could cuff him and get him into the car. He's now trying to apologize for causing any trouble."

"That's Ned. He doesn't always drink, maybe once every couple of months, but when he does he goes crazy."

"Well, unless you want to charge him with assault, I would like to take him home."

"That's a good idea. Would you like me to take him?"

"No, you go back to the precinct, I'll do it. You need to put some ice on that chin."

"Ok, thanks. And Chief, nice job."

"Thanks, Len. Now how about you tell me where Ned lives and I'll see you back at the station."

After getting directions, Andy drove Ned to his house. "Ned, you're home." He was very quiet by this time.

"Thanks, gal. I owe you," He stuttered as Andy helped him from the car and removed the cuffs.

She escorted him to the door and watched him as he entered the house. She walked back to her squad car and waited for a few moments to make sure Ned didn't try to leave again. She proceeded to write up a report, recording everything that happened. Someone would contact Ned Hammer in the morning and make arrangements for him to pay for the damages. Locking him up in jail wouldn't help Ned, and a good night's sleep would. Besides Andy had a soft spot in her heart for ex-Marines. Ten minutes later, Andy headed back to the station. Once there, she entered the precint. It was empty, but she heard voices coming from the break room.

"You should have seen her, Susan, she had the cuffs on Ned before I could sit up. Ned has to weigh over two hundred pounds and what does she weigh? One hundred, if that?" It was Len's voice.

"Hello, anyone here?" She called from the front office. She didn't want anyone to think she'd been eavesdropping.

"We're in here," Susan Nelson, the night dispatcher, answered.

Andy entered the break room to find Len seated at the table, an ice pack held against his chin. Susan was seated across from him eating her late night snack.

"How's the chin?"

"Fine. A little tender, but fine."

"Let's see it." Andy approached him. Len removed the ice pack to reveal a large purple welt on the side of his jaw. "You're going to have a pretty nasty bruise by morning. Keep the ice on it to keep the swelling down."

"Hey Chief, maybe you could show me how you did that tonight. You know, that thing you did to subdue Ned?" Len asked politely.

"It's a form of karate, and I would be glad to show you sometime."

"Great, thanks." He smiled as he spoke to her. Andy smiled in return.

"I'm going to my office to do some paperwork before I head back out. Why don't you stay in the office with Susan the rest of your shift? You could try and get through some of the paperwork on Marta's desk that seems to grow larger and larger every day."

"Sure, Chief."

Andy went into her office and couldn't help but smile. Her skirmish with Len over her capabilities as Police Chief seemed to have been put on hold. Looking at the top of her desk, she groaned. There may not be a lot of crime in Cascade, but the paperwork was endless.

Two hours later Andy left for her last drive around town. She checked her watch and yawned. An hour and a half to go and she would check back at the office to finish her shift.

At eight-fifteen, Andy checked out at work and headed for home. She was exhausted. The extra couple of hours of office work had done her in. She opened her front door and headed straight for her bedroom, shedding her uniform as she went. She rapidly scrubbed her face, brushed her hair, and crawled under her covers into bed. She had one last thing to do and then she could go to sleep. She picked up the telephone and dialed the number she had memorized.

"Hello." It was Jennifer.

"Hi Jennifer, is your aunt up?"

"She's getting dressed. I'll go get her."

"Thanks."

"Chief Andy?"

"Yes, Jennifer."

"You really like my aunt, don't you?"

"I love your aunt, Jennifer." Andy was amazed at this young woman's directness.

"She loves you, too."

"Is that a problem for you?"

"Oh no, my brother and I just want Aunt Jess to be happy."

"I'll do my best to make her happy," Andy pledged.

"I know you will. I'll go get her."

"Jennifer thanks for asking."

"No problem." Andy could hear her calling Jessica to the telephone.

"Hello."

"Hi."

"Andy, you should be in bed."

"I am in bed. I just needed to hear your voice before I went to sleep."

"Are you exhausted?"

"I am, but it was actually busy tonight so I didn't have time to get too tired."

"What if I come over later and you tell me all about your night," Jessica suggested.

"That would be nice."

"I'll come over at four. Will that give you enough time to sleep?"

"Plenty. I miss you."

"I miss you, too. Sleep tight."

"Goodnight."

"Goodnight Andy."

Andy slipped the telephone back onto her night table and curled up. Within minutes she was sound asleep.

Chapter Six

Jessica spent all morning and early afternoon in her studio. Loren's negotiated contract with the new corporate client included several of Jessica's pieces. Since only four were on display at the gallery, she had her work cut out for her. She loved every moment as she steadily chipped, ground, and shaped the wood into intricate designs.

Around three, she cleaned up her studio and herself, slipped into a pair of shorts, a v-neck sweater, and a pair of sandals. She packed a picnic meal for her and Andy, grabbed a jacket, and was out the door. She couldn't wait to see Andy. Jennifer had volleyball practice and dinner at Vicki's so she wouldn't be home until around ten.

Jessica pulled into Andy's driveway and parked her car next to Andy's jeep. She carried her bags of goodies up to the door and knocked, waiting for Andy to answer. She waited for several minutes and then knocked again. Thinking Andy might be in the shower, she opened the door and called to her. There was still no answer. She decided to enter anyway, and went to the kitchen to put the picnic meal on the counter. She checked the living room and smiled as she found Andy's jacket hanging off the end of the couch. She walked down the hall toward Andy's bedroom wondering if she had forgotten that Jessica was coming over. Andy's bedroom door was open, the curtains closed, and the light off. Andy was curled on her side facing Jessica sound asleep. Her legs were twisted in her covers and her arms were tucked under her pillow. She was sleeping so deeply that Jessica didn't want to wake her. She looked so young as she slept, her black hair tousled, her gorgeous eyes closed but ringed with thick black lashes. She had obviously dropped her uniform on the edge of her bed where it lay in a wrinkled pile. As Jessica turned to leave the room intending to let her sleep, Andy stirred.

"Jessica, what time is it, did I oversleep?"

"It's just a little after four and you go back to sleep, you must be exhausted."

"I must have forgotten to set the alarm. I'm sorry." She sat up and ran her hands through her hair.

"Don't worry about it, Andy. Go back to sleep, I can see you tomorrow."

"Jessica, come here, please?"

Jessica walked to the edge of the bed and sat down. She reached out and pushed Andy's sleep tousled hair out of her face.

"What, sweetie?" She smiled at Andy.

"Come here and cuddle with me." Andy requested, reaching for Jessica. She gently tugged her until Jessica was lying on top of the covers next to Andy. Jessica kissed her softly, gently, relishing the taste of Andy's moist, sweet lips. For several minutes they enjoyed slow leisurely kisses before Andy sighed deeply. "I love waking up and finding you here. It feels so right."

"You look so beautiful when you sleep, a beautiful, young woman all curled up. I didn't want to wake you. You need your sleep."

"I've had plenty of sleep. I don't need any more. Besides, I have much better things to do with my time."

Andy grinned roguishly as she pulled Jessica into her arms again, and this time her kiss was not one of gentleness. She captured Jessica's lips with her own her tongue sweeping through Jessica's mouth with such passion that Jessica's body reacted immediately in response. A moan escaped her lips as she returned Andy's kiss with matching passion. She tasted Andy's lips and tongue as she slid her body closer to Andy's, wrapping her arms around her neck. Jessica slipped her hands down her back and underneath Andy's T-shirt her fingers relishing the feel of her warm skin.

After several minutes of heart-stopping kisses, Andy pulled away from Jessica and smiled. "I'm sorry I overslept. I was looking forward to seeing you. I must have set my alarm incorrectly." She slid her fingers through Jessica's hair as she spoke. "I must look like a fright."

"I think you look just perfect, and I'm glad you didn't wake up any earlier. You must have needed the sleep after working such long hours." Jessica reassured her. Andy couldn't have looked more appealing to Jessica than she did right now with her tousled hair, her clear violet, eyes, and her newly kissed lips. "Are you hungry? I brought a picnic dinner over with me."

"That sounds perfect. Thank you. I'll get cleaned up and then we can eat."

"On one condition," Jessica requested. "That you climb back into bed and we have our picnic here. After you've eaten, I'm going home. You need more rest."

"I think I can promise you that." Andy kissed Jessica quickly and hopped out of bed. She looked so cute in her T-shirt and a pair of bikini underwear, that Jessica couldn't resist watching her walk to her dresser.

"I'll go get the picnic started," She volunteered as she got up off the bed and headed down the hall to the kitchen. She had many wonderful things to prepare. She rummaged around Andy's kitchen until she found everything she needed, and finished her preparations. She heard Andy's shower turn off as she began the first of several trips back to the bedroom, her hands full of items. She re-made the bed, straightened the covers, and plumped the pillows. She folded a tablecloth on the lower part of the bed and placed a plate of green grapes, sliced cheese, salami, and crackers on it. On the dresser she placed several lit candles and poured two glasses of wine. Looking around the room, she smiled.

"Perfect." She quickly flipped the overhead light off and sat on the bed waiting for Andy to finish. It was about ten minutes later that Andy came out of the bathroom.

"Wow, isn't this something."

Jessica didn't say a word as she watched Andy enter the room. She had changed into a pair of silk pajamas, emerald green in color. She was barefoot, her face devoid of makeup, and she had tied her hair back in a ponytail. She had never looked more beautiful. She walked over to Jessica's side of the bed and leaned over, kissing Jessica gently.

"Thank you," she whispered softly, spreading kisses all over Jessica's face, nuzzling her as Jessica wrapped her arms around Andy's neck.

"Come and sit down, it's time to eat." Andy did as Jessica requested, finding a place next to her on the bed. "There is a glass of wine on your night table and lots of goodies."

"I can see that. I don't know where to start."

"Here, let me help." Jessica grinned as she plucked a handful of grapes from the plate. She placed a fat juicy grape between Andy's lips. Andy took the grape from Jessica's fingers with her lips, gently sucking on them.

"M'm good."

Andy continued to pay close attention to Jessica's fingers as she took each one into her hot, wet, mouth. Jessica's reaction was instantaneous, and her body flooded with heat. She felt the familiar tingling between her legs. The idea of eating a picnic meal had completely fled her mind. Andy turned Jessica's hand over, palm side up.

"You have beautiful, strong hands. It must be from your carving," Andy said as she reached for her glass of wine.

Jessica was so enthralled with Andy she could not move. Andy took a sip and then dripped a little bit of wine in the center of Jessica's palm. Andy's eyes shined a deep dark purple as her tongue delicately licked the drops of wine from Jessica's hand. What little control Jessica had up to this point was lost as Andy's tongue continued its intriguing path up her arm to her shirt. She tugged on Jessica's arm until Jessica was lying tightly against her.

"I love you, Jessica. I know we haven't known each other very long but I do love you."

"I love you, Andy." Jessica slid her hands under Andy's pajama top and stroked the warm soft skin of her back as Andy trailed kisses along her jaw and neck, making Jessica shiver with anticipation. Andy's hands moved slowly under Jessica's sweater, tantalizing her as they teased along her ribs, before wrapping her fingers around Jessica's breasts. Jessica moaned and her nipples tightened in response. She wanted Andy's hands on her body.

"Andy, I want to make love with you," Jessica whispered. Andy raised her eyes to look into Jessica's as her finger tips massaged and gently squeezed Jessica's nipples.

"Are you sure?"

"I'm sure." Jessica sat up and pulled her sweater over her head. Reaching behind her, she unclasped her bra and slid it off. Reaching for Andy's hands she placed them on her breasts again. Jessica felt a little shy as Andy watched her, smiling.

"You are so beautiful." Andy said as her hands molded themselves against Jessica's breasts again, relishing their fullness.

"Thank you." Jessica felt beautiful when Andy looked at her.

Jessica's fingers began to rapidly unbutton Andy's pajama shirt and push it off her shoulders. Andy turned and pulled the covers back from the bed. Jessica kicked her sandals and shorts off before sliding under the covers, moving over to where Andy leaned against a pillow.

"I'm going to move the food off the bed," Andy explained as she kissed Jessica quickly and pulled away.

She stood up, removed the plates from the foot of the bed, and placed them on the dresser. She came back to the side of the bed and sat down next to Jessica. She gazed at Jessica with a smile on her face.

"I could look at you all night," she admitted.

"Just look at me?" Jessica teased.

She slid her hands around Andy's waist and laid her head next to Andy's on the pillow as she smiled and watched her. Then she slid her leg between Andy's and rolled on top of her, settling her body against Andy's. They fit perfectly. They kissed slowly and deeply, a wet, sensuous kiss, mouths open, and their tongues greedily tasting each other. Jessica's fingers traced Andy's ribs in a slow path, until she cradled Andy's breasts, and they filled her hands. They were full and soft with large rose-colored nipples. She teased them with her fingertips and they puckered in response. Jessica wanted more as she ducked her head and captured Andy's nipple between her lips, teasing with her teeth and tongue. Sharing her attention to both breasts Jessica's hands and mouth could not get enough of Andy's nipples as she suckled with pleasure. She traced a path with her tongue across Andy's stomach, marveling at how firm and muscular and so very feminine she was. She tasted and kissed Andy's navel until she stopped at the top of Andy's waistband. Her fingers continued the journey as they traveled around Andy's hips. She admired the firm taut muscles of Andy's thighs and buttocks, and the heat that radiated from her body. Her hand moved between Andy's legs, feeling the wetness through the silk of her pajamas. A shiver went through Andy's body and she gasped as Jessica increased the pressure of her fingers.

"Jessica," Andy moaned as her legs spread in response. Andy reached down and stroked Jessica's face.

"I need to kiss you," She pleaded, her face flushed with pleasure.

Jessica answered Andy's request by sliding up her body to capture her lips, her fingers still stroking her. Andy's kisses were no longer gentle.

"Wait," She whispered, stilling Jessica's hand with her own. "I want to make love with you at the same time. I want to share our first time. Please?"

Jessica's answer was to push Andy's pajama bottoms down her legs and sit up to remove her own underpants. She lay back down next to Andy, who wrapped her tightly in her arms. Andy rolled Jessica over until she was cradled on top of her, their breasts crushed against each other. She insinuated her legs between Jessica's so their hips were fused. Jessica moved her hips against Andy's, reveling in the feel of their naked bodies touching from head to toe. Andy clasped Jessica's hands in her own, stretching them over their heads, rubbing her breasts against Jessica's. Their kisses were slow and wet and languid as they allowed their bodies as well as their hearts to meld together.

Andy's lips traced Jessica's neck down to her shoulder and across her breasts. Teasing her nipples with her tongue and hot, wet, mouth, Jessica arched her back to meet Andy's mouth, her hips grinding against Andy's. Jessica reached down and clasped Andy's hips tightly to hers, locking her legs around Andy's thighs. Andy raised herself on her arms, rubbing her hips against Jessica's both of them wanted the closest of connections. Sliding a hand between them, Andy slipped her fingers into Jessica's wetness as she moaned with pleasure.

"You are so wet. You feel wonderful," Andy whispered as her fingers were enclosed by Jessica's tightness. Jessica placed her hand between Andy's legs, cupping her gently as she slid her fingers between Andy's tightly muscled buttocks. She stroked Andy's wetness with both hands, her fingers plunging into Andy as she felt the pressure building between her legs. Andy gasped and parted her legs to Jessica's fingers, rocking her hips against Jessica's, while their breathing came faster, their hearts pounding. Jessica could feel Andy clenching around her fingers as she teased her hardened center, her own body responding with matching tremors.

"Andy." Jessica cried as her body jerked. She was immediately flooded with an orgasm that thundered through her body. Andy's body tightened and shuddered as she too enjoyed the ultimate response with wave after wave of pure pleasure. Their hips ground against each other as they prolonged the joy of their intimate joining.

"Oh God."

Andy collapsed onto Jessica, her face pressed tightly against Jessica's. Their explosion of senses had them both overwhelmed and their bodies slick with sweat as they melted against each other. Both shuddered over and over as the aftermath of their lovemaking sent shivers through each of their bodies. As their breathing and their heartbeats slowed down, Andy clung to Jessica's neck, while Jessica held her tightly.

"I love you, Andy," Jessica pledged as she lightly kissed Andy's cheek and neck, until Andy turned to Jessica and returned her kisses.

"What's this? Are you crying, sweetie?" Jessica noticed the tears seeping from Andy's eyes.

"I can't help it." Her beautiful eyes were shiny. "I've never felt like this before. It's overwhelming." She kissed Jessica deeply.

"I have never felt this way either. I feel so close to you. It feels so right, so perfect," Jessica confessed as she ran her hands up and down Andy's back. "You have such a beautiful body, so strong, and so feminine."

"You are the beautiful one, open, so loving, and so perfect. Thank you."

Jessica smiled in response and kissed her gently. If Andy hadn't already stolen her heart, she would have taken it now. "You know, Andy, now you are going to have to marry me." Jessica grinned.

"How about tomorrow, is that soon enough?" Andy smiled in return. "I would be honored, Ms. Jessica Newcomb, if you would become my partner for life." Andy placed her hand over her heart as she spoke.

"Ms. Catarina Andolino, a lifetime with you will not be long enough." Jessica placed her hand over Andy's. "I love you, Andy."

"I love you, my Jessie." Andy kissed her softly.

They lay there in silence, arms, and bodies wrapped around each other, happily sharing this time together. Twenty minutes went by before either one stirred. It was Andy who slipped out of bed, put on her pajama top, and rummaged through her drawer for another shirt for Jessica. As Jessica sat up and put the shirt on, she held it to her face.

The shirt contained Andy's scent and Jessica breathed it in deeply. It was becoming her favorite perfume.

"How about some food?" Andy suggested, as she brought the plate to Jessica seated on the bed.

"I'll be right back," Jessica promised as she stepped into the bathroom to freshen up.

"I get us some fresh glasses of wine." Andy left the bedroom. Jessica cleaned up and climbed back into bed as Andy returned with the wine.

"I'll be right back, love." Andy promised, as she too spent a few moments in the bathroom.

By the time she came back Jessica had straightened up the bed and stacked the pillows so the two of them would be comfortable. Andy slid under her covers and picked up her wine glass.

"I have to honestly say this has been a truly wonderful picnic." She winked at Jessica.

"I suggest we repeat this real soon." Jessica grinned in return.

"I will agree to that."

Andy laughed as she picked up a piece of cheese to nibble on. The two of them shared food and conversation, already very comfortable with each other, like they belonged together.

"Tell me what happened at work last night." Jessica said.

"Let's see, it started out with my meeting where Len did everything he could to question my decisions. He pointed out that Buck didn't work at night. He questioned my scheduling methods, and objected to my order to wear vests while on duty. He made a one-hour meeting last two painful hours, much longer then it needed to be. Even the rest of the unit was unhappy with him. Several hours later as I was just quieting a disorderly drunk down at the Watering Hole Tavern, Len showed up as backup and tried to strong-arm the man into the car. The man resisted and popped Len right in the jaw. Instead of talking the unhappy gentleman into my car and driving him home, I had to restrain and cuff him while Len dusted himself off."

"Is Len okay?"

"Yes, his ego took a bigger beating then his chin did." Andy chuckled. "The surprising thing was after we got back to the precinct, he asked me if I would teach him some self defense moves."

"You're kidding! He asked you for help. That's terrific!"

"Pretty amazing."

"Maybe he's figured out that your being a woman has nothing to do with your ability to do a good job."

"Wouldn't that be something? I just wish he and the others would recognize that talking to someone is usually the better course of action."

"So is your body a lethal weapon?" Jessica teased her.

"Very lethal." Andy grinned. "But I can tell you from experience, your body is a very potent weapon."

"Oh my, why, thank you very much." Jessica laughed.

They were enjoying their conversation as much as their earlier love-making. They visited and giggled for over an hour, sharing their laughter and their lives.

"Let me clean this up," Jessica volunteered as they finished their meal.

"Let's do it together," Andy suggested, and the two of them happily padded down the hallway to the kitchen.

"Have I thanked you for bringing dinner over?" Andy held Jessica in her arms as they stood in the kitchen.

"I don't think so. What do you have in mind?"

"I believe I can come up with a suitable thank you."

Andy proceeded to show Jessica just how appreciative she was. Several minutes of sexy kisses had Jessica and Andy's passion exploding, and the two of them responded with the familiar build up of heat and tension. Andy slowly unbuttoned Jessica's pajama shirt, following her fingers with her mouth as she parted the shirt. Her lips tasted Jessica's breasts, her tongue teasing them into peaks aching with need. Jessica cradled Andy's head in her hands as she leaned back against the kitchen counter. Andy reached down, picked Jessica up and sat her on the counter, stepping between her legs and running her hands up Jessica's thighs, over her ribs, and around her breasts, her mouth sucking lightly until Jessica thought she would crawl out of her skin. Andy's fingers found her wet and responsive as they stroked her to a feverish state. Just as Jessica thought she would explode, Andy's mouth took the place of her fingers, her tongue alternately stroking and plunging. Andy's arms pulled Jessica's hips toward her as she sucked the very center of Jessica. Lightning streaks of pleasure ran continuously through Jessica as her head fell back in pleasure, her body arching to meet Andy's wonderful mouth. The orgasm built with such intensity that Jessica found it hard to breathe, her legs draped around Andy's back. Andy's fingers joined her mouth and as she slid them inside Jessica, Jessica tightened around them in response. She shivered with pleasure as she was once again exploding with complete abandonment.

Andy stood up and hugged Jessica to her as she slowly began to relax and melt around Andy. Jessica wrapped her arms tightly around Andy's neck as her heart continued to pound loudly in her chest.

"You taste so good," Andy whispered as she held her "And I love the way you feel when I touch you, so soft and wet."

"Only with you."

Jessica responded, kissing Andy passionately. She slid off the counter and removed Andy's shirt, stopping to gaze at her naked body. Andy's arms reached for Jessica as their lips joined in a kiss. They kissed hungrily and Andy fitted her frame tightly against Jessica's. Jessica wound her hands in Andy's hair, leaving a trail of hot, wet kisses down her neck and shoulders. She turned Andy slowly around as she kissed and tasted her shoulders and the downy length of her back. Her hands and mouth covered Andy's skin, memorizing the texture and taste. As she slipped her arms around Andy, capturing her heavy breasts, Andy's arms stretched over her head. She leaned against a kitchen cupboard for support, her head leaning back against Jessica's.

Jessica slid her leg between Andy's as her fingers teased her nipples and they hardened with pleasure. Andy tightened her legs around Jessica's, as her hips moved back against Jessica, sliding slowly, her breathing becoming heavy. Jessica dropped her hand to Andy's stomach, spreading her fingers and pulling Andy even tighter against her. Her fingers slowly tantalized Andy, and she let them drift between her legs while Andy turned her head to meet Jessica's lips with her own. Andy gasped as Jessica's fingers entered her. Jessica held Andy tightly, while her fingers stroked her until her body began to shake. Jessica hugged her as Andy's body continued to tremble, her face tucked against Jessica's while she cried softly with her orgasm.

"You are so beautiful," Jessica whispered, as she loved Andy. Andy turned in Jessica's arms and slid hers around Jessica's neck, hugging her tightly.

"I love you," She whispered quietly in return, still trembling.

They stood together in silence in the middle of the kitchen, holding tightly onto each other. It was Andy who broke the silence.

"I'm afraid that I'll never be able to look at a kitchen quite the same way again." Andy giggled.

"I know the feeling." Jessica grinned as she looked at Andy's body. "I have never done anything like this before, but I am certainly not complaining."

"I guess it's a first for both of us." Andy reached down and snagged her shirt from the floor.

"Andy, I love making love with you. You are so passionate, so beautiful." Jessica began buttoning Andy's shirt. "So vulnerable, so loving."

"I have never been like this before. I don't seem to have any self-control when I'm around you." Andy's sudden shyness was so appealing. Jessica just hugged her.

"I don't have any control around you either."

"I do know I am falling madly in love with you."

"I have already fallen in love with you."

"So, are you going to marry me?" Andy asked seriously.

"How's tomorrow sound?" Jessica spoke from her heart.

"I would love to, but maybe we ought to make sure it's okay with your family first."

Jessica could have fallen in love with her all over again. "I'll tell you what, we'll ask them together." She kissed Andy softly.

An hour later Jessica was fully dressed, standing next to Andy's closed front door. Andy stood next to her in full uniform.

"Be careful tonight." She smiled as she placed her hand against Andy's chest.

"I will, and you sleep well. I will call you tomorrow afternoon."

"Andy, Jennifer has a volleyball match tomorrow night and I know she would love to have you come watch."

"I would love to, but check with Jennifer first. I don't want to put her in an awkward position."

"Andy, thank you for thinking about her. I promise you I'll ask her, but I know what she'll say."

"Just ask her first, please."

"Okay, okay," Jessica promised grinning. "I'm going to miss you."

"I'll miss you, too."

They kissed gently and walked out to Jessica's car. She got in, waved, and left, a feeling of euphoria invading her senses. The drive home was short, and sweet. Within minutes Jessica parked her car and went into the house. She quickly took a shower, put her pajamas on, and headed for the studio. She was too happy to sleep. She grabbed her sketchbook and began to work. Jennifer arrived home a little while later, kissed her hello and goodnight, and headed for bed. It was several hours before Jessica decided to turn in.

Andy's night was equally mild, as her town slept quietly around her and the other officers on duty. When her shift came to an end at a little after eight, she pointed her car for home. She pulled into the all night market to pick up a few things when she saw a display of freshly cut flowers. She gathered a large bunch of assorted blossoms and purchased them along with her breakfast. She knew Jessica would love them. She would drive to Jessica's to give her the flowers and then head home for some much-needed sleep. She pulled into the driveway, parked her car, and walked up to the front door, the large bouquet of flowers for Jessica in her arms. She knocked on the door hoping she wouldn't be waking Jessica up.

"Hi, Chief Andy." Jennifer bounced out the front door.

"Hello, Jennifer, how are you?"

"Terrific. Aunt Jess said you are coming to my volleyball match tonight. Cool."

"If it's okay with you. I would love to come watch."

"It's more than okay. Listen, I've got to run, I'm already late for my first class. See you tonight." Jennifer quickly hugged Andy. "I'm glad you're coming."

"I'm looking forward to it." Andy was pleasantly startled by Jennifer's hug.

Jennifer raced down the walkway, her pack bouncing on her back. "Chief Andy, go on in. Aunt Jess is sitting at the breakfast table, and the flowers are a nice touch." Jennifer grinned as she climbed into the Bronco.

Andy grinned and walked through the open door toward the kitchen. "Hello, Jessica?"

"Andy, is that you?"

"Yes, Jennifer said it was okay to come in."

"Hi." Jessica smiled as she walked toward Andy. "I missed you last night."

Andy pulled Jessica into her arms. "I missed you too." She kissed her softly.

"Did you bring me flowers?"

"I thought you'd like them. They're so colorful and vibrant, they reminded me of you." Andy handed the bouquet to her.

"I love them, thank you." Jessica gathered the flowers in her arms. "I love you."

"I love you."

"Jennifer was very excited about your coming to her match tonight."

"She told me. Jessica, she hugged me." Andy had a sweet smile on her face.

"She likes you, sweetie." Jessica grinned at Andy.

"I know, but she doesn't know me very well."

"She knows that I love you." Jessica hugged her tightly.

"I thought about you all last night." Andy kissed Jessica deeply.

"I thought about you, too. Are you sleepy? You haven't had any sleep for awhile." Jessica clasped Andy's face in her hands. "I love this beautiful face, but you look so tired."

"I'm not that tired." Andy grinned as she untied Jessica's bathrobe. Her short nightshirt did nothing to hide her wonderful legs. She slid her hands under Jessica's shirt, sliding them up her back.

"Oh my." Jessica smiled. "Chief Andy, what you do to me." Jessica sighed before she snaked her arms around Andy's neck. Their kisses ignited the passion from the night before as Andy stripped the bathrobe off Jessica.

"Andy, honey, let's go upstairs." Jessica grabbed Andy's hand in her own and led her up the stairway to her bedroom.

"Are you sure about this?" Andy asked as they entered the room.

"I'm sure." Jessica smiled as she unbuckled Andy's belt, dropping it on the floor. Andy started to reach for Jessica but she gently grabbed her hands and held on. "No, it's my turn."

Jessica slowly unbuttoned Andy's shirt, peeling it off her shoulders. Bending down, she removed Andy's shoes and socks, then running her hands up Andy's legs she unfastened her pants and dropped them. She paused, smiling as she admired Andy's well-toned body and generous breasts. She reached up and slid the straps of Andy's bra slowly off and reached behind her to release the clasp. Andy's full breasts and nipples drew Jessica's eyes, and as she traced the waistband of her panties lower and lower teasing Andy with her fingertips. She watched the wonder and anticipation on Andy's face. Her eyes were almost closed as she reacted to Jessica's attentions, her breasts rising and falling with her rapid breathing.

"Please." Andy spoke so softly Jessica could barely hear her.

Jessica pushed Andy's panties off her hips and let them drop to the floor as she leaned over and met Andy's open mouth with her own. Her tongue thrust deeply inside Andy's mouth and her hand reached between Andy's legs. She parted Andy with her fingers, rubbing slowly, as Andy's legs parted wider in response.

"Oh God, Jess." Andy's head dropped to Jessica's shoulder and her arms clung to her neck.

"Andy, you feel so good."

Jessica's fingers entered Andy, feeling her tightness, as her other arm pulled Andy against her body. Her fingers slid in and out as Andy's hips moved in response, her breaths coming in gasps. While her body began to shiver with her climax, Andy placed her hand between Jessica's legs. The front of her panties were wet, her body waiting for Andy's fingers to began their magic. They both came together and they trembled, clinging to each other. It was several minutes before either one of them could speak.

"That was incredible," Jessica sighed, as she pulled Andy onto the bed with her. They lay side-by-side, Andy running her fingers up and down Jessica's thigh and hip.

"I didn't come over here for this," Andy admitted. "I planned on saying hello, giving you the flowers, and going home."

"Are you complaining?" Jessica laughed.

"Absolutely not." Andy followed her remark with a long drawn-out kiss. "I will never tire of touching you."

"I know the feeling," Jessica agreed, as her fingertip circled around Andy's nipples causing them to pucker in anticipation.

Their lovemaking continued in a much more leisurely pace, as they memorized each other's bodies all over again. It was several hours before exhaustion claimed Andy and she slept, her legs draped around Jessica. Watching her sleep, Jessica smiled as she gazed at her beautiful lover. Her heart tingled at the thought that this woman actually loved her. She pulled her legs away from Andy's and slipped out of bed. She tucked the covers around her and kissed her lightly on the cheek, leaving her to get some much-needed sleep. She quickly picked up Andy's uniform and folded it neatly, grabbed some clean clothes for herself, and headed for the bathroom. She was determined that she would not wake up Andy.

Andy woke up slowly and, suddenly realizing she wasn't in her own bed, glanced around quickly to get oriented. As memories returned from the morning's activities, she smiled and looked around the bedroom for Jessica. She had no idea where she'd gone. Andy's uniform was folded neatly on the end of the bed, but there was no sign of Jessica. Glancing at the clock on the bedside stand, she was amazed to see it was after two o'clock in the afternoon. Quickly she climbed out of bed, grabbed her uniform, and headed for the bathroom.

Within ten minutes she had washed and dressed, made the bed, and looked around the room for any of her things before going downstairs. She heard noises coming from Jessica's studio so she headed in that direction. Jessica was seated at her bench, a knife in her hand and a large block of wood in front of her. She had obviously been working for some time, from the evidence of several piles of wood shavings.

"Hi." Andy spoke from the door after watching Jessica for several minutes.

"Hey, sleepyhead." Jessica smiled as she stood up and walked to Andy to kiss her hello.

"I'm sorry I fell asleep. I shouldn't have stayed," Andy apologized.

"Of course you should have," Jessica reassured her.

"Jessica, people are going to see my jeep here and they are going to talk. Think what that will do to you and Jennifer."

"It won't do anything to Jennifer and me. I certainly don't care what they say or think. I love you, Andy. You are the Chief of Police, and I love you. They will just have to get used to it."

Andy grinned as Jessica spoke, her arms hugging her tightly. "I love you, too. Actually, I was worrying more about my reputation when they realize that the famous artist Jessica Newcomb is sleeping with the not so well known Chief of Police. What will they think of that?" She teased.

"Oh, so that's it. Our strong, tough, Police Chief is worried about a little gossip." Jessica kissed Andy as she spoke. It was several minutes before either one said anything.

"I need to go home and change clothes. What time is the volleyball match?"

"It begins at seven. Jennifer has to be there at six, so I can pick you up at six-thirty. That way you can get some more sleep."

"I'll be ready." Andy kissed her one last time. "Thank you for this morning."

"You're welcome, but I believe I have as much to be thankful for as you do."

"Love you, and I will see you later." Andy headed for the front door and home.

At six-thirty Jessica pulled into Andy's driveway. Andy stepped out of her house and Jessica couldn't help but admire the way she looked. Her black hair was loose and straight to her shoulders, a shiny, blue-black mass. She was wearing blue jeans, a bright red sweater, brown loafers, and a navy blue silk jacket thrown over her arm. Jessica thought she looked beautiful.

"Don't you look terrific?" Jessica remarked as Andy got in her car.

"You look pretty wonderful yourself," Andy responded, as she kissed her hello.

"Did you get some more sleep?"

"A little. This is my last all-nighter for a while, so I'll catch up."

"Jennifer is so excited that you're coming tonight. She could hardly sit still on her way to the gym."

"I'm looking forward to watching her. It should be fun."

"Aren't you worried about being seen with me?" Jessica teased as they headed downtown.

"I'll take my chances." Andy grinned in response.

Jessica parked the car in the gym parking lot, and she and Andy walked the short distance into the school gym. Both teams were still warming up as the two of them found seats on the bleachers. Many of the townspeople were there and, as Jessica and Andy climbed the bleachers for good seats, some smiled and said hello. As far as Andy could tell not one of them reacted with the least little bit of unfriendliness or discomfort. She breathed a sigh of relief. The last thing in the world she would want to do was embarrass Jessica or Jennifer.

She had first hand experience on how cruel people could be. She and her previous girlfriend had put up with the harassment when they had looked for an apartment together. One particularly nasty man had made it clear that he wouldn't rent to any dykes. Andy had never forgotten that painful time and she would never let it happen to Jessica and Jennifer. Not if she could prevent it.

They both took seats side by side and Jessica leaned over to speak quietly to Andy. "Relax sweetheart. Look, Jennifer is waving at you."

Sure enough, Jennifer was happily waving to them. Andy smiled and waved back. It was over two hours later when the closely fought volleyball match ended and Jennifer's team was victorious. There was much celebration as Andy and Jessica joined Jennifer after the match.

"Aunt Jess, Andy, what did you think?" She hugged both of them with excitement.

"I'd say the University of Washington was very smart to give you a scholarship. You are really good!" Andy spoke seriously. "I was very impressed."

"You were terrific, Jenn. We're both proud of you," Jessica added.

"Thanks guys, I love you." She hugged them again, a broad smile on her face. "I'll hurry and change my clothes so we can go. Andy, I'm glad you came."

"I wouldn't have missed it for anything." Andy really meant it. Jennifer was finding a place in her heart. She liked this family very much.

"Do you have to work tonight?"

"I do. My shift starts at eleven."

"If you're the Chief of Police, why do you have to work at night?"

"How will I get to know all my officers if I don't work with them?"

"Cool. I'll hurry." She was off like a rocket.

"Jennifer really likes you."

"I like her."

"That's good, because it would be harder to marry me if Jennifer didn't approve," Jessica remarked as Andy grinned at her.

"Hey ladies, what's up?" Buck joined them as they waited for Jennifer. He had the look of a proud parent as he grinned at Jessica and Andy and hugged them both in greeting.

"Buck, we didn't know you were here."

"Just made it for the last twenty minutes or so. Jennifer was her usual terrific self."

"She is good." Andy agreed.

"When are you both going hiking with me?"

"As soon as we have a Saturday or Sunday off. We promise," Jessica pledged.

Buck's matchmaking had paid off and he couldn't be happier. He couldn't help but tease Andy and Jessica that he was the reason they found each other. In Buck's mind and their own, they were a family. The three of them chatted until Jennifer came out and joined them. It was twenty minutes later before they headed home. Jennifer rode with Jessica as she dropped Andy off.

"Thanks for coming, Andy."

"I enjoyed it Jennifer. I'd like to come watch you again, if that's okay with you."

"For sure." She grinned.

"I'll call you, Jess." Andy smiled as she started to get out of the car. Jessica reached out and touched her cheek.

"Be careful tonight," She requested as Andy got out of the car and went inside.

"Aunt Jess, you really like Andy, don't you?"

"Yes, I do, Jennifer. Are you sure it doesn't bother you?"

"Not at all. I can tell Andy really likes you. When you're not looking at her, she watches you, and she has this sweet look on her face when she does."

Jessica smiled as she flushed with emotion. "We both care about each other very much."

"Do you think you might want to live together?"

"We might want to. What do you think about that?"

"I think it would be terrific. There's plenty of room. Besides, I am going away to college next year."

"It wouldn't bother you? You know people would talk."

Jessica had never had any problems about her sexual orientation since she had moved to Cascade to raise her niece and nephew. Over the years she, Tommy, and Jennifer had many long conversations about their feelings and how other people might feel.

"I don't care as long as you're happy, Aunt Jess. That's all I care about."

"Thanks, sweetie, now let's go home and have some ice cream."

"Cool."

Chapter Seven

In the next few months Andy and Jessica's lives began to weave together like a colorful tapestry. Their feelings for each other only strengthened and this allowed the two of them to share a part of their hearts and souls they had both previously protected. Their spirits had touched along with their hearts. Somewhere along the way Jessica, Andy, and Jennifer had become a family. The three of them spent a lot of time together, hiking, laughing, and just plain talking. Jessica and Andy's relationship was one of mutual respect and love. They could talk about anything. The townspeople had not once given them anything but friendship, and life in the town of Cascade smoothly continued.

Andy's job as Police Chief kept her involved in local politics and Jessica's organization of this year's festival made it easy for the two of them to be seen in public together. People accepted them as a couple and moved on. Andy continued to live in her own home, though gradually she spent more and more time at Jessica's. They talked about living together but Andy wanted to wait until Tommy came home for the summer. It was important to her that he be involved in the decision. Andy had never met him in person, but over the months had spoken several times to him on the telephone. He reassured her that he had no objections to her relationship with Jessica and her moving into their home. She remained adamant in her reluctance to make that decision before he had an opportunity to meet her in person, no matter how convincing Jessica and Jennifer could be. It wouldn't be much longer, since he was flying into Seattle that afternoon. Jessica and Jennifer had gone to pick him up at the Seattle-Tacoma Airport. They asked her to go with them but she refused. She wanted the three of them to have some family time together before she intruded. She would meet him in person at dinner later that evening.

Looking around her office, Andy sighed. When she took this job she had no idea how much her life would change. The small police force she led now accepted her as their captain, teasing her, and including her in their lives. Not only did she find the work rewarding, but she also had time to become involved in the community she now belonged to. She had come to love all the characters that made up the town of Cascade and they, in turn, had returned her love.

Her relationship with Jessica, even after several months, astounded her with its depth and strength. Her heart pounded at the thought of seeing Jessica, and when they were together she felt complete and whole. She and Jennifer were her family and they welcomed her with open arms. She had never felt more loved and she counted her blessings every day. Her thoughts were interrupted by a knock on her door.

"Chief, isn't Tommy arriving today?" It was her assistant and biggest fan, Marta.

"He is. Jessica and Jennifer are in Seattle picking him up as we speak."

"He's a handsome one, that boy. It's hard to believe how much both of those kids have grown. Why, it just seems like yesterday when they were little guys, and now Jennifer is graduating from high school. Where does the time go?"

"You've known them all their lives. That is so wonderful. I'm looking forward to meeting Tommy. Jessica has done a terrific job of raising them."

"That she did, but I'm sure glad she found you. She's a special person and needed someone wonderful in her life, someone to take care of her."

"Thanks Marta. I think she takes better care of me then I do of her." Andy smiled.

"I don't know about that. From what I see you both do a wonderful job of taking care of each other," Marta remarked as she handed Andy some folders. "I did come in here for a reason. Here are the files for this year's festival. The permits are in the first one, and the information on the extra uniforms we are thinking of bringing on are in the second folder."

"Great, thanks Marta. As usual you are on top of things." Marta's face reddened with embarrassment. She was very good at giving compliments but receiving them was difficult for her. She grumbled something as she left Andy's office. Andy couldn't help but grin. Marta kept the small police department going with her competence. Everyone knew she was the one who really ran everything. On top of that, Marta never showed any discomfort over Jessica and Andy's relationship. She accepted them as a couple and that was that. In fact, no one, including Len, had shown any adverse reaction to them. Andy felt very lucky that her life in Cascade was so perfect. She loved her family and her job very much.

The next hour Andy spent doing paperwork, which was the majority of her job. It still amazed her how such a small town and police department could generate so much paperwork. At five-thirty she headed out the door; she was due at Jessica's at six-thirty for dinner. Not only were they celebrating Tommy's return for the summer but also Jennifer's graduation tomorrow night.

An hour later, Andy knocked on Jessica's front door. Normally she would knock and enter, but she was feeling quite nervous about meeting Tommy for the first time.

"Andy, what are you doing knocking?" Jennifer asked as she grabbed her by the hand and pulled her inside. "You're family," she declared, hugging her tightly.

"Thanks, honey." Andy hugged her in return. "Where is your aunt?"

"She and Tommy are in the studio. He wanted to see her latest work. Come on in, you sure look nice."

"Why, thank you, ma'am," Andy drawled in her best southern voice.

She had changed twice before settling on a pair of knife-creased jeans, a cream colored blouse, and a navy blazer. As she followed Jennifer into the studio, she could hear Jessica's familiar laughter and a much deeper heartier chuckling.

"Hi sweetie," Jessica said, as she looked up to see Andy behind Jennifer.

A very tall, broad-shouldered man with blond-streaked brown hair stood with his back to Andy. He had on an old pair of faded blue jeans, hiking boots, and a plaid flannel shirt. Andy hesitated before going up to Jessica to greet her with her usual kiss or hug.

"Andy, I'd like you to meet Tommy. Tommy, this is Andy." Jessica introduced them as she reached out to Andy and took her hand.

Tommy turned to Andy, a big smile on his gorgeous face. He had the same coloring as Jennifer, but his face had the faint shadow of a beard. She smiled at him as he moved toward her.

"It's about time I met you in person. You were beginning to sound too good to be true." He chuckled as he wrapped her in a bear hug.

"I'm glad to meet you," Andy responded hugging Tommy back.

"Welcome to the family," he said as he stepped away, still smiling.

"Thank you, I can't think of a better family to belong to." Andy's eyes glistened with unshed tears as her heart reacted to his words. Jessica squeezed her fingers as she too, acknowledged the welcome.

"Let's go into the kitchen and sit down," Jessica suggested, and as Jennifer and Tommy turned to leave the room, she leaned into Andy. "I love you, Andy."

"I love you, Jessica." They kissed lightly before they followed the other members of their family.

"Andy, Jennifer's been telling me you used to be an FBI agent. When you get a chance, can I ask you some questions about it?" Tommy asked as he gently roughhoused with his sister.

"Sure, any time."

The rest of the evening flew by, as the four of them shared experiences and conversation. There was no sign of uneasiness or discomfort. It was just a family sharing and laughing together. It was after midnight before Andy got up to leave. She and Jessica had discussed everything earlier in the week and Andy was insistent that she not stay overnight.

"Thank you for a wonderful dinner and conversation, and it certainly was a pleasure to finally meet you, Tommy."

"I'm really glad to meet you, Andy. Thank you for making Aunt Jessica so happy."

Andy and Jessica walked to the front door. "Are you sure you won't stay?" Jessica asked as she wrapped her arms around Andy. Her rule about no one staying all night in her home had died the moment she fell in love with Andy.

"I'm sure, but thanks for asking," Andy replied, kissing her soundly. "Goodnight Jess, I'll be back tomorrow before we need to leave for graduation."

"You'd better be. Jennifer expects all of her family there," Jessica threatened with a smile. "Call me later, please?"

"I'll be here. I wouldn't miss Jennifer's graduation for anything. And I will call you later," Andy promised as they kissed once more before she left.

Jessica was smiling as she walked into the kitchen. Both Tommy and Jennifer were sitting in front of large bowls of ice cream.

"Aunt Jess, join us for ice cream. We made a bowl for you," Jennifer announced between mouthfuls.

"I don't mind if I do." She grinned as she plopped down on a chair and joined them.

"Aunt Jess, did Andy leave because of me?' Tommy asked, his eyes serious.

"Oh no, honey. She has her own place. She didn't want to intrude on our time together."

"But she wouldn't have," Jennifer interrupted. "She's part of our family now."

"I know, honey," Jessica reassured her. "She just wanted to make sure Tommy is comfortable with our relationship. She doesn't want to be the cause of any problems."

"I think it's wonderful that you have someone who loves you," Tommy stated. "Besides, I like her. Why doesn't she just move in here with us?"

"Tommy, I love you." Jessica couldn't help the tears. "Have I told you both how lucky I am to have you in my life?"

"We love you too, Aunt Jess," Jennifer pledged as she leaped from her seat to hug Jessica.

"Can you believe it, Aunt Jess, our little Jennifer, with ice cream on her face, is going to graduate from high school." Tommy grinned as he dipped his finger in his bowl and plopped a blob of ice cream on the end of Jennifer's nose.

"Oh you!" Jennifer squealed as she attacked her brother. Jessica just smiled as they carried on. They had been doing this since they were tiny.

"I'll be right back," She announced, and she went to the telephone and dialed Andy's number.

"Hello." Andy was never sure who was calling her late at night. It could be the office with an emergency.

"Hi, it's me." Jessica spoke quietly. "I just wanted to hear your voice. I couldn't wait for you to call."

"I'm glad you called. I had a wonderful time. You did a great job with Tommy, he is a doll."

"He likes you too."

"Is that Andy?" Jennifer shrieked as Tommy held onto her tickling.

"Yes it is, and Jenn, she says go to bed, you need your rest for graduation tomorrow."

"She did not, let me talk to her." Jessica handed her the telephone. "Andy, I'm glad you're coming tomorrow. I love you."

"I love you too, Jenn and I wouldn't miss your graduation for anything. Now do what your Aunt Jess said or you will fall asleep during the ceremony. How would it look for the most beautiful and talented kid in the class to be snoring on stage?"

"Oh Andy." Jennifer laughed. "All right, I'm going to bed."

"My turn," Tommy said as he reached for the telephone. Jennifer handed it to him.

"Andy, it's Tommy."

"Hi Tommy, are those girls terrorizing you yet?"

"They're trying, but I'm holding my own. You should have stayed to defend me."

"I think you can take care of yourself." Andy chuckled.

"Andy, I want to know when you're going to move in and take care of Aunt Jess?"

Andy didn't quite know how to respond. "Are you sure it's okay with you and Jennifer?"

"You are part of our family now, and families live together."

Andy found it hard to speak. "Thank you, Tommy. I am honored that you and Jennifer have included me in your family. I love your Aunt Jess and I'll always take care of her."

"Good, and Jenn and I will make sure she takes care of you."

Jessica was having the same difficulty in containing her tears as she took the telephone from Tommy's hand. "Andy, are you there?"

"Yes. You know, those are some kids." The emotion could be heard in her voice.

"They are something," Jessica agreed as she gazed fondly at them. "I'll let you go to bed, but I just need to tell you how much I love you."

"I love you too, Jess. By any chance are you going on an early morning walk tomorrow?"

"I think that can be arranged." Jessica smiled as she spoke. Andy had just asked her to come over in the morning.

"I'm looking forward to it. Goodnight, love."

"Goodnight, Andy."

It was a good hour before Jessica and the kids headed for bed. It had been a wonderful reunion and the three of them were reluctant to end it. They talked extensively about their family and Andy's place in it. Jessica wanted to make sure that both Tommy and Jennifer were secure with her love and that Andy would be a part of that. It continually amazed her that her niece and nephew had grown into such loving and open young adults. Her sister and brother-in-law would be so proud of them.

When Jessica's alarm went off at eight-o'clock, she didn't hesitate as she headed for the shower. Ten minutes later she headed out of her front door, did a few leg stretches, and started her run. It wasn't that far to Andy's home but she needed the exercise. A couple of miles later she opened Andy's front door with her key, a gift from Andy two weeks earlier, and re-locked it behind her. She walked down the hallway to Andy's bedroom, pulling her sweatshirt off as she entered the room.

It always surprised her how soundly Andy slept. Jessica undressed and slid under the covers, snuggling her body up to Andy's back, her arms snaking around Andy's waist. As usual, Andy slept in a pajama shirt and Jessica's hands found their way underneath, cupping Andy's generous breasts. Andy groaned with pleasure as Jessica's fingers teased her nipples, her lips, and tongue kissing Andy's neck until she turned to face her. Jessica was naked to Andy's touch and she pulled Jessica's body on top of hers until Jessica's legs straddled Andy's as she sat upright. Andy's hands and fingers were all over Jessica's breasts and her mouth and tongue left hot kisses on her nipples. Jessica's hips moved in response as the familiar heat spread through her body. She leaned down to capture Andy's mouth with her own, her tongue sweeping through Andy's mouth. Andy's hand moved between Jessica's legs as she began teasing her, rubbing her moist slick lips, until Jessica pleaded for release.

"Andy."

That single plea was all Andy needed as she plunged her fingers into Jessica while Jessica's hips bucked with pleasure. Sliding in and out of

Jessica's wetness was all it took for Andy, and the two of them shuddered with climax after climax. Jessica's body slumped onto Andy's as their breathing returned to normal. Jessica wrapped her arms around Andy's neck, their faces pressed against each other, as they enjoyed the aftermath of glorious sex. Andy's fingers were still inside Jessica and, as she moved them, Jessica's body reacted again. She contracted around Andy's fingers, another orgasm flooding her body. She gasped in pleasure as Andy continued her assault on Jessica's senses, all control leaving her body. Andy held her tightly as her body melted against Andy's with happiness.

"You are going to kill me," Jessica moaned in Andy's ear.

"I hope so." Andy grinned as she gazed at Jessica. "Good morning."

"Good morning to you." Jessica kissed Andy in a long leisurely kiss.

It wasn't much longer before Jessica's attention returned to Andy's kiss-swollen nipples, her tongue and teeth teasing them into hardened points. Her mouth continued a trail of kisses down her stomach and along the lacy waistband of her panties. Her mouth did not stop its heated path as she continued to kiss Andy through the silk. Her mouth and tongue reached the swollen lips between Andy's legs, teasing and kissing her through the now wet silk. Andy's body moved in response, her hands cradling Jessica's head, as Jessica slid Andy's panties off and slowly, deliciously slid her tongue inside her. She stroked her tongue in and out, fingers teasing Andy as her hips rose to meet Jessica's mouth. Jessica could feel Andy's muscles tighten as she whimpered, a moan slipping from her throat. Jessica increased the pressure of her tongue until Andy's body shivered and her hands stilled in Jessica's hair. Jessica waited for Andy's body to stop its tremors before she slid her fingers into her hot, slick cavity, her tongue rubbing Andy again. Andy's body tightened in response, her legs wrapping around Jessica's back. Jessica loved to watch Andy's face, her eyes were barely open, her face taut with pleasure, and her lips swollen with kisses. It made Jessica's heart pound just to watch her, realizing how much she loved this woman. She moved up Andy's body, pressing her breasts against Andy's, enjoying the pleasure of their skin touching from head to toe. Andy bent to meet Jessica in a kiss, their bodies melted together in a familiar embrace. Both drifted off to sleep, hands clasped, and faces tucked against each other. It was an hour later before Jessica woke Andy with a kiss.

"Honey, I have to get going." She apologized as she got out of bed, reaching for her clothes.

"I know," Andy groaned.

"If we lived together, I would already be home," Jessica reminded her.

"How about we take care of that little problem after the festival, when everything is a little calmer."

Jessica leaned over to kiss Andy. "If you can make me wait that long." Her kiss teased Andy with its searing heat. Andy moaned in response as their tongues met with sweet promise.

"You need to go," Andy whispered, running her hands quickly down Jessica's body. It was Jessica's turn to complain as she stood up to leave.

"You know what I want, just one full weekend with you, no interruptions, no jobs, no people, just you and me, some food, and a bed."

"We will honey, we will," Andy reassured her as Jessica left the bedroom.

She wanted that as much as Jessica. No matter how well they planned, their time together revolved around Andy's job schedule, Jennifer's activities, and Jessica's work. Now with the festival in two weeks they had very little time together. On top of everything else, Andy now carried a cell phone wherever she went in order for the precinct to locate her. She essentially was on duty twenty-four hours a day. She needed to do something for her and Jessica, and the sooner the better.

Right now she had to spend some time at her office. The upcoming festival and the increased tourist activity were creating a mountain of work. Since she wasn't officially on duty, she decided to throw on a pair of shorts, a sweater, and tennis shoes. The weather had been warm all week and she wanted to be comfortable.

Forty minutes later she poked her head into the local deli to pick up some treats for the office. "Rachel, how's it going?"

"Wonderful, Andy. How are you and Jess? She must be excited about Jennifer's graduation."

"She is. Tommy came home last night and she is very happy." Rachel and her girlfriend Denise were two of Jessica and Andy's small circle of close friends.

"What can I get for you?"

"How about some goodies for the office, I'm going over there for a while."

"You work too hard, Andy," Rachel admonished her.

"Talk about calling the kettle black." Andy chuckled. Rachel was one of the most dedicated, hard workers Andy had ever met.

While Rachel prepared a plate of goodies, Andy took a seat at one of the tables. It was hard for her to remember a time before Jessica and the town of Cascade. She felt so much a part of everything, almost as if she had always lived there. She knew this is what her life was supposed to be. She loved the small town with its strong characters and friendliness. Included in the townspeople were Rachel and her girlfriend, and many other members of the community, young an old. The small town had adopted Andy as one of their own and closed ranks around her and Jessica. It was a community that thrived on friendship, caring, and good old neighborly support, surrounded by the mountains and the river they all loved. She had much to be thankful for.

While she sat counting her blessings, a group of young men in their twenties loudly entered the deli. They grabbed a table in front of the window next to Andy. One of the older looking men of the foursome stopped next to Andy and looked her up and down, a leer on his face.

"Well, so what do we have here a good looker in this town? How've I missed you, sweet thing?" He pulled out the chair next to Andy and straddled it backwards, his fingers reaching forward to touch her hair.

"I wouldn't if I were you." She warned as she stood up to get away from him.

"This gorgeous kitten's got claws," He drawled as his friends laughed. "I like claws."

"She's not interested, Mike." One of the guys laughed.

"She's interested. She just hasn't gotten to know me." He watched Andy's trim figure walk up to the counter. "Take a look at that package."

"Here you go, Chief." Rachel handed a bag of goodies to her. "I'll put it on your bill." Rachel glared at the men at the table as she spoke.

"Thanks Rachel," Andy responded. "I'll see you later."

Andy quickly left the small restaurant. She had dealt with obnoxious men before and it was the safest policy to ignore them. Besides she wanted backup. Andy immediately got on her radio and contacted dispatch. She wasn't about to leave Rachel by herself to deal with four obnoxious young men. She kept her sharp eyes on the deli while she waited for a patrol car to pull up.

"Hi Chief, what' up?"

"Hey, Randy. I'm not sure if anything is up but there are four very rude men in Rachel's place and I need you to go in there and stay until they leave."

"Okay, boss."

Andy watched Randy enter the deli and greet Rachel. She would continue to observe until the four of them left the building.

"Hey lady, why did you call that fox Chief?" One of the men yelled from across the room as they prepared to leave.

Rachel glared again at the group. This was one part of her job she hated, waiting on rude patrons. "That woman you were speaking about is the Chief of Police."

"Way to go Mike, the Chief of Police!" The men at the table broke out into snorting laughter as Mike, the man who had harassed Andy turned red with embarrassment.

"Isn't she a dyke?" One of the men asked loudly, and the others continued laughing. Rachel cringed at the conversation.

"Hey, watch your mouth!" Randy spoke sharply at the four men.

All of them noisily shuffled out but the one named Mike was extremely agitated. He was obviously very angry and as he stood up he kicked the chair. "Let's get out of here. I need a beer."

Rachel was relieved to see the four of them exit the deli. She had not been looking forward to dealing with them. Thank goodness Andy and Randy had been there.

"Rachel, call dispatch immediately if they come back." Randy requested as he headed out after them.

Andy followed the car as they drove out of town before she headed to her office. Meanwhile, Rachel was breathing a sigh of relief. She could have refused them service, but was thankful it hadn't come to that. Her last thought as she turned to smile at a new customer coming through the doorway was that those men were trouble.

Andy's thoughts were much the same as she entered the police precinct. She was very concerned about the four men and their attitudes. She needed to figure out what kind of threat they brought to her town.

"Hey Chief, what are you doing here?"

"How's it going Mac? I have some paperwork to do. Rachel sent some goodies, will you put them in the kitchen for me?"

"Sure, I'd love to." He snagged the bag from Andy's outstretched arms. He took the time to take a peek in the bag. Rachel's goodies were well known at the office. "My wife would kill me."

Andy laughed, watching Mac groan while he checked out the pastries. His wife had him on a low fat diet, because he was constantly struggling with his weight.

"Mac, there are two low fat bran muffins in there with your name on them, complements of Rachel." His grin was enough to make Andy laugh.

"Thanks, Chief."

"Don't thank me, thank Rachel," Andy reminded him. "Mac, is Len around?"

"Yep, he's on his way back in. We had a complaint by the tavern owner this morning. There was some ruckus last night and Len went to check it out."

"Can you ask him to come see me when he gets here?"

"Sure thing, Chief."

"Thanks Mac, now go enjoy the muffins."

Andy entered her office and sat at her desk. She picked up the top file on her desk and began to work. She was fully engrossed twenty minutes later when Len entered.

"Andy, what are you doing here? Isn't Jennifer graduating tonight?"

"Yes, she is, and I'm just doing a little paperwork this morning. Len, I ran into four men this morning that tripped my radar. The only name I got was Mike. They were all in their late twenties and were not from town. I can't be sure but I think I might have seen one of them before. Have you seen or heard anything lately?"

"As a matter of fact, this morning's mess at the tavern might be connected. You know that construction site thirty minutes out of town where they're putting in that cement firm?"

Andy nodded. She had met the contractor on the job and had checked out the site several times.

"They've got a crew of about 25 men out there and last night several of them decided to celebrate and get toasted at the bar. According to the owner, he cut them off when they got rude, and a couple of them got very angry with him. They threatened him physically, but some of their friends stepped in and calmed them down and they left. This morning the tavern owner found all four of his truck tires slashed. He can't prove they were the ones who did it, but he swears it was them."

"Did you find anything that might prove his claim?"

"Nothing. The tires had been slashed with a very sharp knife, no legible footprints, and nothing left at the scene. Tire marks were too numerous since he leaves his car in the parking lot where all the other cars park."

"What do you think?"

"I think he's right. His cutting them off angered the hell out of them and I think they paid him back."

"Great, just what we need with the festival two weeks away. Any luck finding out the names of these pleasant gentlemen?"

"I'm working to try and get some names from the people at the bar last night. I'm going to make some telephone calls and see what I can come up with."

"Good. Keep me posted, please. I didn't have a very pleasant introduction to this Mike character."

"Did he give you a bad time?"

"Let's just say he thought he was charming the socks off me by sitting at my table. When my reaction was less then overwhelmed his buddies found it very funny. I had the impression that this Mike character was very angry."

"He tried to hit on you? Boy, what an idiot. Didn't he know you were the Chief of Police?"

"I don't think so, and I'm not sure that would have made any difference. Let me know what you find out. I want to stay on top of these guys."

"Will do."

"Thanks, Len."

"No problem Andy, now go home."

"I will in a little while, I just want to finish some paperwork," She reassured him, smiling as he left her office.

It was amazing what a few months had done to Len and Andy's relationship. They not only had a working respect for each other, but also were becoming fast friends. Andy had worked with Len to teach him karate and he was now sharing his skills with the others on the team. He managed things in Andy's absence, and seemed extremely happy with their relationship, and content with his job. Len had returned the favor by introducing Andy to the townspeople and the surrounding area. He had begun to trust Andy and she had returned that trust and friendship. They had found out that they liked and respected each other.

Several hours later, Andy was still working at her desk when Len entered again. “”I have some names for you. According to several people at the tavern there were four men who caused all the trouble. Their names were Mike Chambers, age twenty-nine, Eric Landry, twenty-five, Stan Randall, twenty-three, and Rick Saunders, twenty-six. They all hang out together.”

“Did you run their names through the system?”

“I did, and our boy Mike has quite a record. He’s been charged with assault three times and found guilty once. He didn’t serve much time though. The other charges were dropped. Apparently the witnesses decided not to press charges. He was also charged with attempted rape of a minor, but according to our records the young girl’s parents decided not to press charges either. Did I mention that the girl was only fifteen and he was twenty-six?”

“Well, it sounds like he’s managed to scare everyone off so they won’t testify against him.”

“My thoughts exactly. I think he’s big trouble. The others don’t have anything on record as far as I can find. He has quite a file even as a juvenile. According to what I could find out, he was put into several foster homes after charges of abuse and neglect were filed against his mother. It looks like he took off at fifteen. Then it seems that he started on a life of petty theft and gang activities before he was charged with assault the first time at eighteen.”

“Boy, it doesn’t sound like he got a fair start in life.”

“Maybe not, but it still doesn’t make it right that he hurts women.”

“You’re right. That is lots of good information. Nice job, Len. Let’s think about this for a day or so. In the meantime, let’s keep an eye on this character Mike and make sure he doesn’t hurt anyone.”

"I'll make it my life's work. I hate scumbags who hurt little girls."

"I know the feeling," Andy responded.

"Now, you need to get out of here."

"I'm on my way." Andy laughed as she headed out the door of her office. "Thanks, Len."

"See you later, Chief."

Andy headed for home. She had a little over an hour to get cleaned up, change her clothes, and head over to Jessica's. She had already wrapped Jennifer's graduation gift so she could hurry.

An hour later she was on Jessica's doorstep about to knock when Tommy whipped the door wide open. "Don't you dare knock!" He admonished.

"I was only thinking about it." She flushed with embarrassment, smiling as she entered the house.

"Aunt Jess is in the kitchen and Jenn is running late as usual. You look pretty terrific. Did anyone ever tell you that you don't really look like a police officer?"

"It's been pointed out to me a time or two." Andy chuckled. "You look pretty nice yourself. I like your suit."

"Thanks, Aunt Jess helped me pick it out the last time I was home. I don't get a chance to wear it very often."

He straightened his tie as he spoke. He had on a dark navy blue double-breasted suit with a cream colored shirt. His tie was navy, black, and cream, and he looked like he had just stepped off the cover of 'Gentleman's Quarterly'. He was one handsome young man.

"Hi, sweetie, you look beautiful." Jessica came down the hall to greet her. Andy wore a dark gray silk dress and matching jacket. She wanted to make sure that she looked nice for Jennifer.

"Thank you." She hugged Jessica. "I like your dress."

"Thank you, ma'am." Jessica grinned. She had on a pale yellow knit dress that hugged her body, showing off her figure. "Jennifer, you're going to be late to your own graduation if you don't hurry up!" She called up the stairs.

"I'm coming, Aunt Jess, just one minute."

"One minute, my eye," Tommy responded, rolling his eyes. Jessica and Andy laughed.

Jennifer was true to form, because it was over five minutes before she came tripping down the stairs. "Okay, I'm ready," she announced.

"It's about time," Tommy grumbled.

"You look very nice, Jennifer." Jessica poked Tommy. "Now let's go get in Andy's jeep so we can get to the gym on time. Tommy, grab the camera please." She smiled at Andy and squeezed her hand.

The four of them climbed into the jeep and headed for the high school. Andy parked the car and Jennifer ran to the locker room where all the graduates were readying themselves for the ceremony. Jessica, Andy, and Tommy entered the gym and found seats close to the front. There were many people already seated, and a large number of them greeted the three of them.

"Be sure to save a seat for Buck," Jessica reminded Tommy as they settled in their seats.

"Here he comes." Andy waved at Buck to get his attention.

"Tommy, it's great to see you, son. You look healthy." He hugged Tommy hello.

"I missed you, Buck. How are you? Are you getting any fishing in?"

"Quite a bit actually. You got any time before you start working?"

"I've got all next week."

"How about we head out Monday and hike up into the hills to do some fishing? We can take our time and come back Wednesday night. What do you say?"

"Sounds perfect, Buck. I'd love too." They managed to get several more minutes of visiting in before the lights dimmed.

The ceremony was beautiful, as the graduates in dark green robes received their diplomas. There were speeches by both the principal,

Mayor Little, and several students. Jessica managed to contain her tears until the award for the best athlete was announced and Jennifer's name was read aloud. She held tightly to Andy's hand as Jennifer stepped forward to receive her award.

"I just wish her parents could see how wonderful Jennifer turned out," she whispered to Andy, silent tears running down her face.

"They know," Andy reassured her, as her own eyes welled up with tears. This was her family now, and she couldn't have been any prouder of Jennifer if she had been her own daughter.

The ceremony ended twenty minutes later and the graduates came out to have their pictures taken with their families. The graduates were all going to head off to their graduation party within the hour. Jennifer had brought her pack with a change of clothes, and she was so excited she could barely stand still. Jessica and Tommy took a series of pictures before Todd came over to get Jennifer to go to the party. She kissed Jessica and Andy goodbye and hugged Buck and Tommy.

"Have a great time, honey," Jessica called as Todd and Jennifer left.

"Buck, would you like to join the three of us for dinner?" Andy inquired. "We're just heading for the Falls."

"Are you sure you want an old man to keep you company?"

"Buck, you're not old and we'd love to have you with us. You're family." Jessica kissed him on the cheek.

"Besides, Buck, I won't be outnumbered." Tommy grinned. "If you don't come, I'll have to listen to all this girl talk."

Andy and Jessica groaned. "Sure pal," Jessica teased. "Girl talk. You should be so lucky."

The four of them headed for the parking lot and dinner. Four hours later, Tommy, Andy, and Jessica pulled into the driveway. It was still early in the evening and Tommy had plans.

"Tommy, you be careful tonight," Jessica reminded him.

"No problem, Aunt Jess. I won't drink and drive. I know better."

"Good. Have a great time. I'll be at Andy's if you need me." She hugged him tightly.

"Take care, Tommy." Andy volunteered as Tommy kissed her on the cheek.

"I will, Andy. I'm looking forward to seeing all my buddies from high school and I promise we won't get too crazy so they have to call you. How would it look if my aunt, the Chief of Police, had to come break the party up?" Tommy's eyes twinkled with humor.

"I'll tell you what, if you guys stay home with your partying and be careful, I promise I won't show up."

"It's a deal," Tommy promised as he got out of the car. Andy and Jessica watched Tommy walk into the house.

"He's a good kid," Andy remarked.

"Yes, he is." Jessica smiled. "It's amazing that the two of them have gotten to be such terrific young adults."

"You did a good job, Jess." Andy drove to her home as they talked. The two of them were looking forward to spending the night together. "It has everything to do with how you raised them." She kissed Jessica's fingers as she pulled into her driveway.

"You think so?" Jessica pulled Andy's hand to her mouth, her lips kissing the tips of Andy's fingers "Did I mention tonight how beautiful you look? I love you in this dress."

"Thank you, ma'am, you look very sexy tonight yourself."

"I think we need to take this conversation into the house." Jennifer kissed Andy's lips lightly.

Andy and Jessica held hands as they walked into the house. Shutting the front door, Jessica turned to Andy, pressing her against the closed front door, her hands sliding over Andy's body as she met Andy's lips with her own. Their tongues tasted each other, their bodies pressed tightly together. Jessica's hands cupped Andy's full breasts, her hips sliding against Andy's provocatively, the explosion of passion overwhelming them. Jessica reached down and slid her hands up Andy's thighs and hips, her fingers enjoying the feel of Andy's muscular buttocks. Andy hissed with pleasure as Jessica slipped her hand between Andy's legs.

"Jessica," Andy gasped as the familiar heat began to consume her. In response to Andy's plea, Jessica slid to her knees in front of her. She reached up and began to slide Andy's nylons and panties down her legs, her lips leaving a trail of kisses down her muscular thighs. She pushed Andy's dress up over her hips and her mouth found Andy's moist center. Her tongue slid into Andy, and her arms wrapped around her hips, pulling her tightly to her. Her tongue teased Andy's hardened bud as Andy's legs parted in response, her breathing labored, her hands clenched on Jessica's shoulders. As Andy's hips responded to Jessica's attentions, she cried out with pleasure. Jessica felt Andy's body began to shiver against her mouth as her tongue plunged into Andy. Her fingers reached around and slid into Andy as her mouth and tongue combined to push Andy over the edge, making her legs shake in response. Her gasps pleased Jessica, as did the undulating of her hips.

"Oh, Jessica."

Jessica's fingers stroked Andy, holding her tightly while her body was racked with orgasm after orgasm.

"Oh my God," Andy gasped as Jessica stood up and cradled her arms, holding her tightly, the taste of Andy still on her lips.

"I love you, Andy," Jessica pledged.

"I love you, Jessica." Andy placed her face next to Jessica's. "Do you know what you do to me?"

Jessica smiled as she spoke. "I am just loving you."

"I think it's my turn to love you," Andy reminded her as she led Jessica down the hall to the bedroom.

Andy quickly shed Jessica of her clothes, her eyes traveling over Jessica's body, admiring her wonderfully sexy curves. Equally as rapidly, she removed her own as the two of them tumbled onto the bed together. Andy's mouth latched onto Jessica's nipple as her hands surrounded her breasts. Jessica's legs wrapped themselves around Andy's waist. Her hands were in Andy's hair, cradling her head. Jessica's body reacted to Andy's attentions, her nipples tightening in response. She could feel the wetness between her legs as Andy's mouth and hands created a familiar reaction. She loved how her body reacted to Andy's loving. Never before had she felt such trust and loving faith in another woman. Andy's body slid lower as her lips kissed Jessica's hipbone, her hands feathering over her hips. Jessica reached down and placed a hand on Andy's cheek to capture her attention.

"Andy, I want to taste you while you love me," she pleaded, her fingers touching Andy's lips softly. In response, Andy rose up on her knees next to Jessica's hips and kissed Jessica's stomach, her hands spreading her thighs. Jessica reached for Andy's hips pulling her gently toward her. Andy slid her body down the length of Jessica's, as her mouth teased the tops of her thighs. Jessica returned the favor, nuzzling Andy's stomach with her tongue. Sliding her arms around Andy's hips, her mouth captured Andy's wetness as Andy's tongue found Jessica's center causing her hips to roll in response. Jessica's fingers rubbed against Andy, whose own hips moved with the same rhythm. Andy's tongue and lips drank in Jessica's wetness as a pressure built up in her chest. She slid her fingers into the wet tightness and her mouth pressed against Andy's lips. Andy's body tightened around Jessica's while her mouth teased her, the beginnings of a climax spreading through Jessica's body. She pulled Andy's body tight to hers, twisting, and turning as Andy's mouth sucked the wetness from her body. She moved her fingers rapidly in and out of Andy, matching her movements with Andy's, as they both exploded with feeling. Arching her back to increase the pressure of Andy's mouth, and unable to focus any more, Jessica's arms tightened around Andy's hips. Wave after crashing wave of pleasure consumed her. Her head fell back as she cried out in response.

"God Andy, oh my God."

Her body shuddered and shook as Andy's attentions created one climax after another, until Jessica's body went limp with exhaustion. She cradled Andy while they both lay there reveling in the aftermath of their glorious lovemaking. Several moments later, Andy sat up and pulled the covers over her and Jessica tucking them tightly in then slid her arms around Jessica pulling her tightly against her.

"I love you, Jessica," Andy pledged, kissing her lightly and pushing her hair back from her face.

"I love you, Andy," Jessica tearfully responded, her heart brimming with love. "I can't believe this is the first time you and I will sleep together all night where one of us doesn't have to get up and leave. It's so special." She couldn't keep the tears from falling from her eyes. This woman had become her heart, her life.

"It is special, and the first of a lifetime of nights spent together," Andy promised.

"As soon as the festival is over will you move in with me? We could find some other place to live, if you don't want to move into my house."

"Jess, honey, I love your home and I want to move in with you. Your house is full of love and family, and I'm honored to be included as a member."

"Andy, I never expected to find someone like you to love. I just never thought it was possible for me. You have made my life complete. You are my heart and soul."

"I had resigned myself to never finding someone like you." Andy said. "It's not just about making love, even though I have never had such unbelievable lovemaking with anyone else. I have never reacted with anyone like I do with you. I can share my thoughts and dreams with you. You are my best friend, Jess, my lover, my soul mate."

They shared a brief kiss and Jessica held Andy tightly to, her face pressed against Andy's as they let their love for each other wash over them. Sleep gradually softened their grasp on each other, their breathing becoming quiet and regular. Andy woke up about four-thirty in the morning with Jessica's arms still draped around her waist, her face tucked up against Andy's back, her knees tucked behind Andy's, and her breathing steady as she slept. Andy turned to face Jessica and gazed at her sleeping features.

Even in sleep, her beauty was apparent, her tousled hair and thick eyelashes still sexy, her lips red with moisture. Andy could watch her sleep forever, her heart full of love. She counted her blessings every day that this woman had come into her life. Andy had told the truth when she had admitted to Jessica that she had given up on finding someone to love. In the space of one month she had moved, started a new job, and had fallen madly in love. She would spend the rest of her life loving this woman. Jessica stretched in her sleep, her hands reaching out to Andy as her eyes fluttered open.

"Hi sweetie." She smiled as she moved closer to Andy.

"Hi, did you sleep well?" Andy asked, smiling, as she gazed lovingly at her girlfriend's face.

"Perfectly, and you?" Jessica's hand touched her gently on the cheek.

"Wonderful. I like waking up to find you next to me."

"I like it, too." Jessica grinned as she moved her leg over Andy's hips and settled her body onto Andy's, her hands clasping Andy's tightly in her own.

"Jess, I love the feel of your skin next to mine, your breasts rubbing against mine."

She moved her body slowly against Jessica as she whispered. Jessica and Andy kissed softly, thoroughly, taking their time, leisurely enjoying the pleasure they received from each other in their closeness. This morning there was no sense of urgency in their lovemaking and they slowly awoke their senses with kiss after wonderful kiss. Andy's legs captured one of Jessica's as their lower bodies responded to the building passion. Jessica pressed her leg against Andy's wetness, in turn pressed herself tightly against Andy's leg, grinding their hips together. Jessica's hips continued their movements and she pushed herself up on her arms to pivot her wetness against Andy's as the rhythm became faster. She slid against Andy until the two of them were fused tightly together, their wetness a tight contact with each other. This began a spiraling climax in each of their bodies, and they both shuddered. Jessica's arms refused to support her and she collapsed on Andy, their bodies moist with sweat. No words were needed as they both caught their breath, hands clasped together, faces pressed against one another. Andy's body cradled Jessica's, as their breathing once again drifted to the measured sounds of sleep.

It was after nine in the morning before Jessica and Andy woke up. Jennifer wasn't due home until late afternoon and Tommy had gone hiking with his friends for the day. Jessica and Andy planned to arrive home sometime before Jennifer. They were going to enjoy a leisurely morning. They started with a communal shower, which ended with them back in bed for an hour of lovemaking, before breakfast in bed and another attempt at a shower. Andy and Jessica spent most of the time alternating between laughter and loving. They finally headed back to Jessica's house, Andy with her briefcase in hand. Jessica was going to work in her studio, and Andy was going to get some work accomplished at the kitchen table in the other room. Just being in the same house with each other was a pleasure.

"Honey, do you want something to eat or drink?" Jessica asked after she had changed into her work clothes.

"Nope. Get to work, Jessica."

Andy grinned as she settled herself at the empty kitchen table. She had on a pair of old worn, faded jeans, a bright blue T- shirt, and her hair held back in a ponytail. Jessica quickly kissed her and headed down the hallway to her studio.

"You know where to find me," Jessica called over her shoulder as she entered the studio. Andy couldn't help but laugh, she was finding it equally as difficult to pay attention to anything other than Jessica today.

At three-thirty a happy but tired Jennifer returned home. She excitedly recounted the evening's activities to Jessica and Andy as they listened attentively. Within an hour, Jennifer's eyes began to droop with exhaustion.

"Honey, you need to get some sleep. Why don't you go upstairs and crawl in bed? You can tell us more about it later."

"I will Aunt Jess. It's just so hard to believe I graduated. Just the Senior Ball is left and then high school is all over." Jessica hugged her niece. She too found it hard to believe this young woman was growing up so quickly.

"Jennifer, if you have a moment? I have a graduation present for you," Andy announced.

"A present for me, cool." She turned to Andy excitedly.

"It's something I thought you might appreciate." Andy handed her a a small wrapped package.

Jennifer ripped the paper off to reveal a small blue jewelry box. Jennifer opened the box and gasped. "It's an Olympic Gold Medal!" She exclaimed.

"My father won it many years ago in wrestling. He gave it to me when I went into the FBI Academy. Now I am giving it to you. You are the closest thing to a daughter I'll ever have, and I know you appreciate what it represents," Andy shared with her.

"I can't believe it, a gold medal! Aunt Jess, isn't it beautiful?"

Jessica looked at Andy as she spoke. "It is beautiful and very special."

If she hadn't been in love with Andy before this moment, she was now, after this wonderful gesture. Jessica knew how much Andy missed her parents. For her to share something of such value with Jennifer told Jessica how unique this woman was.

"Andy, I love it." Jennifer threw her arms around Andy's neck, hugging her tightly. "Thank you, I love you, Andy."

Andy hugged Jennifer in return as she looked at Jessica, tears in her eyes. "I love you too, Jenn. I'm glad you like it."

"I can't believe you gave it to me," Jennifer repeated.

"You go get some sleep, Jennifer. You're exhausted," Andy suggested, smiling.

"Thanks again, Andy. I love you guys. I'll see you later. I want to call Todd and Loren and tell them what you gave me." Jennifer bounded up the stairs.

"Andy, you couldn't have given Jennifer anything that would mean more to her." Jessica smiled as she sat down on Andy's lap. "Thank you."

"For what?" Andy asked as she hugged Jessica to her.

"For loving my family and me." Jessica kissed Andy thoroughly.

"My pleasure," Andy responded as she returned the kiss.

"You know they are your family now."

Andy's tears began as her carefully controlled emotions got the best of her. "Jessica." Andy found it difficult to speak as Jessica kissed her tears away.

"I love you, Andy."

"I love you, Jess."

The rest of the afternoon, as Jennifer slept, Andy continued to work in the kitchen while Jessica carved on a piece in her studio. They shared a small quiet dinner together and were just cleaning up the dishes when Tommy returned home from hiking. The three of them visited for over an hour before Andy headed home for the night. Jessica tried to convince Andy to stay but she held to her decision about waiting until after the festival. It was a very lonely drive back home for Andy. She already missed Jessica's company. She needed to concentrate on getting the festival safely behind her so she and Jessica could pay attention to their moving in together. Just a couple more weeks and they would make that commitment. Andy knew it was the last time she would ever move. She was that sure of Jessica and their love for each other.

Chapter Eight

The next two weeks were a flurry of activity for both Andy and Jessica, beginning with Jennifer's Senior Prom and preparations surrounding the festival, and it kept the two of them running in all directions. The festival was officially going to open on Monday morning and Andy was putting the final changes on the schedule for police coverage. It was late Saturday night and she was exhausted. She and Jessica had managed a few stolen kisses but any meaningful time would have to wait until after the weekend.

Right now, Jessica, Jennifer, and a large group of volunteers were putting the final decorations on the booths and the fairgrounds. An unofficial party was scheduled Sunday evening to kickoff the festival. Andy was heading to the fairgrounds as soon as she was done in order to offer her services. She had the Sunday afternoon schedule at the festival and she wanted to spend a little time with Jessica before the horrendous week began. Grabbing her cell phone and radio, she headed out her office door, schedule in hand.

"Marta, go home, it's late, re-introduce yourself to your family."

"There's plenty of time for that after the festival. Did you finish the schedule?"

"I did, and it can be published tomorrow. Now I am serious, go home. You need to get some rest. I'm depending on you to keep the place running next week. Now scoot."

"Okay Andy, but I'm going to say the same thing to you. You've been in this office until after midnight for two weeks. You need as much rest as everyone else," Marta informed her sternly. "You lose any more weight and you will disappear."

"I promise, I'm heading home right after I pick up Jessica and Jennifer from the fairgrounds. They've been working since seven this morning."

"Good, say hello to the girls." Marta hugged her quickly. "I'll see you tomorrow."

"Thanks, Marta. I appreciate all your hard work."

"No one works any harder then you do, Chief. Now get out of here."

Andy grinned as she left the office. Jessica, Jennifer, and Tommy weren't the only members of her new family. Marta and the rest of the officers on her crew had adopted her as one of her own. They watched out for each other very carefully and Andy couldn't have a better group to work with.

She climbed into her jeep and headed toward the fairgrounds, yawning as she drove. She was so tired and Jessica and Jennifer must be even more exhausted. Tommy was working long shifts as a park ranger up in the mountains so they rarely saw him. He worked three twenty-four hour shifts and then had forty-eight hours off, loving every minute of his job. Jennifer would also begin working full time at the deli after the festival ended. Rachel had offered her the position and at first Jennifer felt guilty thinking about it. Jessica encouraged her to try the deli instead of spending her summer at the gallery and Jennifer was excited to try something new. It also helped her add to her school money, and since she had officially enrolled at the University of Washington, she was going to need all the spending money she could make.

Jessica and Andy were going to try to get away for several days after the festival concluded, somewhere all by themselves. They had been running steadily for two weeks and missed each other's intimate company. Andy pulled into the fairgrounds and parked her car, her eyes scanning the parking lot while she locked the jeep and began to walk toward the booths. She caught a cigarette flair and noticed a small crowd on the edge of the parking lot. She recognized the young man, Mike Chambers, who had given her a bad time earlier in the month. She and Len had been watching him carefully for several weeks but so far he had done nothing illegal or anything that concerned them.

He was standing with two other young men next to a picnic table. A young woman was draped around him, her hand on his thigh. She looked very young, and Andy decided to check it out. Turning her radio on she notified dispatch what she was up to then approached the group. All four of them watched her carefully.

"Nice uniform," One of the young men commented. "Nice body."

Andy ignored him as she pulled her flashlight out of her belt and turned it on. "What's up folks? May I please see some identification?"

A cigarette butt was flipped against her pant leg as she waited for them to provide their paperwork. She showed no reaction to their behavior.

"Sure, officer, we have no problem showing our paper. Or should I call you Chief?" Mike Chambers sarcastically remarked.

Leering at Andy, while he nonchalantly pulled out his wallet, his other hand slid under the woman's shirt as he brazenly dared Andy to say anything. For some reason he had to prove something to the woman police officer standing in front of him. He hated the fact that she looked at him with such contempt. All women were the same, just like his mother. They all manipulated and used the men around them.

He still could remember the first time his mother had locked him in his room after strapping him within an inch of his life for stealing a dollar from her purse. He had been four years old, but it hadn't made a difference with his mother. First she beat him on his hands until they bled and then pounded his backside and legs before throwing him into his bedroom. He had cried himself to sleep, the first of many painful lessons his mother had taught him. When she began to loan him out to older men to have sex for money, his heart filled with hate. It had never gone away and as he grew up he found his hate spreading to all women.

He could feel the anger bubbling up inside of him as he reacted to the command in Andy's voice. No woman gave him orders.

Andy turned to the young woman and repeated her request for identification. The young woman pulled her driver's license from her pocket. Andy took her license and shined the flashlight on it. Seventeen, the young woman was seventeen! She quickly checked the other's identification to see that they were all over twenty-one. She returned all the identifications and spoke to the young woman. "Would you come with me, Alice?"

"What for?" She belligerently asked, still hanging onto Mike.

"I would like to speak with you in private. These gentlemen won't mind, I'm sure." She looked Mike right in the eye, challenging him.

"You go ahead, sugar. I'll catch up with you later." Mike kissed the young girl sloppily. The girl was way too young and stupid to do anything but follow Mike's every command. Besides she knew he would punish her if she didn't do everything he demanded. He lazily walked away with his buddies, staring at Andy as he left. "What I wouldn't give to have that cop's legs wrapped around my waist." There was only one thing women were good for and that was fucking, nothing else.

Andy chose to ignore the remarks and the ensuing laughter. She focused her attention on the angry young woman standing in front of her. "Alice, the man you were just kissing is more then ten years older than you and very dangerous."

"He is not, he loves me."

Andy sighed loudly. "I'm calling a police unit to take you home. I really suggest you stay away from Mike for your own safety." She called a unit on her radio and then waited for them to arrive. Once a very disgusted Alice was safely stowed away in the car on her way home, she was finally able to go locate Jessica and Jennifer. It bothered Andy that she could nothing about Mike Chambers. He had not broken any laws even dating a seventeen year old wasn't illegal. It just worried Andy that he was in her town. Something about him was off. She shivered as she walked. He was dangerous. She just knew it.

"Hey, honey," Jessica called as she caught sight of Andy. She and Jennifer were stapling bunting along the roof of a booth.

"Hi, how's it going?"

"We're just finishing the last booth and then we're done. I was getting worried about you," Jessica admitted as she gazed at Andy. "You look exhausted, sweetie."

"You and Jenn must be tired. You both have been working since early this morning."

"We are," Jenn admitted. "I just want to go home and crawl in bed."

Jessica stapled the end of her bunting. "That's it, we're done. Let's get out of here."

"I second that." Jennifer cheered.

Jessica loaded up her toolbox and closed it. "Let's go." She grinned at Andy. No matter how tired she was, seeing Andy always made her smile.

"The security guards have been patrolling regularly, haven't they?" Andy inquired. She would do what ever it took to protect her family.

"Yes, they just walked by not ten minutes ago," Jessica answered as she gathered her things. Andy picked up her toolbox and the three of them headed for Andy's jeep.

"I think by mid-morning tomorrow we'll be ready," Jessica announced as she climbed into the front seat. Jennifer settled in the back seat, unusually silent.

"That's great," Andy responded as she drove them home to Jessica's.

They pulled into the driveway and started to get out of the car. Andy poked Jessica and pointed to Jennifer in the back seat. She was sound asleep, her body curled up against the car door.

"I hate to wake her, she's worked so hard all week," Jessica whispered.

"Come on sweetie, we're home." Andy gently shook her awake.

"I'm so tired." Jennifer yawned.

"You go crawl in bed. We will get this stuff. Go, honey." Jessica shooed her into the house. Jennifer did not argue.

Andy and Jessica followed her into the house with Jessica's gear. They left it in the front hallway. "Honey, you look so tired," Jessica remarked as she hugged Andy.

"I'm not working any harder then you are." Andy held her in her arms.

"Let's go crawl in bed," Jessica suggested.

"I shouldn't stay, honey. Jennifer is here," Andy reminded her.

"Andy, you're moving in here in a couple of weeks. What's two weeks going to do to change things?" She grinned at Andy.

"You've got a point." Andy chuckled.

The two of them climbed the stairs to Jessica's bedroom. They shed their clothes, cleaned up in the bathroom, and climbed into bed. Andy and Jessica kissed goodnight and curled up against each other, Andy on her side, Jessica tucked up against her back, her arm around Andy's waist. Within minutes, the two of them were sound asleep.

Chapter Nine

The next seven days went by in a blur, as the festival took on a life of its own. Jessica and Jennifer worked from early morning until late in the evening, while record-breaking numbers of tourists enjoyed the activities. Andy's schedule was much more erratic, while she covered all different shifts. She and Jessica managed to spend one night together in that time, neither one having the energy to do anything more than snuggle with each other as they slept. Tonight they all decided to take the evening off and enjoy the festival themselves. Tommy and Jennifer were meeting friends, and Jessica and Andy were going to spend their time together. It was the last of the evening festivities for the festival. It was all but over.

Andy managed to get home around seven to change out of her uniform into a pair of jeans and a sweater, and then was on her way to meet Jessica at the security booth. Even though she was officially off duty, Andy still carried her radio, cell phone, and gun. Things had gone very smoothly the whole week and she wanted to keep it that way.

She parked her jeep and began to enter the fairgrounds, when the faint sounds of fighting reached her ears. It was coming from the woods to the right of the fairgrounds parking lot. Flipping her radio on, she notified the dispatcher of her activities. Just to be on the safe side, she left her radio on. She quickly ran to where the noises came from.

Entering a clearing in the woods she saw Todd, Jennifer's boyfriend, lying on the ground obviously badly beaten. There were four young men standing around him including Mike Chambers, who had his arms around Jennifer. Her blouse was torn as if she had been struggling, her mouth bound with what looked like a bandana.

"Well, who have we here?" Mike said as he ran his hands over Jennifer's breasts, a knife glistening in his hand. "If it isn't the Chief." His eyes were cloudy with anger and something else.

"Let her go, Mike," Andy ordered as she took in the details around her. Pulling her gun would probably not be a wise idea since she was currently outnumbered and Jennifer could get badly hurt. Her only choice was to keep the situation from escalating until help arrived.

"I don't think so, Chief Andy." Mike responded. "In fact, I want you to throw your gun down, please. I would hate to have to cut this pretty young woman's face." He grinned and slid the large hunting knife along Jennifer's cheek.

Andy did as she was asked. Jennifer's eyes betrayed her terror, as Andy tried to reassure her with her calmness. Andy would not allow anything to happen to her.

"Eric, Stan, bring the Chief over here, please." He continued fondling Jennifer's breasts as he watched Andy's reactions. Inwardly Andy was sick, but she knew not to show any response; it would just egg him on.

"Rick, come here and hold onto this young thing," Mike demanded.

Andy's arms were forced behind her back, her radio, and cell phone stripped from her belt. She prayed that dispatch was monitoring her radio long enough to send help.

"Well, Chief, it seems we are meant to be together," Mike drawled, sliding his knife along the bottom of Andy's sweater, slowly lifting it up. "I think your being a dyke is going to change. It just takes the right man to show you what you are missing."

His eyes gleamed as he cut Andy's sweater up the middle, revealing her bra. 'Well, well, look what you've been hiding under that uniform. It appears that I am going to have my hands full."

He laughed and roughly grabbed Andy's breasts. She couldn't help but flinch with pain. She resisted the urge to react to Mike's actions as her stomach rolled with displeasure. She heard Jennifer cry against her bandanna and glanced quickly at her to check on her. She noted that a young man, whose attention was focused on Mike's next move, loosely held Jennifer. Andy wasn't worried about the two men who held her arms. Her only concern was the knife currently in Mike's hand and her gun on the ground. While she continued to assess the situation, her eye caught some movement behind Jennifer. They had all but forgotten about Todd, and he had been able to rouse himself and was within arm's length of her gun.

As Mike slipped the knife against her skin intending to cut through Andy's brassiere, she made her move. Her knee came up and slammed between Mike's legs, causing him to collapse in pain. Her elbow caught the nose of the young man on her left as her right hand knocked the knife from Mike's grasp. She turned to face the man on her right his fist caught her face as she slammed her foot into his knee breaking his kneecap. She leaped the few steps to where Jennifer was being held and slammed the heel of her hand into the third man's nose. He dropped in a heap on the ground.

"Jennifer, are you all right?" she asked as she removed the binding from her mouth.

"Andy, watch out!" Jennifer cried out. Andy turned to face her attacker as he lunged at her with his knife, catching her on the ribs. It drew blood and it spurred him on as he lunged again at Andy.

"I'll take care of you, you dyke!" He shouted, his knife plunging toward Andy's chest.

Andy heard Jennifer scream as she met Mike's attack head on. As Mike's knife arced toward Andy, she rushed headlong into him, forcing him to grab at her with his other arm as she deflected the knife from its deadly course.

"You bitch!" He shrieked, his fist catching Andy's chin and snapping her head back.

Mike swung the knife once again toward Andy, aiming for her stomach. She brought her hand down in a vicious chop to Mike's wrist, knocking the knife from his fingers. His hand slammed against the side of her face as he tried to grab her. Her other hand met his chin and she knocked him backwards. She snapped her leg around, catching him in the chest and slamming him to the ground. He sprang up, rage clearly showing on his face, as he threw his body at Andy knocking them both down.

Andy knew she couldn't wrestle with him, he was too big. Rolling quickly away, she stood and prepared to defend herself as he rushed her again. Snapping her leg around again, she caught Mike in the ribs, causing him to hesitate before renewing his attack. It was all the time Andy needed, as her foot connected with his chin, and knocked him down. Before Mike could move, Andy grabbed his arms and pinned him to the ground.

"Do not move or I will break your arms!" she warned.

She quickly grabbed the knife and looked around the clearing. Todd had managed to grab the gun and moved to Jennifer, his arm around her in protection.

"Todd, bring me the gun," she ordered as she pocketed the knife in her jeans. "If any of you try to move, be assured that I will shoot you where you stand." She took the gun from Todd.

"Good job, Todd, thanks. Are you okay?" She asked as she pointed her gun at Mike. None of the four men were moving too quickly.

"Yeah, I'm fine."

"Now, can you go grab my radio on the ground over there and bring it too me?"

Todd did as she asked as Jennifer huddled in shame. Andy knew she needed to get to her soon; the shock would soon hit, and she needed to know Jennifer was okay. She spoke into the radio and was told two units were on their way. She could hear them pulling into the parking lot. Less then a minute went by before Mac and another officer burst into the clearing, their guns drawn.

"Keep your eye on the four men on the ground for me," She ordered as she walked over to Jennifer. She looked her right in the eye, buttoning Jennifer's shirt around her. "You did great, Jennifer. You were very brave. Everything is fine now, you are going to be just fine."

"I know," Jennifer whispered, and she threw her arms around Andy's neck, hugging her tightly. "I knew you would save me." She whispered as she began to cry. Andy held her tightly as her own tears filled her eyes. Now was not the time to lose it.

Len ran into the clearing, stopping abruptly as he saw the men lying on the ground being handcuffed by police officers. He rapidly glanced around for Andy, a look of fright on his face.

"You okay, Chief?' He called.

"I'm fine, Len. Could you clear this garbage up for me? I'll explain what happened later."

"You got it, Andy."

The two officers and Len roughly dragged the four men from the clearing as they read them their rights. Andy continued to hug Jennifer as she cried softly on her shoulder. Todd's battered face was tucked in Andy's other shoulder for comfort, as Andy allowed herself to think about the last ten minutes and what had almost happened.

"Andy, we need to get the three of you checked out by paramedics," Len gently reminded her as he re-entered the clearing.

"Okay, Len. Will someone locate Jessica and Tommy, and call Todd's parents?"

"Already done. Now, let us take Jennifer and Todd and you let these paramedics look at you, please?"

Andy found it difficult to let go of the two young people. Len took her arm as Jennifer and Todd were attended to. When Len saw the condition of Andy's sweater, he immediately removed his jacket and covered her.

"Andy, honey, you are injured," Len exclaimed as he supported her. "Get a paramedic over here, now!" He yelled.

Andy looked down at her bloody sweater as he fussed over her. "It's just a small scratch," she reassured him.

"You could have been killed by those assholes!" Len raged. "I don't know what I would have done if something had happened to you. You are my best friend." His voice choked with emotion. Len hadn't realized until that minute how close he and Andy had gotten.

"I love you, too, Len." She smiled as she patted him on the cheek.

"Andy, where is she. Let me see her!" Andy could hear Jessica's frantic voice.

"I'm right here Jessica, I'm fine." Andy smiled as Jessica rushed to her, throwing her arms around her neck.

"Jennifer told me what happened. You could have been killed!" Jessica kissed her quickly. She could care less who saw them.

"I'm fine, honey. You should be with Jennifer. She was pretty badly shaken up."

"Tommy's with her. Len, where is the paramedic? Andy is bleeding very badly." Jessica's voice was full of panic.

"I was just taking Andy to them Jess. They are on their way." He reassured Jessica, as he supported Andy's other side.

Jessica and Len slowly walked with her. Andy was amazed at how difficult it was for her to move; she seemed to have run out of energy. Two medics and a gurney met her halfway to the parking lot and insisted that she lay down so they could examine her.

"It's not that bad," she insisted as they removed Len's jacket and pulled her sweater away from the wounds on her ribs.

"Oh my God!" Jessica gasped as she and Len saw the extent of Andy's injuries.

"I'm afraid you're going to need some stitches," one of the medics stated. He cleaned and began to pack the wound. The other medic was busy starting an IV in Andy's arm

"Jessica, please check on Jennifer and Todd for me. Todd was pretty badly beaten." Andy winced with pain. Her body was beginning to react to the abuse inflicted upon it.

"Todd is on his way to the hospital to be checked out and Jennifer refused to go with out you. She and Tommy are waiting in the ambulance." Jessica held tightly to Andy's hand as she and Len escorted the gurney to the waiting ambulance. She was not leaving Andy's side.

"Jennifer has a few bruises, but otherwise physically she seems okay. She's very concerned about you."

"I'll be fine, Jessica. I'm sorry I didn't get there sooner."

"Andy, you saved both those kid's lives. There's no telling what might have happened if you hadn't gotten there when you did." Jessica shuddered as she spoke. She didn't want to think about what might have happened.

"Andy, you did good," Len reassured her. "I don't know anyone who could have handled it better." He patted her on the leg.

"Len, you are now the acting Police Chief. Can you get this mess cleaned up so the festival is not disrupted?"

"I can do that. I'll meet you at the hospital to take your statement and clarify some things with Jennifer and Todd. I'm going to have Mac take care of things here."

"Good. And Len? Thanks."

"No problem, Andy. Don't worry about a thing." He grinned as she was lifted into the ambulance. Jennifer was laying on the gurney next to her. Tommy was seated by her side, holding her hand.

"Jennifer, are you okay?" Andy asked as she gazed at her pale face. Jessica and the two paramedics climbed in with them.

"I'm fine, Andy. How are you? I know you were hurt." Jennifer's eyes filled with tears.

Andy reached over and clasped her hand. "I'm going to be fine, kiddo. As long as you're okay, I'm going to be perfect. Jennifer, I'm so proud of you. You were so brave."

"I love you, Andy."

"I love you, sweetie."

Jessica sat next to Andy holding her other hand. She gazed at Andy and Jennifer as they held hands, and reached across to grab Tommy's. The four of them were very lucky.

"Jessica, we need to get in here and look at Andy before we head to the hospital." One of the paramedics climbed in, and removed the remains of Andy's sweater and covered her with a drape. Another one inspected Andy's face as the scrapes and bruises were showing an angry red.

"Tommy, how about you and I follow the ambulance in Andy's jeep? Jessica asked as she moved out of the way. "Jennifer and Andy will be fine on their trip to the hospital." The ambulance was much too small for all of them. She was reacting calmly and rationally right now. It was not the time to fall apart. She could do that later.

"Okay, Aunt Jess." Tommy's face betrayed his fear. He bent and kissed his sister on the cheek. "Jenn, we'll be right behind you."

"Okay, Tommy. We'll be fine." She still clung to Andy's hand.

"Andy, thanks for taking care of Jenn." Tommy spoke softly and kissed Andy's cheek. "I can't believe what you did!" He looked at her with something akin to awe.

"I just did my job, Tommy. Besides, Jennifer is family." She smiled up at him. Jessica leaned over and kissed her lightly on the lips.

"I love you, Andy." She smiled deeply at her.

"I love you, Jessica."

"Jennifer, you take good care of Andy for us, and we'll meet you at the hospital." Jessica knew Jennifer needed something to focus on.

"I promise, Aunt Jess. I'll take really good care of her."

"I know you will, honey. I love you." Jessica kissed Jennifer and hugged her tightly.

"Love you, Aunt Jess."

Jessica smiled as she and Tommy climbed out of the ambulance. She loved these women very much and she was so glad they were going to be okay. "Come on, Tommy. I have Andy's car keys. Let's check with Len and get out of here."

After a few moments of conversation with Len and the other officers, Jessica collected Andy's cell phone and she and Tommy headed through the large crowd to Andy's car.

"Jessica, Andy, and Jennifer are going to be okay," a voice from the crowd called.

"They will be just fine."

"You tell them we're thinking about them."

Friends and neighbors of Jessica, and now Andy, offered their prayers and good wishes as she and Tommy headed out of the parking lot to the hospital.

"Aunt Jess, Andy's going to be okay, isn't she?" Tommy asked, his face pale in the passing headlights.

"She's going to be fine. The paramedic said she needs some stitches, but she's going to be okay." She reached for Tommy's hand and squeezed it. "She was very lucky."

"I can't believe what she did! She took out those four guys and one had a knife. She's so small, and those were huge guys."

"I know, Tommy, but she is very well trained. I'm just glad she arrived when she did. She saved Jennifer and Todd's lives."

She and Tommy both became silent, as thoughts of what could have happened played in their heads. Someone had been looking out for all three of them. Jessica silently thanked God for saving them.

"Everyone was very lucky," Tommy remarked.

"Yes, they were."

Aunt Jess, do you think I should tell Andy how much she means to me?"

"I think she would love to know how you feel." Jessica smiled as she spoke.

Jessica pulled the jeep into the hospital parking lot and parked. She and Tommy rushed to the emergency exit. As they entered the hospital, Buck met them at the door.

"Oh Buck, I'm so glad you're here!" Jessica threw her arms around him.

"I just got here, Jess. From what I understand, Jennifer and Andy are in the emergency room and Todd is in another hospital room. What the hell happened?" He led her and Tommy to seats in the hallway.

"I'm not totally sure, Buck. Tommy can fill you in on what we know. I'm going to go in with Jennifer and Andy."

She walked swiftly through the doorway of the emergency examining room, as Tommy began to explain to Buck what he had been told. Jessica found Jennifer being examined by Doctor Swift.

"Abe, is she okay?" Jessica asked as she approached the side of the bed.

"She's fine, Jessica. A few bruises and scrapes, but physically she is just fine." Jessica breathed a sigh of relief.

"I'm going to have the nurse clean and bandage her scrapes and then you can take her home." He patted Jennifer on the arm. "I'm awfully glad you're okay, young lady." Doctor Swift had known Jennifer since she was born.

"Thanks, doc." Jennifer grinned.

"Nurse Connolly, can you take care of my favorite patient here while I go check on Andy? Jennifer gave me my orders." He again patted Jennifer on her arm. "I'm going to take good care of her and Todd, don't you worry."

Jessica grinned at the exchange. Obviously Jennifer was recuperating rapidly, especially if she was giving the doctor orders. "Honey, do you want me to get Tommy to come sit with you? I'm going to check on Andy. I'll be right back."

"No, I'll be fine, Aunt Jess. Can you find out how Todd is doing?"

"I will, sweetie. I'll be right back."

Jessica stepped through the curtains into the next examining room where Andy was being worked on. Doctor Swift was intently looking at the wounds on her ribs while another doctor was working on her face.

"Well, young woman, I would say you were very lucky," Doctor Swift said to Andy. "These wounds could have been much worse. I'm going to have this nice young doctor stitch you up once he's done repairing your face. He does a much better job of stitching than I do. Then I'm going to prescribe some antibiotics and some pain pills and send you home with this very worried woman behind me. Judging by the extent of your injuries you are going to be one very sore patient."

"Thanks doctor. How are Jennifer and Todd?"

"Jennifer is just fine. She has a few scratches and bruises but other than that she'll heal very quickly. You might want to get her into counseling right away. She has been through a very frightening ordeal. Todd is also going to be okay. He has two black eyes, extensive bruising on his face, and has some heavy bruising on his ribs and back. Nothing was broken and he'll heal up just fine, but he's going to be pretty sore for a couple of days. I've seen worse on that kid from playing football, so he'll be okay. He's feeling pretty bad about not being able to protect his girlfriend, though. Someone ought to talk to him about that."

"Thanks doctor, I will. Where is he?"

"He's just getting ready to head home with his parents. I believe Len is getting his statement."

"Can I see him for a moment?" Andy asked, as the doctor began to stitch her wounds. Jessica remained silent, watching from the door. Her face was white with worry as she watched the two doctors work on her lover.

"I'll bring him in." Doctor Swift slipped through the curtains.

Moments later, Todd stepped into the room. Jessica couldn't help but gasp at the sight of his badly beaten face. His eyes were almost swollen shut and his lips were bloody and split in several places.

"Hey, Chief Andy, are you okay?" He asked as he approached the bed.

"I'm just fine Todd. How about you?"

"I'm okay. I just saw Jenn and she's okay, too."

"Tommy, I wanted to thank you for helping me tonight. I couldn't have done it without you." Andy reached out and clasped his hand.

"I let them beat me up and do what they did to Jenn. I wanted to kill them, but I didn't do anything." His head dropped in shame as he spoke, his voice breaking with emotion.

"Tommy, look at me." Andy spoke gently as she held his hand. "The key to being brave is knowing when to do something. It was four against two. You had no way of winning."

"But you stopped them." His eyes were red with unshed tears.

"Tommy, I had your help and years of police training. You were terrific and very brave and I'd work with you any day." Andy smiled.

"Thanks, Chief." Tommy grinned in return. His shame had turned into instant honor.

"No problem. Now you go brag to your friends about how you, Jenn, and I beat the stuffing out of those guys."

"I'm glad you're okay, Chief."

"Todd, call me Andy. After what we've been through I think it's appropriate."

"Thanks. Andy. I got to go now. My parents want to take me home."

"Good, thanks again Todd. I couldn't have done it without you."

Jessica couldn't hold her back tears. Andy continually amazed her. Even with everything she had gone through today, Andy was still able to think of other people. She loved the beautiful woman who went out of her way to make everyone in her life happy and safe.

"Okay, Andy, we just need to slap a another bandage on you and take that IV out and then you can go," the young doctor announced. "You aren't going to have any scars."

"Thanks, doctor."

"Have I told you lately just how much I love you?" Jessica spoke softly as she walked up to Andy, smiling at her battered partner.

"I love you, too, Jessica." Andy's face was beginning to darken with bruising.

"You're done here," the doctor announced. "I want to see you early next week to check the stitches. Keep them dry tonight and tomorrow, and no sit ups for awhile."

"Okay, doctor, and thanks again."

"My pleasure, and I'm sure glad you were able to protect those kids."

"Thanks. I am too." Andy gingerly sat up. "Do you think I could get something else to wear home? My sweater seems to have disappeared and this blanket isn't going to work."

"Sure, I'll grab you a surgical scrub shirt. I'll be right back." The doctor hurried off to do as he promised, while the nurse finished bandaging Andy's scrapes.

Andy reached out and pulled Jessica closer. "I'm so glad Jennifer is okay. I've never been so scared in my life." She held Jessica as close as possible.

"I'm glad you're both okay, and according to everyone involved, you did everything right, Andy. I don't know what I would have done if something worse had happened to either of you." She slipped her arms around Andy's neck. "In case you haven't figured it out, I want to spend the rest of my life with you."

"It's a good thing, because I'm not going anywhere." Andy reassured her as she rested her head on Jessica's shoulder. "I am committed to you for life."

"Here you go." The doctor stepped back into the room with a shirt in his hand. "There's quite a crowd out there waiting for you."

"Great." Andy grumbled, grimacing as she tried to put the shirt on. Jessica helped her get into it. Andy was already becoming stiff and sore.

"You ready?" Jessica inquired as Andy was helped into a wheelchair and the orderly prepared to push her out of the door.

"Yes."

Jessica opened the door for her and held her hand as she slowly proceeded down the hall. Jessica was amazed at the size of the crowd that waited for Andy. She could see Rachel and Denise, Vicki and her family, the mayor, Buck, Tommy, and Jennifer, along with Todd and his family.

It also appeared that every single police officer in town was there in uniform. As Andy reached the center of the group, they broke into applause and continued to clap as she stared at all of them in surprise. Her officers, one after the other, snapped to attention and saluted her, showing their support and recognizing her extraordinary job. Andy showed confusion and embarrassment as Jessica smiled at the reception. Len approached Andy, as the crowd grew silent.

"We're sure glad you're okay, Chief and we want you to know that we'll handle things for you while you take it easy. You don't need to worry about anything. We're very proud to be a member of your police force." Len's voice cracked with emotion as he smiled at his friend and mentor.

"Thanks, Len, I know you will. I am so very proud of all of you. I consider it an honor to be your Chief." Andy found it hard to speak she was so close to tears.

"Chief Andy, we want to thank you for protecting our son." Todd's father approached Andy to shake her hand.

"I couldn't have done anything without Todd's help. He was a very brave young man," Andy told Todd's parents. "You should be very proud of him."

"We are, Andy." Todd's father hugged his son tightly as Todd grinned.

"Come on honey, let's get you girls home," Buck suggested. He could tell Andy was exhausted and in pain; her face was pale and beaded with sweat. He and Tommy walked with Jennifer as Jessica and Len assisted Andy out of the hospital, pushing her wheelchair.

"Len, do you need me to fill out my report tonight?" Andy asked. Many of the townspeople shook her hand as she slowly moved through the crowd.

"No, we'll take care of it tomorrow. We have plenty of charges to hold the four of them on. I'll come over to Jessica's tomorrow afternoon and we'll take care of it then. Now you go home and get some rest, you earned it. That's an order." Len grinned. Andy shook her head in acknowledgement. She was rapidly running out of energy. "Thanks, Len."

"Come on, Andy." Jessica and the orderly pushed her out of the exit and up to the waiting jeep. "Tommy's got the jeep right outside the door." Andy allowed Jessica to help her into the jeep. Moving was becoming very painful and she had no energy.

"Buck, do you want to come over to the house for awhile?" Jessica asked. She knew he was very concerned about Jennifer and Andy.

"If you don't mind?" he responded.

"We want you there. You're family," She reassured him as she climbed into the jeep next to Andy. Tommy and Jennifer were in the front seat.

"I'll follow you."

Tommy slowly pulled out of the hospital and headed for home. No one said a word as the short drive was made. In the backseat Andy leaned heavily against Jessica with her eyes closed. It was Jennifer who spoke first.

"Tommy, will you fix some grilled cheese sandwiches for me for dinner? I'm starving."

Jessica couldn't help but laugh. Jennifer was already behaving in her typical fashion. Andy's hand closed over Jessica's as she too smiled at Jennifer's remark. "She's going to be okay," she whispered.

"Thanks to you," Jessica reminded her as Andy once again rested her head on Jessica's shoulder.

Moments later Tommy pulled the jeep into the driveway and parked. Jennifer and Tommy immediately got out of the car and entered the house while Jessica and Andy slowly followed. Jessica could see the pain on Andy's face as she moved.

"Let's get you into bed," she suggested.

"I think that might be smart," Andy agreed through clenched teeth. She slowly climbed the stairs with Jessica's help and entered the bedroom. It was all she could do to get to the bed.

"Why don't you sit down and I'll help you undress," Jessica suggested as Andy winced in pain when she started to bend over.

"Thanks, I seem to have gotten a little stiff," Andy responded with a slight smile.

Jessica squatted down and removed Andy's shoes and socks. She then stood up and gently pulled the surgical shirt off. She reached behind Andy and unhooked her bra, sliding it softly off her shoulders. Jessica could have cried when she saw the cuts and bruises on Andy's chest and back along with the bandages. She bit her lip in order not to cry.

"Can you stand up so I can get your jeans off?"

Andy was too sore and too tired to even answer, as she struggled to get off the bed. Jessica assisted her in slowly standing up. She removed Andy's jeans and helped Andy sit back down. Andy scooted back onto the bed and slid her legs under the covers. All she wanted to do was sleep. Jessica went to the bathroom for a minute, and returned with a warm wet washcloth and a glass of water.

"Andy, here's your pain pill." She handed it to her. "Now let me wash your face and then you can go to sleep," she promised as she gently washed Andy's beautiful face. Jessica's heart ached as she bathed her lover's wounds. "Now slide down under the covers and rest."

"I love you, Jess." Andy kissed her as Jessica leaned over to kiss her goodnight.

"I love you, Andy. Now you go to sleep. I'll be back up shortly to check on you." She kissed Andy again and pushed her hair out of her face. Andy's eyes were already shut.

"Okay."

Andy did as Jessica asked, pulling the covers up around her shoulders and rolling slowly onto her side. Jessica stared at her for a few minutes before turning out the light and leaving the room. She paused in the hallway and leaned against the wall, tears slipping from her eyes. She couldn't stand the thought that her niece and Andy had been hurt tonight. She was so glad it hadn't been any worse. Andy looked so badly injured, and she just couldn't handle it. She always told herself she wouldn't allow anyone into her heart that she might lose. Now she was in love with a police officer. One who would never avoid protecting her family and her town. Jessica could no more give Andy up then stop breathing. She was a part of her, the best part of her. She had saved Jennifer and Todd's life because it was what she was destined to do, just as Jessica was driven to carve. Their love was just that kind of need, deep in the soul and filling their hearts. She cried out of grief and love, and a need to cleanse her fear.

While she quietly grieved, she could hear Buck and Tommy's voices carrying up the stairs from the kitchen while they talked. Their voices soothed the ache that still throbbed in her chest. It was several minutes before Jessica could stop the tears and get control of her emotions. She wiped her face clear and walked down the stairs to join the others. Jessica entered the kitchen and, going to Jennifer, she immediately hugged her tightly.

"Do you know how much I love you, Jenn?" Jessica buried her face in Jennifer's hair as she held her. Tears were threatening to fall again.

"As much as I love you, Aunt Jess," Jennifer replied happily as she returned the hug, oblivious to Jessica's emotional state.

"How's Andy?" Buck asked. He and Tommy were preparing the grilled cheese sandwiches Jennifer had requested.

"She's sore and very exhausted." Jessica responded as she gradually got control of her emotions. "I'm hoping she will go to sleep. I gave her a pain pill. The doctor said she could take it right away and she could go to sleep. There was no concussion or anything."

"She's one very smart and tough lady," He remarked. "I'm very proud of her. How are you doing?" Buck looked at her with knowing eyes. He recognized the effort Jessica was putting forth to stay in control. He felt the same way. This was his family and he was angry that someone had tried to harm them. He also knew Jessica well and saw how her emotions were battling with her heart.

"We're all very proud of her, and I am doing fine, Buck. Thanks for asking." Jessica looked at Buck as she spoke.

If she admitted how she felt out loud she would burst into tears again. She smiled to reassure him and a yawn escaped her. Glancing at the clock, she was amazed to find out it was after one in the morning. No wonder Andy was exhausted. It had been a very long and emotional day.

"Jenn, I want you to sleep in tomorrow. Loren is handling the booth and there is no need for either of us to go to the festival."

"But Aunt Jess, it ends tomorrow night. What about the Fourth of July and the fireworks?"

Jessica had assumed Jennifer would not want to be there after what she had gone through. "I'll tell you what. Depending upon how Andy's doing tomorrow, we'll see if we can't get there to watch the fireworks, okay?"

"Cool."

"Now let's eat," Tommy suggested, as he and Buck handed out the sandwiches and glasses of milk.

It wasn't too much longer before Jennifer began yawning and decided to go to bed. Kissing her brother and Buck goodnight, she and Jessica walked up the stairs together.

"Jenn, are you going to be okay?" Jessica asked as Jennifer entered her bedroom.

"I'm fine, Aunt Jess," she reassured her.

"You come wake me up if you need me?" She requested. "You and Andy are going to need to talk to the counselor next week about what happened, honey. But if I can help with anything you let me know."

"I will. Is Andy going to be okay?"

"She's going to be just fine. You know she asked me the same thing about you?"

"She was amazing, Aunt Jess."

"I know, honey. She loves you, like I do. She would never let anything happen to you. She would give up her life to protect you." Jessica reached over and pushed Jennifer's hair out of her face.

"I love her, too." Jennifer smiled.

"Good, now you go crawl in bed and think good thoughts."

"Goodnight."

"Goodnight, sweetheart." Jessica watched Jennifer for a few minutes to reassure her heart before she headed to her own room.

Jessica silently entered her darkened bedroom. She changed into a nightshirt, washed her face, brushed her teeth, and crawled into bed, trying very hard not to disturb Andy. She turned on her side and laid her head on her pillow, intent on staying as far away from Andy as possible in order not to jostle her. Andy would have nothing to do with that, as she slid over and tucked her body tightly against Jessica's, slipping her arms around Jessica's waist. Jessica smiled as she hugged Andy's arms to her chest, tears filling her eyes. She was moving Andy in tomorrow and she wasn't going to take no for an answer. From now on, the two of them were going to sleep in the same house and the same bed every night. Jessica drifted off to sleep her fingers meshed with Andy's; Andy's steady breathing reassuring Jessica that she would be fine.

Andy didn't wake up until the clock read ten-twenty and she certainly didn't feel fine. She tried to sit up and immediately hissed at the pain that shot through her body. She breathed slowly, nausea causing her to swallow quickly, her head pounding. She rested a minute to get her bearings, and then very slowly moved to a sitting position, still taking slow, deep breaths. She slipped her legs off the edge of the bed and hesitated before trying to stand up. Fighting dizziness, she made her way to bathroom. She glanced into the mirror and was shocked at the sight of her bruised and scraped face. The dark circles under her eyes did nothing to hide how pale she was. She gently washed her face, trying hard not to pull on her chest bandages. Dressing right now was not an option as she struggled with her nightshirt. At least she could wear that. The idea of putting on a bra made her cringe. As Andy stiffly walked down the stairs, she could hear Jessica and Jennifer talking in the kitchen.

"Good morning," she announced as she entered the kitchen. She headed for the nearest open chair, barely making it before her knees buckled.

"Andy, what are you doing out of bed?" Jessica exclaimed as she watched her try to sit comfortably.

"It's time to get up," Andy answered, not too convincingly. She was debating whether to head back upstairs and crawl back into bed.

"How are you feeling, Andy?" Jennifer stared at Andy's face, fear evident in her voice.

"Not as bad as I look," she reassured Jennifer as Jessica took her hand.

"How are you really feeling?"

"Really, not bad. I just have a few cuts and bruises, no big deal. I know I look pretty bad but I feel okay."

"Should you be up?" Jessica watched her carefully as she spoke.

"The doctor didn't say I had to stay in bed. Besides the quicker I'm up and around, the faster I'll heal." She tried to rationalize as she read the look of irritation on Jessica's face. She didn't want to worry Jessica any more than necessary.

"I don't think he meant that you would immediately be up and about, honey. I think everyone would understand if you spent some time recuperating," Jessica seriously suggested, her voice still carrying an undertone of irritation.

"I will, I promise," she pledged trying to smile. "Now what does a person have to do to get a cup of coffee around here?"

"I'll get it," Jennifer volunteered. "Do you want some breakfast?"

"How about some toast?" Andy suggested. Her stomach was still too jumpy for anything else. As Jennifer busied herself with Andy's breakfast, Jessica sat down next to her.

"Andy, how do you really feel?" She asked quietly.

"Like I've been run over by a truck."

"You can take another pain pill the doctor gave you."

"I think that might be a good idea." Andy agreed, clasping Jessica's hand. "Jess, could you help me get dressed after I have some toast? I don't think I can do it by myself and I don't want to be in my nightshirt when Len comes over." Andy blushed with embarrassment. She was having a difficult time asking for help.

Jessica smiled. "Of course I will, honey. How about I go get you some jeans and a loose T- shirt. You can change down here so you don't have to climb the stairs."

"Thanks."

"Honey, you don't have to thank me," Jessica whispered, kissing her gently on the cheek. "I'll be right back." She hurried out of the kitchen.

"Here's your coffee, Andy. Do you want some jam on your toast? I can make cinnamon toast."

"Just butter would be perfect, Jenn."

Jennifer rapidly buttered Andy's toast and, placing it on a plate, she carried it to Andy, setting it on the table in front of her.

"Andy, can I ask you something?" Jennifer's serious tone and the look on her face told Andy the question was very important. "Were you scared last night?"

"I was scared to death," Andy admitted.

"You didn't act like it."

"I didn't want those guys to think I was."

"They were going to rape me." Jennifer whispered. It was a statement, not a question. "They said some pretty awful things." She hung her head as she spoke.

"I know, Jenn. But I wouldn't have let them hurt you." Andy clasped her hand, squeezing it gently. "Jenn, I think we are both going to need to talk to someone about what happened. Jessica made an appointment for us to go see a counselor. Will you go with me?"

"Okay, Andy. I'll go with you." Jennifer held onto Andy's hand. "I can still feel that guy touching me. It makes my skin crawl."

"Honey, it will go away. I promise you, it will eventually go away." Andy hugged Jennifer tightly. "I'm sorry this happened to you. I would give anything to make it go away. There are some very bad people in this world and you and Todd were exposed to some extremely dangerous guys."

Jessica started to enter the kitchen, but hesitated as Jennifer continued to speak. This was between Jennifer and Andy.

"Andy, he touched you, too. Doesn't it make you sick? I couldn't go to sleep last night." Jennifer was close to tears.

"Yes, it still makes me ill, and I did wake up with bad dreams several times last night. That's why I need to talk to someone. Do me a favor, Jennifer. If you wake up with a nightmare you come find me or Jessica and we'll talk about it. Will you promise me?"

"I promise."

"Jennifer, what those men did was wrong and violent. When someone touches you it should be with gentleness and love. You are going to be fine. The memories of what happened will eventually fade away. I promise."

"Thanks, Andy. I love you."

"I love you, too, Jenn."

Jennifer quickly darted out of the kitchen, speaking over her shoulder. "I'm going to change my clothes and head over to Todd's."

"How's he doing?"

"He's says he's pretty sore, but he's doing okay."

"Say hello to him for me."

"I will."

Jessica waited until Jennifer raced up the stairs before she entered the kitchen. She slipped her arms around Andy, hugging her gently, trying to hide her tears.

"Thank you, Andy." Jessica kissed her sweetly on her bruised lips. "She trusts that you will always tell her the truth. She needed to talk to you."

"I needed to talk to her. My skin still crawls from that man's hands," Andy admitted. "I'm lucky I have you to replace those feelings with your touch. I just don't want Jennifer to think any of this was her fault. That guy was looking for trouble for a long time. I just wish I could have prevented the whole thing."

"I love you, sweetie." Jessica kissed her again.

Andy sighed. "If only I wasn't so sore." Even though Andy was battered and bruised, her violet eyes had the familiar twinkle that Jessica recognized quickly.

"Oh you, just eat your toast." Jessica laughed, kissing Andy softly.

They sat in companionable silence while Andy finished eating. Afterwards, Jessica helped Andy get dressed and then assisted her as she took a seat on the living room couch, cell phone in hand.

"Marta, this is Andy. Is Len around?"

"Hi honey, how are you doing, Len's at the festival? I can reach him for you."

"I'm fine, Marta. Would you have Len call me on my cell phone when he gets an opportunity?"

"I sure will, Andy. Now you take care of yourself, we need you back here healthy. I miss you."

"I will, Marta, and thanks. I miss you too." Andy sat back on the couch to wait. She needed to find out how Len and her team were doing. Jessica was on the kitchen telephone talking to Loren at the fair. It wasn't two minutes before the cell phone rang shrilly.

"Hey, Chief, how you doing?"

"I've felt better," She admitted.

"I'll bet you have. Are you going to be around for awhile?"

"I'm not going anywhere, I'll be at Jessica's."

"I'm on my way."

Andy placed the cell phone down. She needed to write her report and collect her thoughts. She started to get up off the couch and it took her two tries to stand up steadily. Jessica met her as she entered the kitchen.

"Where do you think you're going?"

"To get some paper and a pen." Andy's impatience could be heard in her voice.

"I'll get it. You go sit down, and if you need something let me know."

Andy meekly returned to the couch. "Since when did you get so bossy?" she grumbled.

Jessica just grinned as she handed her the tablet and a pen. She also held out a pill and a glass of water. "Please take your pill." Andy did as she was asked. "Thank you."

"You love this," Andy mumbled.

"I just never knew you would be such a miserable patient." Jessica grinned.

"I hate not being able to do anything."

"Andy, it's only for a short time."

"I know, but it's embarrassing. I'll try to be better."

A knock on the front door kept Jessica from responding. It was Todd's dad. "Hi Jessica, I'm here to pick up Jennifer."

"She's getting ready. I'll go get her. How's Todd doing?"

"He's doing pretty well. He's awfully sore, and he looks pretty damn scary."

"We're just glad he's okay."

"How's Andy doing?"

"She's pretty sore herself but she's going to be fine. She's sitting in the living room, if you want to talk to her. I'll go get Jennifer."

Todd's father walked into the living room as Jessica went to get her niece. "Chief Andy, how are you doing?"

"Pretty good, Judd, how's Todd?"

"He'll be just fine, thanks to you."

"Your son helped. He was very brave."

"He's a great kid."

"Hi." Jennifer burst into the living room.

"Hey, Jennifer don't you look nice?"

"Thanks Mr. T. Aunt Jess, I'll be back after the fireworks are over."

"Okay honey, you guys have a good time."

"They'll be fine, Jessica. I won't take my eyes off of them." Judd conveyed his emotions without another word. He would guard Jennifer and Todd with his life, just like Andy had.

"Thanks, Judd."

"No problem." He and Jennifer headed out the front door.

"Jessica, can we go to the fireworks?" Andy asked.

"Are you sure you are up to it?"

"I'd like to go to our first Fourth of July celebration together, please?" Andy pleaded.

"Okay, honey, as long as you bundle up and take it easy."

"I promise." She grinned. How could Jessica say no to her? Her face may be bruised and swollen but she was so damn cute and Jessica couldn't refuse her anything.

"I'm going to do some paperwork at the kitchen table. Do you need anything?"

"Just you." Andy grinned wickedly. Jessica laughed as she kissed Andy and left her seated on the couch.

Andy concentrated as she began to write her report, and for twenty minutes she wrote steadily. Once she had it down on paper she re-read her words, correcting a few here and there until she was satisfied. She was wishing she had a computer right about now.

"You know what I need?"

"What?" Jessica answered her from the kitchen.

"A portable computer."

"Well, let's go find you one next week." The answer seemed to satisfy Andy, and she remained silent. "Andy, will you move in with me next week?"

"I thought you would never ask, but I don't think I'll be able to pack for a couple of days."

"We'll worry about that next week."

Andy again fell silent. They both worked quietly until a knock on the front door interrupted them. Jessica answered the door and let Len in. He grinned happily at Jessica.

"Hey, Jessica, where's the Chief?"

"Hi Len. She's in the living room."

"Thanks. How are you doing?"

"I'm okay. I'm just glad everything turned out the way it did."

"So am I, Jessica. So am I. Those guys never had a chance against Andy." He grinned as he followed Jessica into the living room. Jessica couldn't help but think it was amazing that in a few short months Andy had filled many people's heart.

"Wow, Andy, no wonder you're sore. You look awful."

"Thanks Len, don't remind me. Here, I wrote my report. Can you review it and help me fill in the blanks?"

"Sure."

"Len, have a seat. Can I get you something to drink?" Jessica inquired.

"No thanks, Jessica, I'm fine."

"Then I will leave you two to your work."

"Thanks, Jess," Andy said as Jessica left the two of them in the living room. "Len, I think I've got all the facts down, but read it and let me know what you think." She handed him the tablet.

"Andy, two of the scumbags confessed this morning. They have all been charged with attempted rape, aggravated assault, and the Chambers fellow with attempted murder of a police officer. I think the two are going to plead guilty of assault and attempted rape and will testify against Chambers. They don't want to be charged with attempted murder of a police officer. The prosecutor is still reviewing their statements and the evidence."

"Good. I think there are a few other charges we might be able to add to Chambers' list."

"The prosecutor from Seattle is coming back out tomorrow to work on the case." Cascade was too small to have a full-time prosecuting attorney.

"Maybe I'll come in and talk to him," Andy volunteered.

"You stay right here. If he needs to talk to you he can come over here." Len was adamant, his face red with emotion.

"Read my report." Andy had no intention of staying home. It was her town, her department.

"Yes, boss." Len grinned.

Obviously Andy was finding it difficult to be a patient. She wasn't her usual calm self. He did as she asked. After reading it for several minutes, he took out a pen and began asking Andy some questions.

"Okay, let's clarify a few things here. You saw Chambers place the knife against Jennifer's neck and threaten to hurt her?"

"Yes."

"He was fondling her sexually?"

"Yes, and he talked about what he was going to do to the two of us. He described explicitly how he was going to rape us."

Len's face grew dark with anger but he checked his reaction. "You threw your gun down because he threatened to harm Jennifer with his knife?"

"Yes."

"Did he cut you before or after you tried to disable him?"

"After. He used the knife to cut my sweater off, but he didn't cut me until after I knocked him to the ground. I thought he was knocked out. It was due to my carelessness that he attacked me again with the knife. I had gone over to check on Jennifer when he came after me the second time."

"And where was Todd?"

"He was barely conscious. He managed to grab my gun while I subdued Chambers."

"I think that answers all my questions. It matches Todd and Jennifer's statements. If I have any other questions I will call you. Andy, you know those kids were lucky you found them when you did."

"How did they get Todd and Jennifer in the first place?"

"According to Jennifer, she was waiting for Todd to park his truck. She had seen him pull into the parking lot. They were planning on going on some of the rides at the festival. Chambers and his buddies grabbed the two of them when Todd got out of his truck. I don't think it was a planned abduction. I think they all ended up in the same place at the same time and things escalated. Two of the men admitted that they were surprised at Mike's actions. They dragged Todd and Jennifer into the woods and when Todd put up a fight, they beat him up. The Chambers fellow showed Todd the knife and threatened to castrate him if he didn't stop fighting. As near as I can tell, they were planning on raping Jennifer and were going to make Todd watch. I don't know what their plans were after that. I hate to think of what might have happened. It looks like Jennifer and Todd were in the wrong place at the wrong time. Like I said, those kids were very lucky."

The two of them looked at each other. Both knew how close it had been to a horrible tragedy. "Do you need anything else from me, Len?"

"No, I don't think so. The prosecutor may need to talk to you, but I think we've covered everything. Considering what happened last night, the festival has been calm and quiet, even with the record crowds. We have two shifts covering the fireworks tonight, but I think everything is going to be fine."

"Good. You're doing a great job, Len. Thanks."

"No problem, Andy. I have a good mentor."

Andy flushed with embarrassment. "Go on and get out of here." She smiled.

"Okay, boss." Len grinned.

"Call me if anything comes up."

"I will. Now, will you get some rest?" Len reminded her as he prepared to leave. "Goodbye, Jessica. Take good care of her, I kind of like her."

"I will, Len." He went out the front door with a grin.

Jessica had heard bits and pieces of their conversation and was shocked at what she heard. The reality of what happened was setting in. She got up to check on Andy and found her slumped forward on the couch, her head in her hands.

"Andy, are you okay?" Jessica sat down next to her.

Andy's tear-stained face looked up at her. "I just realized how close we were to Jennifer and Todd being seriously hurt or killed. What if I hadn't gotten there in time? What if I hadn't been able to stop them?" Andy's shoulders shook with sobs and Jessica held her tightly as she cried.

"But you did get there in time and you saved them, Andy." Jessica tried to reassure her as she continued to cry. "It's okay, Andy. It's all over now."

Jessica continued to speak softly to Andy, and her sobs lessened. Jessica held Andy while she dealt with her emotions. She needed to let it all go. They sat there for a long time as Andy allowed Jessica to comfort her.

"I'm so tired," Andy finally said, her voice hoarse from crying.

"How about I get you a pillow and blanket and you rest for a while? It will be good for you."

"Okay." Andy didn't have the energy to argue.

Jessica went to the hall closet and returned with a blanket and a pillow. She slid the pillow behind Andy's head as Andy stretched out on the couch. Tucking the blanket around her, Jessica kissed Andy deeply. "Now you get some rest."

"Thanks, honey."

"You're welcome, doll." Jessica went back into the kitchen. Within minutes she could hear Andy's even breathing and knew she had fallen asleep. Jessica turned back to her work. She also needed time to think about how closely Andy and Jennifer had come to being badly hurt or worse. Her heart ached as she thought of the injuries Andy had gotten saving Jennifer and Todd. She knew it was all part of Andy's job, but she could never lose this woman. She meant the world to her.

It was several hours when before Jessica answered the knock on her front door. Andy was still sound asleep on the couch, even though it was well after four in the afternoon. She'd been sleeping heavily since Len left.

"Hi, Buck, come on in." Buck had called earlier to see how Andy was feeling. Jessica had warned him she looked pretty bad. He had been very angry, having spent the morning at the police station. Mike Chambers was still spewing his hatred of women.

"Hey Jessica, how you doing?" Buck hugged her tightly.

"Not too bad, considering all that's going on. Come into the kitchen, Andy's asleep on the couch and I don't want to disturb her." Jessica returned the hug, recognizing the sheen of tears in Buck's eyes.

"Andy is not asleep." Andy's hoarse voice echoed from the living room. Jessica rolled her eyes and grinned at Buck. When Buck looked at Andy he shivered. He realized just how close they had all come to losing three people he loved.

"Hey girl, how are you feeling?" Buck asked as he joined Andy in the living room.

"Much better then I felt earlier." She slowly sat up to face Buck. Her face actually showed more bruises and swelling. "I am not a nice person to be around today," she admitted.

"I find that hard to believe." Buck laughed as Andy just looked at him, impatience written all over her face.

"Can I get you something to drink? Andy, I'm making some tea if you would like some?"

"I'd love some tea," Andy responded, smiling at Jessica.

"Nothing for me," Buck said.

"Andy, while you were sleeping some flowers came for you. I have them sitting in the kitchen, if you would like to see them," Jessica announced as she walked into the kitchen.

"Buck, how about you and I go sit at the kitchen table? I need to move."

"Fine with me."

Andy slowly walked into the kitchen, still extremely stiff and sore. Buck followed behind her.

"I came from the station. It looks like three of those fine gentlemen are looking to make deals with the prosecution in order to get lesser charges, and the prosecutor is going to throw the book at Chambers. He's got himself a lawyer, but right now they've got him cold on some charges that will keep him in jail for a long time."

"Good, that's where he belongs," Andy snapped. "Wow!" she exclaimed as she caught sight of three large bouquets of flowers. "These are beautiful."

"Honey, the cards should be attached somewhere."

Andy pulled the cards from each bouquet. "This one is from Todd and his family, and this is from the office. These are from the town council, isn't that nice of them? That is so sweet of everyone. They're beautiful."

"That was very thoughtful. Buck, please sit down. Andy, please have a seat." Jessica placed a cup of tea in front of Andy.

"Thanks, Jess. She's taking good care of me, Buck."

"I knew she would. You take it easy, young lady, you gave us all quite a scare."

"I know, Buck." She patted him on the hand.

"I was talking to Tommy and he says you're planning on moving in here next week?"

"I was. I made arrangements with the realtor to be out by the fifteenth. I guess I should call and tell her I won't make it."

"Why do that?" Jessica wanted Andy close to her. She didn't want to wait any longer to live with her. She just needed to convince Andy how much she meant to her.

"Buck, I can't pack and move right now. I can't even dress myself."

"Between Tommy, Jennifer, Jessica, and myself, we could have you moved in a couple of days. What do you think, Jessica?"

"The three of us spoke this morning and we thought we could take care of the packing and moving this Tuesday and Wednesday."

"We can wait a week so I can do the packing. I don't think I can do much lifting by this Tuesday."

"Andy, you are not lifting anything, period." Jessica's look made Andy's response die in her throat.

"Good, I'll bring my truck and meet you there Tuesday morning," Buck added.

Andy looked at Jessica and Buck in amazement. "Andy, are you okay with this?" Jessica was wondering if Andy might be having second thoughts.

"I am more than okay about moving in." Andy grinned. "It's not like I ever really unpacked."

"Good, it's all settled then. I'll leave you two alone, but I'll call Monday night to check," Buck responded. "Andy, you take it easy. We all love you, girl." Buck bent and kissed her cheek.

"I love you Buck, and thanks."

"No problem. I'll talk to you later."

"So long Buck, thanks for stopping by."

"You're welcome. And Jess, don't take any lip from Andy." He grinned as he left.

"Oh boy," Andy grumbled as Jessica grinned at her.

"Andy, are you sure about moving in next week?"

"Jessica, I'd move tomorrow if I could. Are you sure?"

"Positive. I want to go to sleep with you every night for the rest of our lives."

"Doesn't that sound wonderful?"

"Now let's get something to eat. We have fireworks to watch. That's if you still want to go?"

"I do. Can I help with dinner?"

"Sure, you can watch me make it." Jessica chuckled.

"Jessica," Andy moaned.

At quarter to ten, Andy and Jessica pulled into the fairground parking lot. They were dressed warmly and Jessica had brought two blankets.

"Are you sure about this?" Jessica asked as Andy struggled to get out of the car.

"I'm sure," Andy sighed, as she gingerly stood upright. She was so stiff and sore that bending was a major effort. The two of them made their way slowly through the park where many people were seated on the ground awaiting the fireworks display.

"Hey, Chief, glad to see you're okay."

"Hi Andy, Jessica, how you doing?"

Several people spoke to Andy and Jessica as they slowly made their way to a clearing in the crowd. Andy acknowledged their greetings while Jessica laid one of the blankets on the ground. Andy stiffly sat down.

"I'm probably going to need your help getting back up," Andy whispered wryly.

"No problem, sweetie. Here, put this blanket around you." Jessica snuggled next to Andy.

Many other people stopped by to say hello and offer good wishes to Andy before the show started. It was amazing to Andy that so many people approached her. She didn't think she knew that many people in the town.

"Jessica, I don't know all these people."

"I know honey, but they know you and they just want you to know how much they appreciate what you did." Jessica smiled and hugged her startled girlfriend. "You saved Jennifer and Todd's life while risking your own."

"It was my job," Andy responded, uncomfortable with the conversation.

"I love you, sweetie." Jessica smiled at her battered and bruised girlfriend. Andy had no clue that she was her job. She was honorable, dedicated, and well trained. She also was a very valuable member of a close-knit town, one that welcomed her as a member.

They heard the first explosion, as the sky lit up with brilliant colors. Jessica and Andy sat side by side, a blanket around their shoulders, their faces tilted skyward to catch the show.

"Our first Fourth of July together," Andy whispered to Jessica, as they held hands under the blanket. "I love you, Jess."

"I love you, Andy."

They smiled at each other. At that moment the previous night's activities faded from memory as they enjoyed this time with each other. The show lasted for forty-five minutes, volley upon volley of fireworks filling the sky. As the two of them walked to their car along with the rest of the crowd, everyone agreed this was the best festival ever, despite last night's incident. They thanked Jessica and Andy over and over for their hard work. Jessica and Andy headed for home, feeling exhausted, as their busy schedules, Andy's injuries, and Jessica's worrying took their toll. They just wanted to crawl immediately into bed. Tommy was already home and heading for bed himself.

"How are you feeling, Andy?" He asked as they came in the front door.

"Not too bad, Tommy. Thanks for asking."

"I'm glad. Andy, I just wanted to tell you, I'm really happy you're part of my family." Tommy flushed with embarrassment as he shuffled from foot to foot.

"Tommy, I feel very blessed to be a part of your family."

"Thanks, Andy. Hey, I'm working until seven tomorrow night, but I'll be able to move your things Tuesday and Wednesday."

"Thanks, Tommy. I really appreciate your help."

"No problem, you are family. Besides, you guys are going to help me move when I go back to school." He grinned evilly.

"I haven't told her yet, Tommy." Jessica grinned.

"Oops. I'm going to bed, goodnight." He loped up the stairs.

"I'll tell you what he was talking about later," Jessica explained to Andy.

"Good. I'm too tired to think about anything more tonight. He's awful sweet, though."

"I know the feeling. Tommy loves you, honey. Let's get you to bed." Andy didn't argue.

Andy was already in bed and Jessica was in the bathroom, when Andy heard a knock on the bedroom door and Jennifer's voice. "Can I come in to say goodnight?"

"Of course you can," Andy called from the bed.

"Hey, how are you doing?" Jennifer flopped onto the end of the bed on her stomach, her chin resting in her hands.

"Good, how about you?"

"Good."

"How's Todd?"

"He's fine. All his buddies think he's real cool, so he's good."

"Jennifer, you come wake me if up if you have any bad dreams."

"Only if you do the same."

"Deal."

"Cool, thanks Andy."

"Hey Jenn, honey, what did you think of the fireworks?" Jessica asked, as she entered the bedroom rubbing lotion on to her hands.

"They were the best ever. It's going to be hard next year to top this year's festival."

"I don't know about that. We make a pretty good team." Jessica was glad her niece was looking forward to next year.

"We do," she agreed. "Well, I'm tired and I'm going to bed. 'Night, Aunt Jess, 'night Andy."

"Goodnight." Jessica smiled as Jennifer bounced out of the bedroom.

"She's going to be just fine," Andy spoke softly.

"I know she is." Jessica climbed into bed and turned out the light. "All because of you."

"I think you and Tommy have a lot to do with it. She's a pretty smart kid."

"I think between you and me, Jennifer and Tommy are going to be much loved."

"I just can't thank you enough for sharing your family with me."

"Honey, I'm not sharing them. They are as much your family as they are mine."

Andy began to weep softly as Jessica folded her in her arms. "I seem to be crying a lot lately."

"You've been through an awful lot, Andy. It's normal for you to feel this way." I am glad you and Jenn are going to see a counselor."

"So am I, it will help us both. I love you Jessica. I wish I wasn't so tired and sore. I would very much like to make love with you."

"Andy, we have all the time in the world for that. I would just love to hold you while we sleep. We have a lifetime of nights."

"Jessica, I'm so glad you found me. I can't imagine what life would be like without you, Jenn, and Tommy."

"I'm just glad we didn't lose you."

"Never." Jessica and Andy sealed their love with a kiss. Despite everything that had happened, their life couldn't be more perfect.

Jessica turned onto her side and Andy curled up against her back. Her arm draped over Jessica's hip where Jessica held her hand. "Good night Andy."

"Sleep tight, Jess."

"I will forever, with you."

Their breathing softened and their bodies snuggled even closer together. As sleep quickly claimed them, they were secure that they would be doing this for many years to come.

Chapter Ten

"Aunt Jessica, Andy and I are back," Jennifer yelled from the front door as she entered.

Andy followed her a little bit slower. Her body was still stiff and sore from the beating she took. Her face had turned purple and blue from the bruising, her eyes still swollen. She and Jennifer had just come from Andy's office. Jennifer had volunteered to go in with her for an hour or two. Andy had gone back to work almost immediately to handle the huge amount of paperwork and legal requirements to build a case against all four men. She had worked with her officers and the prosecutor. Along with Jennifer and Todd's testimony to record the facts, Mike was all but assured of being found guilty. It helped that three of the men involved had turned on Mike Chambers to save themselves. Mike Chambers was rapidly falling apart in jail. His hatred for his mother, and by association all women, along with the abuse he had been subjected to, ate away at what little control he had left. His lawyer was recommending that he be tested by a psychiatrist for mental illness. It was a good bet the psychiatrist would find one.

"How is the office doing?"

"Marta is running everything perfectly, as usual. It was pretty quiet after all the activity in the last two days. I am sure Len appreciates some quiet time." Andy met Jessica with a hug. "What time did you get back?"

"About twenty minutes ago." Jessica had headed to Seattle earlier in the morning for a meeting with a client of the gallery. "Andy, did you talk to the prosecutor?"

"Yes, and he doesn't need much more from me right now. Actually, it looks like Chambers' lawyer is negotiating a lesser sentence if he pleads guilty to attempted murder of a police officer, so I don't even know if there's going to be much of a trial."

"I hope not too much of a lesser sentence."

"I don't think he'll get less than twenty years, but we'll have to wait and see."

"Andy, there's a present for you in the kitchen."

"For me?"

Andy followed Jennifer into the kitchen where a wrapped box sat on the table. Andy proceeded to tear the wrapping off the package. "Is this from you?" Andy asked.

"No, actually it's from the town council. I spoke with them this morning and they agreed it was a good idea."

"Andy, it's a portable computer! Cool!" Jennifer squealed.

"Wow, it is a portable," Andy exclaimed as she pulled it out of the box.

"I told them it would make it easier for you to stay on top of things while you were recuperating and they agreed. I picked it up in Seattle today. It's supposed to be one of the best!" Jessica smiled at Andy as she spoke.

"I'm speechless." Andy grinned back.

"I figure while we're packing and moving you tomorrow you can work on your computer, sitting in a chair somewhere," Jessica teased her. "It should keep you out of trouble for a while."

"Thank you." Andy hugged her tightly. She knew who had talked the council into purchasing the computer. "Come on Jennifer, let's see what this thing can do."

"Cool!"

Jessica grinned widely as she watched the two of them sit at the kitchen table, their attention focused on the computer. They had developed a strong bond in the last few days as they recuperated from everything. They both had started seeing a counselor the day before to talk about what happened to them. It was a necessary part of their healing. They also talked to each other, something that Jessica found especially heartwarming. They were a family.

"Girls, I'm going to change my clothes and work for awhile in the studio. How about I order pizza for dinner tonight?"

"Perfect!"

The two of them would have agreed to anything. Their attention was centered on the computer and nothing was going to interrupt them. Jessica smiled to herself. Life was getting back to normal, and Andy would be moved in a matter of days. Jessica thought life was close to perfect herself.

The next two days flew by as Jessica, Jennifer, Tommy, and Buck packed and moved all of Andy's things into her new home. Jessica did allow her to supervise but she wasn't allowed to lift one item. No matter how much Andy grumbled the moving crew would not relent. They were pretty adamant and Andy finally gave up the argument.

"Well, that's the very last box unpacked and put away. You are officially moved in," Jessica announced as she closed the closet and flopped onto the bed next to Andy.

"You know, I could have helped," Andy grumbled.

"You did, sweetie." Jessica kissed her quickly. "Now it's time for bed. It's after midnight and I'm going to go clean up."

As Jessica went into the bathroom, Andy stood and went to the dresser. Changing from her shorts and T- shirt to a silk nightshirt, Andy flew back into bed. She planned to celebrate her moving in and she knew exactly how. "Jessica, aren't you done yet?" Andy called from the bedroom.

"Yes. What's up with you?" Jessica asked as she joined Andy in bed. "You've been planning something all night. I know you."

"I thought I could talk you into a little celebration with me on account of my moving in." Andy's eyes twinkled as she smiled.

"A little celebration, huh? Now what do you have in mind, if I may ask?" Jessica rolled onto her side, her hands reaching for Andy's.

"Jessica, I need to make love with you. I miss that part of us." Andy moved closer to Jessica until they were inches apart.

"Well, I think we should do just that," Jessica agreed as she closed the gap between their bodies. They met in a hungry breath-stealing kiss, their mutual passion for each other unleashing itself.

"I just don't want to hurt you. Your wounds are still healing," Jessica whispered as she covered Andy's neck and shoulders with kisses. Unbuttoning Andy's nightshirt, she continued her attentions.

She was going to wash away any bad memories Andy had and replace them with loving ones. Andy gasped as Jessica's fingers touched her in a thousand places, skimming her nipples, grazing her wounds, and loving Andy's body with her touch. Her lips followed the trail left by her fingers. She suckled on Andy's nipples until they ached with pleasure, while Andy moaned with passion. Her body began to move against Jessica's, as Jessica's fingers found their way to the swollen wet lips that waited for her touch. Unable to wait, Jessica plunged her fingers into Andy as she continued to bite and nibble on her nipples, Andy's legs widened in encouragement thrilling Jessica with their response. While Andy's body began to react with a tensing of muscles, Jessica slid down to fuse her mouth to Andy's swollen flesh, alternately plunging her tongue in and out of Andy as her fingers teased her into a frenzy. Andy gasped as she climaxed, her hips pushing against Jessica's mouth, her hands flung over her head as her body unraveled.

"Jessica, oh, oh my God!"

Andy could barely speak as her body shook with wave after wave of pleasure. When it started to subside, Jessica renewed her efforts, and

Andy was again caught in the throes of one climax after another, unable to respond with anything but gasps and moans.

"You taste so good," Jessica whispered as she continued to enjoy her lover's response to her enthusiastic lovemaking.

"Enough, I think I am going to die," Andy said quietly. She reached down and pulled Jessica up until she lay on top of Andy.

"Andy, be careful of your ribs," Jessica reminded her.

"I know how to fix that."

Andy pushed Jessica onto her back and placed her now naked body on top of her. Andy's hands found their way to Jessica's breasts as the two kissed wildly. They didn't need slow and leisurely lovemaking, frantic, wild, and heated was what they needed. Andy's hands rubbed and teased Jessica's nipples, her hips rocking against Jessica's. In response, Jessica spread her legs and met her hips with matching movements. Jessica had come to bed nude and the feel of Andy's naked body against her own was wonderful. The familiar heat began between her legs as Andy's wetness rubbed against hers. She grabbed Andy's hips, pulling her tightly as she felt the pressure build.

"Andy, please."

Andy responded to Jessica's request, her fingers finding their way between Jessica's legs, rubbing her until Jessica's fingers again found Andy's wetness. Andy slid her fingers into Jessica as she rocked against Jessica's hand. Jessica's legs wrapped around Andy's thighs, her body tensed and then unleashed a series of orgasms that shook her to the core. Andy could feel Jessica's response, as she loved her thoroughly.

"Oh, I have missed this," Jessica cried softly.

"I love you, Jess."

"I love you, Andy."

They held each other tightly, unwilling to let go, as their breathing slowly returned to normal. They slipped into exhausted sleep almost immediately, their bodies wrapped around each other and their hands clasped together. They had been asleep for several hours when a knock on the bedroom door awoke Andy.

"Andy, are you awake?" It was Jennifer.

"Yes, just a minute, Jennifer." Andy pulled the covers up around Jessica as she grabbed a bathrobe and went to open the door. "What's up, sweetie?"

Jennifer stood in the hallway, obviously upset. "I keep having a nightmare," she cried.

"Come on sweetie, let's go get some warm milk and talk about it."

Andy threw her arm around Jennifer's shoulders and directed her down the stairs and into the kitchen. "Here, have a seat, while I warm up some milk. Now tell me what your nightmare is about."

"I keep having the same nightmare over and over. That creep keeps grabbing me, you know, and telling me what he's going to do to me. I can feel him touching me," Jennifer whispered.

"Honey, it's okay. You're safe and he can't touch you again." Andy sat next to Jennifer.

"What if I can't ever forget?"

"You will, honey. One day when you are ready you will fall in love and the two of you will learn together what making love and touching each other is all about. I promise you it will be wonderful and special, and you will never have another thought about that creep."

"You promise?"

"I guarantee it, sweetie."

"Andy, do you have bad dreams?"

"Sometimes, but your Aunt Jess tells me how much she loves me and the nightmare stops." Andy held Jennifer's hand.

"You two are lucky you love each other so much."

"Yes, we are. Now I want you to do what our counselor suggested and write all your feelings down."

"Okay. Andy?"

"What honey?"

"I don't want any warm milk. I don't like it."

"Okay, then what do you want?" Andy grinned.

"I think I want to go back upstairs and try to sleep again."

"Good idea."

"Thanks, Andy."

"Thank you, Jenn."

"For what?"

"For being such an important part of my family." Andy smiled.

"I love you, Andy." Jennifer smiled in return.

"I love you, too. Now, let's get you upstairs."

The two of them walked up the stairs together. Andy stood in the doorway of Jennifer's room while she crawled back into bed.

"Goodnight honey, and come wake me if you have another nightmare."

"I will, and thanks again, Andy."

"No problem, sweetie. Goodnight."

"Goodnight."

Andy slipped into the bedroom she shared with Jessica and quietly removed the bathrobe.

"Is she okay?" Jessica asked as Andy crawled under the covers.

"She will be," Andy responded. She turned to Jessica. "She will be fine when that special man enters her life and her bad memories are replaced with wonderful, pleasurable ones."

"Kind of like what we did tonight?'

"Just exactly like that."

"How about if we make sure we've made enough memories?"

"My thoughts exactly." Andy smiled as the two of them reached for each other. "It might take several hours, maybe even days," Andy teased.

"I think I'm up to the task." Jessica laughed.

"Oh, I know you are."

Andy and Jessica kissed slowly and deeply as all thoughts slipped from their minds except for their love for one another. They had years and years to create more memories.

The End

About the Author

Jeanne is a forty eight year old woman born and raised in the Pacific Northwest where she currently lives with her partner in their home in West Seattle. She has been writing on and off for over twenty years and this is her second book to be published. She will soon follow this one with eight new books along with many more stories just waiting to be written. As you can tell she believes in happy endings and hopes that you enjoy them as much as she does.

Printed in the United States
22654LVS00005B/301

9 780595 205998